To Carole —
Remember the barn!
And thanks for the tree

D1527327

Return in Kind

by

Laura C. Stevenson

(signature: Laura C. Stevenson)

Separate Star Publishing

New York

©2010 by Laura C. Stevenson
ISBN 0-9712872-5-9

Published by Separate Star Publishing, Inc.
New York, NY, U.S.A.
www.separate-star.com

Cover photo by Laura C. Stevenson
Book design by Blackthorn Studio

To F.D.R. with love.

Prologue: A Legacy

Letty Hendrickson was dead. The funeral would be held in three days.

It was incomprehensible.

Helena paused as the first rays of the sun touched the tulips in her garden, then eased herself into the Mercedes and negotiated the ruts down to the mist-filled village below her. It wasn't the funeral arrangements that were incomprehensible, of course. Thoughtful even in grief, Joel had suggested that the ceremony be held the day after Commencement, so the trustees, already summoned to the College a day early to discuss the legacy, wouldn't be further inconvenienced by having to return in later weeks. Nor could it be the death, given the years Letty had been fighting cancer. And while she'd been only sixty-one…well, after one passed one's eighth decade, the demise of friends far younger than oneself ceased to be occasion for remark. No, it wasn't the end of a life that was incomprehensible. It was the end of the past a presence had made present.

She turned left at the church and followed Route 100 south, looking abstractly at the spring landscape and reflecting how much it had changed since she had driven to Mather College for her first Trustee meeting, over fifty years ago. Route 100 was paved now, of course, but the once-prosperous Vermont farms between Westover and the Massachusetts border were faded and mostly for sale; and further east, the tentacles of the malls and industrial parks that extended from Lawrence and Lowell were creeping alarmingly close to Whitby and Mather's Georgian campus.

There were still, however, a few familiar landmarks. Over the years, their associations had become shadowy, demanding only a smile of vague recognition, but today they thrust themselves through the wisps and sworls of mist with startling immediacy. The clock on the squat-towered Adamsville church—and Letty at fourteen, standing sullenly on the steps of the President's house next to Nathaniel, into whose bachelor existence she'd suddenly been catapulted by her father's death. The hairpin turn over the brook—and Letty on the eve of her high school graduation, tearfully insisting, over Nathaniel's puzzled but gratified objections, that she wanted to stay at Mather and make her role as College hostess into her life's work. The gray thoroughbred standing in the lee of its master's barn—and Letty, many years older now, watching with silent affection as Nathaniel circled a puddle of brandy in his snifter, his face lit by after dinner candles and the poetry he was discussing with Joel. The Colraine steeple rising out of the river valley, and Letty, elevated to the Board of Trustees after Nathaniel's death, arguing passionately against…no, those scenes were best forgotten. Letty's passing opened possibilities that the trustees could only welcome, but it marked the end of an era many of them had long held dear. Dwelling on the later years of wrangling rendered that era doubly lost.

Still, she'd always been able to forgive Letty for her obsession. However exasperating it might have been to deal with, her determination to extend Nathaniel's public influence beyond the grave had been an expression of love, not of ambition. And in a peculiar way, that misconstruing devotion had also preserved the private man

2

Letty had never understood. The Nathaniel who had cared deeply for Joel Hendrickson. The Nathaniel with whom she, Helena, had for forty-five years shared a friendship that could have existed in no generation after their own.

And that, of course, was why it was difficult to believe Letty Hendrickson was dead: her death had completed Nathaniel's. Helena nodded as she followed the road downhill between flowering apple orchards and turned east on Route 2. She was driving to Mather College to attend not one funeral, but two.

Letty Hendrickson was dead.

Eleanor closed her mailbox and looked across the valley at the delicate spring colors of the mountains.

Amazing. Incredible. But here was the evidence in her hand—David's scrawled apology for postponing the supper she'd planned to welcome him and Charlie for the summer. *Can't get to Vermont Saturday night. Have to go straight to Mather College after picking up Charlie at Logan—must attend AMAZING trustee meeting Saturday P.M. Momentous legacy. Commencement Sunday, funeral Monday. Rain check, okay?*

Well, the rain check was no big deal. They'd be here Monday night, full of gossip, and dinner could easily be arranged for Tuesday or Wednesday, before they got swept into the social round of summer people. But Letty Hendrickson...

An insistent German shepherd muzzle nudged at her hand, but instead of starting out on the promised walk, she wandered to the house and sat on the front steps. The dog established himself at her feet, dislodging the cat from the thyme in which it had curled up; unperturbed, it moved next to her on the warm stone, and she stroked it absently.

Letty Hendrickson. Some passings resurrected the assumptions of an age, and just for a second there David's letter had shoved her back thirty-five years into the world of her childhood. The post-war world that created academia's Golden Age at the same time it destroyed hill-farming in Vermont. College professors from Massachusetts to Ohio who, like her father, could suddenly afford abandoned farms. The world of summer gentry. How certain, how natural, how wide-ranging it had seemed. And yet, how cloistered, how limited it had been. Amidst the stimulating talk that had seemed to reflect widely different viewpoints there had not been one black or Asian voice to be heard. And the distinguished scholars who had discussed Nathaniel Brantford's forward-looking educational ideals had all been men. The women had listened silently or begun side conversations about gardens, recipes, or the achievements of the precocious children who were playing fiercely competitive croquet.

Thirty-five years. And here she sat on the front steps of the same house. Who would know that she and those other competitive croquet players had grown up to revolt against the society that had produced them? And who would know that *their* new world was as lost to her as the world of Nathaniel Brantford...

No, she wouldn't let herself think that way. Her book was slowly progressing—on a computer, even, courtesy of David's gratitude for all the time Charlie had spent here the last two summers. The few academics she still encountered reminded her that the intellectual world, with all its bright ideas and pretentious ideologies, was still there. But she no longer belonged to the remnants of Vermont summer gentry. She'd become what as a child she had secretly longed to be: a full-timer.

And it wasn't—it *wasn't*—a bad life. Cleaning houses was tedious after its initial sociological interest wore off, but it was honest work. And if her income hovered just above the poverty line, that was her own fault. She'd inherited half a summer estate, after all. It had had nothing but sentimental value when she and baby Hattie had stayed here while Stanislaw went on tour, and no more in the stunned summer after his death. But now...well, if she had any doubts about its worth, all she had to do was think of the eight hundred grand that

4

the schized-out shade of her brother had netted last March from the deal he'd secretly closed with Hume and Rickerts for his share.

Reluctantly, she raised her eyes to the familiar, rock-strewn hillside across the road. It looked just as it always had, until—her gaze dropped to the root-filled scar that cut through the grass. She followed its ugly line up the rise to the demolished hand-laid wall and the gate that leaned uselessly against it. Beyond the wall, three gnarled trees lay on their sides in piles of shredded blossoms; the others were heaped together in a bulldozed mass of dirt and branches, their roots stretched to the sky. The Cherry Orchard—never mind that they were apple trees. The principle was the same. The world of summer estates was as antiquated as the world of Nathaniel Brantford. Only hopeless sentimentalists like herself and Letty Hendrickson tried to preserve it.

But unlike Letty Hendrickson, she was still alive, and there were important matters to attend to. That event horse Charlie had said she was schooling this summer, for example—and which was due to arrive tomorrow afternoon. If Charlie was going to be spending the weekend at Mather College, there might be trouble settling him in. She'd better go down to Ray and Connie's place and assure them that she'd lend a hand. It would be good to see them, anyway. She hadn't talked to anyone for days.

She fished in her pocket for her hearing aids, put them in, and stood up, surprised by the sudden clamor of peepers. "Come on, Derri," she said to the delighted dog. "Let's go for a walk."

⚉ ⚉ ⚉

Letty Hendrickson was dead. David was going to be stuck at Mather College.

Couldn't the wretched woman have held on just one more day?

Charlie set down the phone and padded to her room—quietly, so her mom wouldn't ask what was up. It was essential to keep things cool on the day she switched from *mater* to *pater*. Recrimination was a drag, and besides, this wasn't David's fault—or, to be fair, Letty Hendrickson's either. It wasn't like you got to choose a time to die.

But for Pete's sake. Letty Hendrickson had interfered with so much for so long, she couldn't even *die* without causing trouble. Twenty-four hours later, and the news would have broken after David had dropped her off in Vermont—no problem. Twenty-four hours earlier, and she could have called Cocoa's owners and asked that he be sent on the next van East. But as things were, he must be on the far side of Gary by now. And tomorrow, when that enormous van turned up at Ray and Connie's barn, and she wasn't there...well, the guys were competent, but they were guys. Faced with a six-year-old Hanoverian-Thoroughbred who had been cooped up for two days, they'd probably strong-arm him when he shied and pranced—disaster. Connie had the right attitude, but she was sort of timid. As for Ray, unless something went wrong, he'd just sit back and enjoy the rodeo...oh, why why why couldn't Letty Hendrickson have died tomorrow?

She sat down on the bed, looking first at her two stuffed suitcases, then at her watch. Half an hour—everybody said that since the Gulf War, security had gotten really slow. She had half an hour to figure out how that horse could be gotten into Ray and Connie's barn without injuring him. Or traumatizing him. Or hurting someone. Or...

She jumped up. Eleanor. Of course! Eleanor could handle a big, spooky horse without turning a hair. Sure. One phone call and—no, wait. The last few months, Hattie had been taking care of the phone calls, and she'd been worried about how Eleanor was going to manage when she left. So forget it. But if she phoned Ray and Connie...she smiled, picturing Connie in her pink sweatshirt, calling Ray from the porch, and Ray climbing on his tractor and spinning off (much too fast) down the road to find Eleanor.

Great. That took care of that. All she had to cope with now was a weekend of ceremonies at Mather College. Commencement amongst the lilacs on Sunday. A funeral amongst the gravestones on Monday.

The same dark-suited men. The same inspiring words about the Next Life. The same inattentive reverence. Talk about putting a funeral in perspective. Or maybe it was Commencement it put in perspective.

Still, it would be kind of interesting to see the last major college in the East that still excluded women. You had to wonder how that was legal—though come to think of it, didn't Smith and Mount Holyoke exclude men? Yeah, but Mather was different. Nathaniel Brantford had been the great spokesman for classical knowledge—which was to say [male] Liberal Education as the tool of informed [male] democratic action. The whole shtick. Not that there was anything inherently wrong with the old Greeks, as David had commented when she'd wondered if she should apply for Yale's Directed Studies Program. It was just a matter of remembering there were Asians, Native Americans, and African-Americans who had had good ideas too. And of course places like Yale had been shamed by the Revolution into upgrading their gender assumptions, while in spite of David and Helena's best efforts on the Board of Trustees, Mather College was still groping around in the Dark Ages of Patriarchy. And all, if David's stories were even half true, because of Letty Hendrickson.

A couple of years ago, she'd wondered how one person could have so much influence, but she knew now: Money talked. To colleges. To Vermont farmers who learned that if they sold their land for development, they'd never have to work again. To Eleanor's worthless brother, who'd had just enough marbles left to realize that selling off his half of the Randall property would support years of addiction. Tears, heartbreak, ecology—heck, even justice—forget it. All that mattered was money. It was sick.

But here she was, being paid $1500 a month to make a $100,000 horse into a $250,000 horse. Going to Yale in the fall. Spending her summers at her prodigal father's estate in Vermont. As Hattie had pointed out last summer, the two of them were *products* of the inequality they hated. But look at the product Hattie was! After all these years of lonely, fanatical practicing and Eleanor's unquenchable support, she was in London, on scholarship at Goldsmith! How could you say something that awesome meant caving in?

Later. She'd think about it later. Meanwhile, she'd get a glimpse of the college Letty Hendrickson had done so much to destroy—and, if she were lucky, a glimpse of the infamous Letty's long-suffering husband, Joel. David's horror stories had led her to picture the poor man as a Walter Mitty who'd married Venus, spent the first half of his married life playing second fiddle to the Great Nathaniel, and spent the last half saying "Now, dear..." every time his wife had a run-in with the Board. But last summer when she'd said that, Helena had squashed her with a look only Helena could give, and David had positively *turned* on her and said that Joel Hendrickson was the last gentleman of the twentieth century. So now she'd see for herself.

First, though, there was a phone call to make, an airport to get to, a goodbye at O'Hare, a hello at Logan, and waves of barely concealed intra-parental hostility to ignore in between. But this was the last time. Next summer she'd be eighteen, and her years as a joint custody kid would be over. No more tolerance of militant feminism in Chicago. No more tolerance of "adult relationships" in Vermont. No more mediation. She'd be *free*.

She'd gotten halfway to the phone when she realized there would still be the problem of money. Well, she'd take that fence when she came to it.

Letty Hendrickson was dead. The funeral had come to an end, the appropriate hands had been shaken, the appropriate sympathy endured.

It should all be over now, but it wasn't.

Joel sat in his office, his elbows propped on his desk and his forehead dropped into his hands. In a few minutes he would go home, but "home" meant, among other things, confronting so many quietly-left casseroles that he was going to have to call the homeless shelter to deal with them all. And next to the phone, the answering machine would be blinking with consoling calls it would take him an hour to return. Here, at least, nothing broke the vacation silence of the corridor beyond his door, and everything he looked at was his. It was such a god damn relief.

Everybody who had been through this sort of thing had warned him about relief. Perfectly normal, they said, in someone who had cared for A Loved One during a long illness. Perfectly normal, their eyes added, in someone who had mediated between his wife and his college for over a decade. Perfectly normal. A casserole of reassurance. And occasionally sustaining—as when he jerked awake at the door of Letty's room and realized he no longer needed to be sure she was still breathing. Or when arguments and strategies spun through his mind at three in the morning, and he realized they would no longer be needed. Perfectly normal.

Relief from the daily consciousness that the intellectual heritage of Nathaniel Brantford was being lovingly distorted. Relief from the hopeless sense that with every compromise, the promise of Nathaniel's college was being destroyed. Perfectly normal. Sure. All through time, the collaborators of the world had been relieved by the end of the conditions that had made them betray their values. And like him, it was only when the pressure was off that they realized how far political wrangling had driven them from the ideals they had sought to preserve. Perfectly normal.

Oh, Letty, Letty, Letty.

Local gossip had it that her legacy was proof that she'd realized what she'd done to the college. But apparently his patience, his tolerance—his love, damn it, his love—had sheltered her from realizing what the legacy would do to him.

If she'd only *thought*, for God's sake…!

But then, thoughtfulness—in any sense of the word—had never been one of her virtues. And he shouldn't complain. It had been her very lack of rationality, as conspicuous as her beauty in the sterile world ruled by thesis, antithesis, and synthesis, that had drawn him to her. The touch that turned seven flowers into a breathtaking arrangement. The incandescence that made people stop and watch when she danced with him. The instinctive sense that a social affair was about to go wrong; the invisible graciousness with which she changed its direction. No, no, in her own sphere she'd been a genius. What a tragedy her appointment to the Board had thrust her into a sublunary world for which her skills were so unfitted.

In any case, he couldn't expect thought. And if *he* had thought, he might have realized that she would choose to go out with some grand gesture. Well, she'd done that, all right. Above the dreary conformity of those dark suits, every face surrounding the grave had been transformed by wonder and awe. It was the victory she'd always desired, and he was the only one aware of its crowning irony. Unless he was wrong, of course...

He pushed himself back in his chair and gazed unseeingly at the lilacs outside his window. "I leave to the Corporation of Mather College unconditionally and in perpetuity any and all the personal and movable property left to me in the will of Nathaniel Brantford." She'd known the approximate value of the stocks, of course. But not the rest...unless she had had it appraised, and it seemed very unlikely that she had. In 1977, when she had inherited what she called "Nathaniel's old stuff," she'd actually refused to have it appraised. Who cared about its value? she'd said when Helena had urged her to get an updated statement for insurance purposes. All she cared about was its association with Nathaniel. And presumably it was that association, not a new sense of its value, that had led her to leave it to the College. Presumably.

No, certainly. If Letty had discovered the 1991 value of the "stuff" Nathaniel had salvaged from the ruined Europe of 1918—the first editions, the Renaissance furniture, the early Cubist paintings— could she have kept quiet? Unthinkable. She would have been too upset. Hell, *he* had been upset. Even Helena had been disturbed, and Helena knew that "appreciation" had a double meaning. To the people who had loved Nathaniel Brantford, the possessions that had once filled the President's house had become the last remnant of his presence. Considering them in terms of cash profaned the man's memory.

He couldn't be wrong. So far as Letty was concerned, her bequest was only a gesture—whether of conciliation or of triumph, who could say? There was the irony of which no one was conscious but himself. Letty Hendrickson had left Mather College one of the largest collegiate legacies in Massachusetts history without knowing what she did.

Father, forgive them... But wasn't fourteen years of forgiveness, of enduring political compromise, of ignoring personal rumors— wasn't that enough? Apparently not. The need for forgiveness was fated to dog the rest of his life. Well, that was one less relief to feel guilty about.

Oh, Letty, Letty, Letty.

"I leave to my husband, Joel T. Hendrickson, any and all real estate left to me as a beneficiary of the Ward Trust." The Ward Trust, it materialized, was an investment in Vermont ski country land. All the young lawyer at Smith and Sons knew was that it had been drawn up four years before their marriage, presumably by the part of her family she'd never talked about. Like everything else connected to her pre-Nathaniel past, it had been obliterated from her consciousness until, after thirty-two years, legal necessity had resurrected it in all its appreciation or degeneration (depending upon your point of view). And she had left it to him.

Jesus H. Christ. Hadn't she'd realized how that would look? *Everything she cared about to Nathaniel's college, and only a stray investment to Joel. We always **said** Nathaniel was first in her heart. Poor old Joel. Let's make him a casserole.*

That was unfair. Businesslike people—Helena, David—doubtless thought that she had left him the land (which was surprisingly near their summer places) as a recompense for the loss of Nathaniel's possessions. It was a point Helena would probably suggest when she came to visit him this evening, and for reasons of his own, he wouldn't argue. But the Letty who had been unaware of the true value of Nathaniel's estate would hardly have checked into the value of the Ward Trust. No, the second clause in her will was at best an afterthought, at worst...

He wouldn't think of that now. Instead, he would try to think positively about David and Helena's plan to get him out of Whitby, Massachusetts to Draper, Vermont during the time Sotheby's removed Nathaniel's possessions from his house. It was a kind thought, one that would save him a world of sympathy—and the sight of colleagues, friends, and neighbors who just happened to be passing by when the van arrived.

For of course everything would be sold. The resulting cash would be the salvation of the college. New buildings. New academic fields, with new young professors to teach them. Computers, not just for the staff, but for the library, which needed the digital catalogue every major university would soon have installed. The Revolution, decades in arrears, just as a new wave of technology broke over their heads. It was good. He had no complaints. For godsake, even in his present stunned state he hadn't sunk to greed. And if, facing the prospect of going to a state he'd never set foot in to appraise a piece of property whose very existence humiliated him, facing the prospect of returning to a house denuded not only of his wife but of the furniture, books, and pictures he had treasured for fourteen years, he felt dispossessed...well, as his friends would say, that was perfectly normal.

1. Introductions

J oel leaned against the doorjamb of the living room, looking across the boxes at the renaissance chair Helena Woodhouse had been sitting in the evening after the funeral. Nathaniel had used it as a desk chair, and even now it was haunted by the shade of the man himself, bent over the book before him, his fingers delicately touching the pages. Helena must have been as conscious of the memory as he was; in all the years she had seen the chair in this room, she had never sat in it. But she had chosen it that evening, and when he looked at it now, he saw her shade superimposed on Nathaniel's, her silver crown of braids rising barely to his shoulders, but her habitual refined detachment, as always, making her presence larger than herself.

Until you see it, she had said, *it will be only a clause in a will.*

At the time, he had considered the remark only in its obvious economic context: a tour of his property would enable him to get some sense of its value and decide how to market it. But recently he had realized that the message she had called up Nathaniel's ghost to deliver had a subtext. Come to think of it, the same text had possibly lurked behind David's words when he'd called yesterday morning to confirm arrangements. *You'll be staying in a scholar's paradise—overrun with books. Heard of Robert Randall? Right, the classicist. Well, Eleanor Klimowski's professional name is Eleanor Randall. She's Randall's daughter, and the room you're renting is in Randall's old summer place. The real thing. Not one of the ten-acre "vacation" parcels that are turning Vermont into a forest of second growth and second homes: a farmhouse, fields, woods. Part of the landscape.*

Part of the landscape. There it was. To sell Vermont land, either as a whole or in ten-acre parcels, was to replace the summer estates created by the great humanistic generation of Nathaniel Brantford and Robert Randall by "developing" the pastoral countryside they had preserved. To collaborate further, in other words…

No, he was letting guilt make him unfair. David shared Helena's lack of sentimentality in business matters—which was undoubtedly why she had had gotten him onto the Board of Trustees. There was probably nothing more behind their remarks about Vermont real estate than their regret for the passing of another tradition.

He stood up straight and checked his watch. Almost eleven. He'd better close the windows. The plane David was meeting came into Logan at nine o'clock, and he and his friend were due to swing by "on the way" to Draper at any minute. He paused, listening, as a car came around the corner. False alarm: David wouldn't drive the Jaguar fifty yards with its muffler dragging. This sounded more like a new suitor for the neighbor's daughter, and if so, one with a considerable chance of success. Most of her knights still arrived by skateboard; no doubt their charms would look paltry indeed to a maid who could have an older man of, say, sixteen. He smiled as the car back-fired into silence nearby. At nearly forty years past sixteen, one could afford to be amused.

Upstairs, he threaded his way to the bedroom window between the boxes that flanked the emptied highboy and armoire, closing out the familiar sounds of lawn mowers, children's voices, and distant traffic. One hundred fifty acres. The Ward Trust. He wandered down the hall to Letty's room and paused, letting his gaze rise slowly from her stripped canopy bed to the Chippendale mirror over her dressing table. Gradually, Letty's face, its bone structure still exquisite in spite of the ravages of chemotherapy, appeared in the wavering glass, looking anxiously at itself with an expression that dissolved into years of conversations, opinions, queries, evasions. Evasions. He crossed the hall to the guest room, dusted the Whitby grit off the empty renaissance chest, and reached for the window behind it.

The thump of the closing sash mingled with a long, familiar jangle. He ran down the stairs and wrenched the front door open. "Hello, Dav—"

But it wasn't David. It was a girl so beautiful that for a moment he thought she was a creation of his overtaxed mind. Or maybe—he gazed at her, transfixed—maybe a goddess. One needed only to imagine a shell beneath the sandaled feet, the beautifully curved calves, the slender, muscular thighs that rose into shorts that began just at the level of her hands, both of which were slightly grubby. Smiling a little at the detail, he looked up past the graceful, virginal hips, the soft breasts chastely covered by an embroidered tank top, the hooped silver earrings that dangled on both sides of the perfect neck, to the face. And there his gaze stopped, ashamed. For the hazel eyes that met his own were completely devoid of the coquettishness that characterized the modern-day goddesses on the covers of supermarket magazines. There was nothing in them but intelligence and straightforward friendliness.

"Dr. Hendrickson?"

Like her eyes, her voice and manner were far more deferential than her beauty would have led him to expect. A colleague's grown-up daughter? A student's girlfriend? "That's right."

The girl gave him a lovely smile. "I'm Charlotte Reynolds, David's daughter. Logan was socked in this morning, and the plane David was meeting was rerouted to Hartford. So he asked me if I could come get you instead."

Socked in. On a perfect day in May? "Oh, that's very kind of him—and of you."

15

"No problem! I'm just sorry to spring it on you like this. But the whole thing crashed on us about seven this morning, and we didn't want to wake you." She glanced over her shoulder. "Otherwise I'd have warned you you'd have to make the trip in a rust spot with wheels, not the Jag. I hope you're not terribly disappointed."

He was, a little; David's Jaguar was a beautiful machine. But as he looked past the girl at the Toyota that huddled next to the curb, he found himself smiling. "It's the wheels that count," he said. "Besides, student cars are exciting in their own way."

"A student car? I'd always thought of it as a mutation, not one of a species. But it certainly has its excitements, as you probably heard when I drove up. The hanger on its muffler broke just before I turned the corner. That's why my hands look like this; I was trying to fix it, but it was too hot."

Wonderful. There was nothing he liked better than crawling around under an old car just before a trip. "Okay, just let me change, and I'll see what I—"

"—No way!" The chestnut hair swished over her bare shoulders as she shook her head. "Once it's cool, I can fix it in a jif if you have a piece of wire."

He pushed away the temptation of suggesting that her earrings, unwound, would do the job nicely. "I might," he said. "Let's take a look." He led the way into the kitchen and opened the everything drawer. "How about picture wire? It's heavy gauge."

She tested it. "Hey, this is terrific! Much more flexible than electric fence wire."

"Delighted to be of service. Need pliers?"

"No thanks. They're standard equipment in student cars. But—" she looked down at her tank top and shorts— "if you had a tarp or something I could lie on, that would be great."

The obvious jocular answer was coarse, so—somehow unable to think of another—he fetched her the doormat from the back porch in silence.

"Awesome!" She gave him another lovely smile and disappeared down the hall.

16

Charlotte Reynolds. David's daughter. He strolled to the front door and watched as half her exquisite body disappeared under the car. She certainly made up for the absence of the Jag. And quite apart from her loveliness, it would be a relief not to spend the journey chatting with David, who would have insisted on regaling both his passengers with a blow-by-blow account of the trustees' reaction to Letty's legacy. In his present mood, any subject this girl might choose was preferable, and surely, she'd have lots to say. With her forthright competence, she was exactly the kind of woman Nathaniel Brantford had hoped to bring to Mather twenty years ago, and would have, if Letty had only—but that was over now. Within the next year or two Mather could attract many girls like Charlotte Reynolds. Meanwhile, her company would provide insight into the workings of the Contemporary Female Mind—a badly needed lesson, since the last young women he had talked to at length had been the artificially deferential creatures with whom he had endured Fifties mixers at Yale. With luck, the experience would cure him of the disgraceful sexism with which he'd looked—Good heavens, she'd gotten it on, in 'a jif,' just as she'd promised. He hurried upstairs and collected his suitcase, smiling with a weariness he wished he didn't feel. Three hours in a rust spot with wheels. God help the poor girl: sexism aside, the part of him that had conversed effortlessly with students for years was in the same shape as her muffler.

Charlotte was emerging from the kitchen when he came down, drying her hands on her shorts. "All set," she said, pulling the wire out of her back pocket and handing it to him. "At least I think it is. I couldn't get it to hang just right—the whochicky is beginning to rust."

There was still, it seemed, such a thing as a woman's ear for terminology. "Hm. Maybe we should take the wire with us, so you can perform further surgery if the whochicky fails us."

She glanced up but decided not to risk a smile. "Oh, thanks a lot."

"Don't mention it," he said, deadpan, enjoying her perplexity. He could tease her a little, then; that was something. He looked around the silent house. "Well, shall we go?"

"Sure. Only…if you don't mind…" she glanced at him awkwardly. "When we were down here for Commencement last week, Helena said the stuff your wife had left to the College was very beautiful. I was just wondering if I could take a quick look."

"Of course." He gestured to the living room, and she walked slowly through, admiring Nathaniel's chair and its companions, stopping appreciatively in front of the Picasso, smiling at the little Duchamp study. He followed her, pulling down the shades. In the dining room, she touched the Louis XIII table almost reverently, then looked over the six matching carved chairs to the sideboard. But she said nothing, and when they returned to the hall, she reached for his suitcase with an expression he couldn't quite interpret. "I'll load this into the car while you lock up, if you'd like."

He let her take it, since she seemed to want to. When she was gone, he checked the bolt on the back door, walked through the darkened dining room to his study, and looked at the beautifully-bound volumes that awaited Sotheby's special packing. Caxton's *Golden Legend*. Erasmus's *Adagia*. The First Folio. Spenser, Milton, Sir Thomas Browne. Each had long grown intimate with the location in which he had reverently put it years ago; by now, they'd become so much a part of his being that he could lay a hand on any one of them without hesitation and open it to a desired passage. Yet there they were, unaffected by the changes of the past weeks, indifferent to the upheavals of the coming two. Would he could be the same. He surveyed them one last time, then collected his tweed jacket off the newel post, locked the front door, and walked down the steps without looking back.

The girl was leaning against her car, apparently absorbed by the scolding of two squirrels who were chasing each other around a tree. Looking at her silent, purposely-turned face, he was suddenly touched. He would not have expected to find such tact in David Reynolds' daughter.

18

Eleanor vaulted over the stone wall and pushed through the blackberry canes between her and the old logging road. It must be nearly six, and David had promised to deliver Joel to her house at five-thirty, after a late lunch at his place. She really should have called. If only she weren't so useless on a pay phone…if only she weren't too proud to ask the guys at the garage to phone for her… On the other hand, she would only be a few more minutes, and she'd put the old wooden chairs out on the lawn, so there was a place for them to sit. And if she was sweaty and scratched when she met Joel Hendrickson, well, he was supposed to be a forgiving man.

She ran down the old road at a good clip, smiling at the apple blossoms at the edge of the woods. It was going to be a good year. Maybe she should celebrate it by learning some forgiveness herself. The Ward Trust had always been peculiar, and the Ward Place, with its mountain views and lake frontage, must be worth over a million bucks. It was absurd to expect a man whose wife had left all their furniture—even their car—to the College not to sell it.

The other night, Charlie had argued that he wasn't the sort of man who did that. And David (after pointing out that her opinion was based on one look across an open grave) had agreed. Any man who had lovingly kept up the Great Nathaniel's '36 Dodge for fourteen years instead of trading it in on something more practical cared about the past. That *was* promising, but surely it was a matter of personal commitment. He had no commitment to the Ward Place; so far as he was concerned it was just a piece of property. *Her* affection for Mary Ward and her farm had no effect on the way *he* perceived its value. She would have be forgiving as she watched him sell it off.

And he might be easy to forgive. *Not bad looking, if you go for that sort of looks*, David had admitted judiciously. *A Roman god who's let himself slide a bit.* The qualification suggested a fortunate absence of the god's-gift-to-woman assurance that had to be forgiven in most good-looking men (David included). What was the phrase Charlie had used? Darn. Without Hattie to repeat things, the simple act of hearing took such effort that it eclipsed her memory of what people said. But all that was secondary. The real stunner was who he was. It shouldn't have been; there was no way David could *not* have mentioned that the "Joel" of David's Letty Hendrickson horror stories was J.T. Hendrickson, the great critic of Spenser and Milton. The fact lent the stories too much zest. But she'd missed it, and along with it the possibility that a certain academic envy might lurk behind David's narrative voice. Because whatever Joel's relationship with his wife, his books were brilliant. No vapid theory masked in incomprehensible prose. No tortured readings. Absolutely lucid. Full command of new philosophy and traditional historical and literary research. It would be small not to forgive a man for selling the Ward Place when his intellectual achievement was as rare as Caxton's *Golden Legend*.

She turned off the road on to the narrow path that led into her mowing—and stopped, staring, at the top of the first hill. Derri, whom she had carefully shut into the barn, was bounding through the grass halfway between her and the house, a few yards from a solitary man who was leaning over to pick up a stick. Not David; David would never wear a sportcoat up here, and besides, he and Derri tolerated each other only out of mutual affection for her. She watched as the stick left the man's hand in a long, graceful arc. It must be Mather College's Roman god, complete with latter-day discus—but where was David?

As she moved left to look for the Jag, Derri caught sight of her and streaked up the mowing, barking. Turning, the man shouted and started after him at a run, but his chivalry was unnecessary; after two hundred noisy yards, the dog recognized her and subsided into a series of embarrassed sneezes. She returned his shame-faced welcome, then hurried down the field to meet her guest. He was panting; it had evidently been a while since he'd put that long distance runner's stride to work. But you could hardly say he'd let himself slide, for heaven's sake.

"Sorry we worried you," she said, twenty feet before she had a hope of hearing a reply. "Derri didn't expect me from this direction."

He smiled and extended a hand, saying something gracious that included "Joel Hendrickson" and her own name.

She took the hand, noting it was softer than her own. "Yes, I'm

Eleanor. I meant to be here when you arrived, but my car got a new water pump today, and when I went to collect it, the guys at the garage had found a suspension problem they didn't have time to investigate until tomorrow morning. So I had to take the shortcut home."

He said something that inexplicably included "jinx," but instead of trying to decipher it, she reflected that David needed an art history lesson. No Roman god, this. The face was right out of Titian. A study for a Christ on the cross, maybe, or for one of those portraits of aristocrats whose pensive expressions undercut their aura of virtu. Amazing, seeing that kind of sadness off a canvas. But he was waiting for a reply.

"I'm surprised you managed to let Derri out of the barn," she said, as the dog trotted up to them with a hopeful stick. "He usually doesn't cotton to strangers."

"I didn't let him out." He threw the stick in a long, easy motion as they started down the mowing together. "David's daughter *mxmx* school her horse *mxmx* left hours ago *mxmx* but showed *mxmx* room and introduced Derri. *Mxmx mxmx* read *mxmx* wonderful library. But *mxmx* beautiful evening *mxmx* take a walk."

Charlie had brought him here? Hours ago? How on earth? No doubt he'd explained it, but it was excruciating to make people repeat things. Better to let it ride for now and respond to the only sentence she'd understood. "So you like Vermont, do you?"

As she looked up to see his reply, she caught the familiar expression of perplexity that told her that the bulk of what he'd said had warranted a response far different from the one she'd given. God, she was such an idiot.

"*Mxmx* very beautiful," he said. "*Mxmx* hadn't realized *mxmx* so many different shades of green." He smiled and added something about Calidore and Mount Alcidale.

A literate reply flew to her lips, but she silenced it and merely nodded. If she replied, he would. And she'd be hopelessly lost.

Joel stopped as they reached the yard and studied the house. "David told me *mxmx* your father *mxmx* Robert Randall *mxmx* classicist *mxmx* this place."

She put the statement together and answered cautiously. "Yes, he bought it in the Fifties; it was run down, but we fixed it up, planted the garden, and mowed the fields."

"*Mxmx* georgic preoccupation," he said, smiling. "I'm very fond of his book."

Fond. It was a peculiar word to apply to a scholarly treatise on the *Georgics*, but her father would have been delighted. As for herself, back in the days when conversation had been a pleasure (not to mention, a possibility), she would have enjoyed talking to this man. As it was— "You'll want meals as well as the room, won't you?"

There was no mistaking the surprise in his face this time. And who could blame him? She'd responded to what she was thinking, not to what he'd said. She stooped down to tie her shoe so he wouldn't see her wince.

"Just breakfast and supper. *Mxmx* fend for myself. *Mxmx* pay you now?"

All the warmth had gone from his voice, and as if that weren't bad enough, she had to think before she understood what he'd said. God. Forget intellectual conversation; she could barely negotiate a contract with a tenant. And when she could no longer manage that, what would she do? "It can wait. Write out what you want to eat, and I'll figure everything up." She forced herself to smile. "I'll get supper soon. Just give me a few minutes to get cleaned up."

"Don't *mxmx* on my account. *Mxmx* happy," he said, reaching for the doorknob of the east wing.

'Happy' was the last adjective she would have chosen, but this was no time to prolong their mutual embarrassment by playing with words. "I'll call you when it's ready," she said hastily, and fled, shooing Derri into the kitchen. Inside, the dog looked at her with an anxiety that irritated her. All right, she was upset, but he needn't advertise it. Especially after he'd sucked up to a stranger with only Charlie's introduction. Whatever Charlie had been doing here.

And when she could no longer manage—? She couldn't manage *now*. It wasn't just a matter of not listening carefully. Joel had told her how he'd gotten to her house, just as David's stories had said who Joel was. In spite of her friends' efforts to protect her from the knowledge, she was no longer a participant in the world about her. Without Hattie's assistance, she was just an observer of events that came and went without explanation. Well, in a way it would be a relief to stop fighting. After Joel Hendrickson left, she could just take out the damn aids and clean houses for the rest of her life. It wouldn't be so bad. There was Hattie's glorious scholarship and all it promised. There was the farm—what was left of it. And the dog and cat. And the hope that the rest of her life wouldn't last too long.

Oh, for Pete's sake. Was she really going to let herself despair like this over a few awkward moments? Humiliation was just an adjunct of deafness: repetition, confusion, misinterpretation came with the territory. All she had to do was tough it out, and she could manage Joel Hendrickson's tenancy fine. She took a quick shower, put on clean jeans and a decent sweater, and hurried back into the kitchen. There was nothing in the refrigerator but the basic ingredients of a vegetarian spaghetti sauce; she'd planned to go shopping on her way home. But it would be a good sauce, and as for the rest of the meal, there was the bread she'd made last night, some decent cheese, and the rest of the rhubarb pie she'd made for David and Charlie.

When everything was ready, she set the table, then stopped and looked at it. She had laid it for two, since he was really a guest, not a kitchen-privilege tenant. But if he and she ate together, she would have to watch every gesture, every lip movement, every expression of politely concealed annoyance as she asked him to repeat unreadable words over and over. She took out one of the places and went to call him, praying that he would be clothed and awake.

He was both. But though he was sitting in the leather chair with an open book, he wasn't reading; he was staring out the window. She moved slightly, hoping to attract his attention without startling him. "Joel?"

He turned his head; and in the moment before he comprehended who she was, his face was so full of pain that she could hardly bear to look at it. A Job face. *That* was the phrase Charlie had used. A face of suffering.

"Supper's ready."

"Oh, thank you." He closed the book, but he didn't stand up. *"Mxmx* right there."

She went back to the kitchen and dumped the spaghetti in the colander. Maybe she should eat with him. It would be good for him to talk. All she'd have to do was look attentive and draw him on, a technique that didn't require hearing. And the friendly gesture might assure him of her sympathy, which was certainly real enough.

She turned to the silverware drawer to reset her place, and startled as she saw him standing in the door. She hadn't heard it open? She checked behind her ears. Yes, both aids were turned on. Sometime in the last few months, she must have lost the ability to hear sound behind her. She pushed the drawer shut. "Here you go. The spaghetti's in here, the sauce is there. The bread and cheese are on the table, and there's pie up here in the cupboard."

He looked from her to the single place. *"Mxmx* you *mxmx* eat?"

No, it was impossible. "I've eaten, thanks. But let me know if you need anything."

He looked as if he were going to protest, so she called Derri and escaped upstairs. Some busy sound would be convincing; she booted up her computer and began to type. *Dear Hattie: So you have been passed up the ladder to the Grand Old Man! The news had Charlie and me dancing in streets.* It had come to this. She couldn't even help a sensitive man who was devastated by his wife's death. *Across the road, they cut down the Pilgrim Maple...*

When she tiptoed downstairs half an hour later, his solitary plate was sitting in the dish rack, dripping. So were the spaghetti pan, the saucepan and the colander. Pulling out a chair softly, she sat down at the carefully-wiped table and cried.

2. A Trust

Joel blinked slowly awake and looked up through mote-filled shafts of sunlight at thousands of books. Not his books. Not his room. He half sat up, then remembered: Eleanor Randall Klimowski's East Wing. He clasped his arms behind his head and lay back, surveying it.

Letty would have said it was shabby, and she would have been right. The worn Caucasian rug had been tucked back under itself on the far side of the ell; the curtains were as faded as the unframed prints thumbtacked into the wall; the arms on the deep leather chair were worn nearly white; and the roll-top desk had needed refinishing for half a century. But its shabbiness was the result of intimacy, not neglect, a sort of annotation, as if the Randalls had left part of themselves in their library the way they'd left their marginalia in their books. The atmosphere permitted a privacy and peace he had long forgotten. It had been years since he'd slept straight through a night, and the sun was not usually this high when he awoke.

Swinging his feet out of bed, he picked up his watch and saw that it was well past nine. He shaved quickly and hurried into the kitchen with an apology on his lips, but none was necessary. His place was laid, and a village of brown muffins was waiting by the stove, but except for the huge yellow cat curled up on a sun-lit kitchen chair, the room was empty. He poured himself a cup of coffee from the waiting thermos and transported it and two of the muffins to the table. There was a note on the plate, written in a gracefully indecipherable hand. Slipping on his reading glasses, he started to puzzle it out. *Derri's in the barn. You can let him out if you want company, but please don't take him if you go see your place; the contractor across the road is afraid of him.*

No surprise there, given the way Derri had reacted to him before Charlie's introduction had converted protectiveness to aloof acceptance, but it would be sad to leave such a magnificent animal languishing in the barn. When he got back, he'd make amends by taking a stick-chasing stroll in the other direction. He smiled at the thought, then at the cat, who had jumped down from its chair and was sniffing his knees. Derri-dog and Fou-cat: apparently, Eleanor didn't think much of post-structuralism. Readjusting his legs as Fou leapt into his lap, he returned to his paleographical excursion. *I'll shop this afternoon; leave a list of things you like to eat. Rent for May 24–June 7, $100 plus whatever food comes to. No hurry. Eleanor.*

May 24–June 7—*how* much? He held the paper a little further from his eyes, scrutinizing the number again. The first digit was almost certainly a one. Incredible. In Whitby, $50 a week wouldn't pay for a fifth floor walk-up in the part of town where nobody dared to walk. He looked up from the note to the insistent yellow dandelions that punctuated the fields outside. She could charge three times as much for that wonderful lair of books, shabby or not.

So why didn't she? She certainly didn't want company; every movement she made in his presence indicated how much she'd rather be alone. *I've eaten, thanks. Leave a list.* As if the very prospect of conversation scared her off. Peculiar. One had to look no further than the library to see breadth of interest, no further than the dog and cat to detect wit, no further than Charlie's laconic account of summer life with David to detect years of quasi-maternal support extended to a daughter's best friend. From such a person, one would have expected…well, it wasn't his place to speculate. He lifted Fou off his lap, washed his dishes, and stepped out into the sunshine.

The walk to his property was not the quiet stroll he'd envisaged when Charlie had pointed out the path that started across the road. For one thing, though the rise across the way hardly qualified as a hill, it winded him, just as his two hundred yard dash after Derri had winded him yesterday evening. Vermont apparently had little sympathy for ex-cross-country stars who had given up running at fifty. Beyond that, though, when he reached the top of the rise and looked about him, he was no longer in the country. The mountains still loomed in the distance, but the foreground had been bulldozed into suburban conformity, only the muddy remnants of walls and piles of charred tree roots attesting to its former identity. The very air was citified, filled with the sound and smell of machinery. He sighed as he thought of the obliterated georgic past. Even if the grieving shade of Robert Randall called on Athena to stop the construction of the three houses Charlie said were soon to be built, it would be decades before the land was fruitful again.

He crossed the barren plot and started down a bulldozer track into the woods. The noise of machinery grew louder as he progressed, and after a few minutes he emerged, blinking, in a clearing. On the side nearest him, a burly white-haired man looked up from the felled maple he was limbing and shut off his saw.

"Morning. You Joel Hendrickson?"

"Why—yes."

The man smiled. "Ray Walker," he said. "Charlie Reynolds rides at our place down the road. She said you'd probably be along, and since we've wiped out the path to the Ward Place since last time she was here, I figured I'd better stick around."

Joel looked at the chaos of fallen trees ahead of him. "That's very kind. I would certainly have been lost on my own."

Ray shrugged. "Have to mark out a new path anyway, and I'd rather do this kind of work than the big-time felling they're doing up on the ridge." He pulled a roll of luminous orange streamer out of his back pocket and started into the woods. "Hate to see the Randall Place being carved up like this," he said, tying a length around a spruce branch. "It'd been in the family a long time, and it meant a lot to Eleanor. She talk to you about it yesterday?"

"We hardly talked at all—just settled some details about the rent."

Ray shook his head. "I keep trying to tell her, if she'd just let on she was deaf, people'd help her out, but—"

"—Deaf!"

"Yup. Can't remember the condition's fancy name, but her hearing nerves die off a few at a time. That's why she lives up here full time, now. Five or six years back, the college she taught at said 'no hear, no job.'" He shook his head. "Real tough."

Real tough. The end of a job; the end of teaching. If it had happened to him, it would have been the end of life.

"It's not all that hard to talk to her, though," said Ray. "You just have to remember to look at her right in the face, so she can see what you say. Makes you think, when you realize how much you don't look at folks you talk to, usually." He looked back over his shoulder as they skirted a degenerating stone wall. "Like now."

Or like last night, when he'd looked at the view, the house, the dog—at everything but Eleanor. Come to think of it, he could hardly remember what she looked like, beyond an impression of a slim, vigorous figure, a face no longer young, and gray eyes that somehow refused access. "I wish I'd known that."

Ray shrugged. "Might not have helped. These days, with new people, she just skitters away. And even with people she knows, if you yell, or look peeved because she didn't get something, she sort of curls up. Worth getting to know, though, if you got the patience. There's not many people with that much to them." He tied a final streamer around a branch and followed the wall out of the woods. "Coming back, all you need to do is follow the wall and you'll— Hey, there's Charlie."

Joel looked where he pointed; not too far away, a horse and rider were trotting along some kind of track. The horse startled as Ray let out an ear-splitting whistle; Charlie steadied it, then waited while they fought their way through the hard-hack and choke cherries.

"Bush-whacking," she said as they stumbled out on the path. "Never know what you'll take up next, Ray."

"Smart aleck," said Ray. "You'd have been bush-whacking yourself in a few yards if you'd kept on." He pointed up the trail; near its top a huge hemlock swayed, creaked, then disappeared with a crash that made the horse snort.

Charlie stared at Ray. "They're taking down the *hemlock* grove?"

" 'Fraid so. There's going to be a house above it, and the trees block the view. They probably won't take them all—Colleen Rickerts is doing it, and she knows new places sell better if you leave a few old trees. But they're cutting where the trail was, so we had to make a new one. I got streamers up now, but I'll have to run through with a brush hog and saw before you can ride it, so you'll have to turn around. Maybe you could show Mr. Hendrickson his place while I get back to work."

Charlie looked anxiously at Joel. "That okay with you?"

He smiled. "Fine. You trot, I'll follow your tracks."

"Okay, then," said Ray, chuckling. "I'd better get going. Glad to've met you. Come down to our place after work some day. There's always a cold beer."

"Thank you," said Joel automatically; but when he looked at Ray's sunburned face, he realized the offer was genuine. He was suddenly, unaccountably pleased. "I'd like that."

"Yeah? Make it about five tomorrow, then," said Ray. "Charlie teaches this horse to dance at about that time, and it's kind of interesting watching her try." He grinned at Charlie and pushed back through the brush.

"Isn't he great?" she said, as they watched him disappear into the trees.

Joel nodded. *There's always a cold beer.* Strange how the phrase implied a sort of masculine companionship: Monday night football, meaty sandwiches, comfortable conversation about cars, sports, women. It was half the world of his adolescence, and one he still occasionally missed—for its certainties, if nothing else.

"So," he said as they walked back the way she had come, "you board your handsome fellow with Ray and his wife?"

"He's not my handsome fellow," she said. "He belongs to a syndicate that buys and sells horses ordinary mortals can't afford. My job is to turn him into a major league eventer—which I'm doing partly by letting him see the world outside a suburban paddock. It's a bit of a shock to him, but he's pretty steady for a guy his age." She smiled. "Think you could open the gate?"

He examined the two electrified strands that crossed the gap in the wall before them. It seemed that he should unhook the plastic handles from the wire loops.

"Thanks," she said, riding through. "And welcome home."

He looked down the rocky pasture to the smoother, south-facing fields that rolled towards a distant grove of maples. A hawk burst out of the trees, coasting over the fields and rising into the cloudless sky; he watched it float in circles above the mountains, then let his eyes drop gradually to the still surface of the lake that lay at their feet. Behind him, the machinery had stopped, and everything was perfectly quiet. "This is...mine?"

She nodded. "Just about everything you can see this side of the lake. Your land ends at the road on this side of it—see it down there?—and at the far side of the sugar grove over there, at this fence, and at a stream somewhere in those spruces. The house is at the end of the mowing, behind that little hill."

The house. Good God. He'd had no idea there would be a house.

"Would you like me to introduce you to the Wards on the way down?"

Again, his ignorance. "The Wards?"

She smiled. "The Ward family owned this place until 1959. They're still here, resting peacefully inside their stone wall." She pointed to a family graveyard a little way to their left. "Want to see?"

He looked from the weather-bleached stones to the mountains, seeing in a double image the iron fence of the Whitby cemetery and the maze of roads that led past crowded graves to the plot where Letty lay in the shade of Nathaniel's monument. "Sure."

Charlie started the horse towards it. "It's a wonderful graveyard," she said over her shoulder. "Not just because of where it is, but because of the Wards. When we were kids, Hattie and I used to sit here for hours, working out their history from the graves. Some of what we worked out is even accurate; Eleanor got us other information where she could."

He looked over the beautifully built dry-stone wall into the plot, noticing with a pang of sadness the care with which it had been kept up. To somebody, evidently, the Ward Place was much more than a clause in a will. He turned to ask Charlie if she had done the work, but she was busy trying to tie the fretting horse.

"Guess I'll have to perform the introductions from out here," she said, after two unsuccessful attempts. "Cocoa, here, had never seen cows before this morning, and we met the whole herd on our way up the hill. I'm afraid he hasn't forgotten."

"Cows?" Joel looked around.

"You look just the way Cocoa did," said Charlie, grinning. "Sure. Mr. Wolfington always puts heifers here in mid-May. But they won't bother us; they're pretty shy. Okay, go through the gate and start over there in the corner. The stones you can hardly read belong to the first Wards, who cut down the trees and started the farm in the early 1800s. Their son Robert—over there—built the house in around 1840, and his son—Henry Ward, with the big stone—was a Town Father in the 1870s and '80s. Late in life he married Alice Boyd and had two sons. She was lots younger than he was, and after he died in 1890, she ran the farm — not to mention, the sons—until she died in 1911. The older son, Henry, seems to have escaped matriarchal tyranny by leaving the farm as soon as he could; but the second son, Robert, waited patiently, inherited the farm at 31, and— get this—married Mary Bartlett within months of his mother's funeral."

Joel surveyed Alice Ward's unoffending stone with some compassion. It was on the tip of his tongue to say that neither son's action was necessarily proof of maternal tyranny in an age when the only road to advancement lay away from rocky hillsides, and when no farmer married until he could support a wife. But it seemed a shame to interrupt the vigor of the narrative. "And so," he asked, "did Robert and Mary enjoy a long era of post-matriarchal bliss?"

"No such luck. Look over there."

He walked obediently to three little gravestones that rose out of the violets.

Robert Ward II: 1913–1918
Henry Ward: 1915–1918
Peter Ward: 1917–1918

"Robert died in 1918, too," said Charlie. "There was a flu epidemic that year, and they all got it. At least, that's what Mary Ward told Eleanor."

He felt as if he'd been catapulted into the present. *"Eleanor* knew Mary Ward?"

"Sure." Charlie pointed to the newest of the graves. "Mary Ward didn't die until Eleanor was thirteen. They were very close, in that funny way kids get with old folks. I guess she was really special. Eleanor says she was beautiful even when she was old, and dignified— though you have to wonder where that dignity came from."

"Well," he hazarded, "at the turn of the century you could still speak of yeoman aristocracy."

"Oh, sure you could! And the Wards were definitely members of it. But Mary wasn't. Her father was the Draper Rake. Handsome, I guess, but so wild when he was drunk none of the local girls would have him. So he married a sixteen-year-old mill girl named Clara Rogan, and gradually sank from rakishness to steady inebriation, while *she* had a baby every year and supported the family by making dresses for the respectable women in town. Knowing the Rake, they paid only half the money to Clara, and gave the other half to the general store. Mary told Eleanor she and her brothers used to stop by the store on their way to school, eat breakfast, and change into decent clothes. But Clara died having her eighth baby, and since Mary was the oldest and the only girl, she dropped out of school and took care of the others."

He shook his head. "And with a background like that, she ran a farm single-handed for forty years?"

"Not all of that time. Two of her brothers helped her until the war. But by the time Eleanor's family got here in the early fifties, one brother had died, the other had left, and Mary had shut out the world. See, her daughter Clara—her one surviving child—died of appendicitis in 1943. Shouldn't they have been able to fix that, even then?"

"If they got to it fast enough," he said. Which they hadn't, in his mother's case. "Is Clara Ward buried here, too?"

"Right over there." She pointed.

"What did she do to deserve the brambles on her grave?" he asked, smiling. "Besmirch the family honor?"

Charlie looked at him indignantly. "They're not brambles; they're roses!" Her face softened. "I suppose they don't look like much now. The only roses that can survive in Vermont are the kind with fierce thorns. But when they bloom, they're gorgeous."

"How did they get here?"

"Eleanor asked Mary that once, and Mary said to let the dead lie easy. Just like that. The end. So she never dared ask again. She told Hattie and me that when I was ten or so, and we promptly gave Clara a wildly grieving lover who planted roses by her grave and beat his head against the cold, hard stone." She looked at him sheepishly. "We were a bit gone on *Wuthering Heights* at the time. But last summer, when we were laughing over our story, we admitted we half believed it. You'll see why, when the roses bloom. They just *breathe* regret."

That he could believe, no matter who had planted them.

"Maybe we should get on down to the house," she said after a short silence. "Cocoa really shouldn't eat grass with his bit on."

The house. The house. "Sure." But as she tightened her girth and mounted, it was the graves that filled his mind. He looked back as he pushed the gate open. Alice. Mary. Clara. Letty couldn't possibly have been more different from the strong, solitary women who lay buried here. What—? How—?

"All set?"

Charlie was waiting for him. "All set," he said.

Charlie looked over her shoulder at Joel's pre-occupied face as Cocoa minced down the hill. His wife had been dead two weeks, and the first place she'd taken him was a graveyard. Not the most brilliant of moves. All that care *not* to talk to him about the Ward Place in the car, all that planning to show him the history of the place this morning so he would realize how important it was for him not to sell it—and she had blown it. Sighing, she dismounted and opened the gate into the yard. "Well, here we are."

Joel closed it behind him and looked at the house, first with surprise, then with an appraising eye she wouldn't have expected in a man who wore a sport jacket and Oxfords in the country. She slipped Cocoa's halter and lead-rope out of her waiting backpack, tied him to the ring she and Hattie had driven into the oldest maple tree, then took off her helmet and hurried to the lawn, shaking out her hair. "Well, what do you think?"

"I think it needs a coat of paint," he said mildly.

That was somewhat wanting, as a total reaction.

"But it's in a lot better shape than the barn," he went on. "That needs to be taken down immediately."

All of a sudden, she saw the Ward Place not as she knew it but as he saw it: a faded house with boarded-up first-floor windows and an ell of sagging sheds, standing next to a barn with half its south side gone and a caved-in roof of rusted metal sheeting. When its history, real or imagined, was taken away, there was very little left of it.

"You won't have any trouble with the barn," she said. "Ray'll know somebody who'll take it down in return for the beams and siding. That's what everyone else does with barns like this."

"Are there so many of them, then?"

"Oh, yeah. Some people who buy the land fix up the old places, but most of them want something more upscale, so they have them taken down. It's sad, but it's better than letting them fall down and get covered over in trees so nobody even knows they've been there. That happens faster than you think—only thirty years, Eleanor says, for a farm house nobody keeps up."

"Mmm. I would have said fifty for total collapse, though I suppose some of the old places weren't kept up well to begin with. In any case, unless my arithmetic fails me, this house has been empty for thirty-two years. That means, by Eleanor's reckoning, it should have fallen down entirely; by mine, it should be roughly in the same state the barn's in. But look at it."

She straightened her back. "It doesn't look so bad."

"That's my point. There's the paint, of course, and the roof, but a few jack posts would fix the porch, and the house itself seems pretty sound. It might even be possible to salvage the sheds, though you'd have to get in there to see."

"You sound like Ray," she said. "Where did you learn about fixing up old houses?"

"My father was chief groundsman at Exeter Academy," he said. "I grew up helping him repair elderly buildings. So I know an old house doesn't look like this unless somebody has kept it up. Who has kept this one up?"

Talk about embarrassment. Here she was posing as the expert on the Wards, and she couldn't answer this obvious, simple question. "Well, the Wolfingtons—they're the ones who put their heifers in the pasture—hay the mowing. Maybe they do a bit of upkeep in return. I'm sure Eleanor knows."

The expression on his face was unfathomable. Down at the end of the long driveway some crows cawed, and the sound of a car drifted up from the road. "Well," he said finally, "let's see if we can get in. I suppose it's not house-breaking if I own it."

She followed him up the steps, practically holding her breath.

He studied the door, then put his shoulder against it, turned its handle, and shoved. To her surprise—and his, obviously—it gave a little. Steadying himself with one hand on the wall, he placed a deft kick between the knob and the jamb, and it burst open in a squeal of hinges. He stood in its frame, staring. "My God," he said softly.

She peered around him and saw…amazing.

Opposite the door was an overstuffed brown sofa with three doilies on its back and two on its arms. There was a braided rug in front of it, and on the rug was a rocking chair with a dingy embroidered cushion. Between the sofa and the chair, a small table held a basket of rags and what might be a sewing box. On the other side of the sofa, a quilt-covered reclining couch pointed towards a Fifties television on a sagging wire stand; beyond that loomed a big Glenwood stove. And that was it, except for faded drapes, a framed picture of Niagara Falls that looked like it had been bought at some tourist shop, and a home-sweet-home calendar open to September 1959.

"Ho-ly shit," she whispered. "It must be just the way it was."

He nodded. "The executors must have assumed the heir would clear out the furniture."

Executors. Heirs. That was a pretty mundane explanation for what was like stepping into a time warp. But their presence didn't make things any less weird. Why *hadn't* the heir cleared the house out? He'd had thirty-two years. No, not "he"—"she." Joel's wife had inherited the house. So why hadn't she, or he—?

She drew a breath to ask, but he spoke first. "You really don't know who has been looking after this place?"

"I'm clueless," she said, trying to keep the indignation out of her voice. "Cross my heart."

"Of course, of course," he said hastily. "I just thought that as somebody local—"

"—Hold it, hold it, hold it! I'm not local."

"No?" His eyebrows rose.

"Absolutely, no. I'm a summer person. People like me float on top of a base of people like the Wolfingtons, who have lived here for generations. They accept us because we keep up the old places—which puts us in a very different category from skiers. But they're the real Draper, and when it comes to getting things done, they've got agreements that go way back, rules that everyone takes for granted, and you've got to be a *real* local to be in on it. Even Eleanor has only one foot in the circle, and that's only because she knew Mary Ward." She paused, conscious of the care with which he was listening. "It's... it's sort of complicated."

"Oh, yes," he said quietly. "But not altogether surprising, if I'd thought about it." Then, after a little silence, "Well, let's look around. Maybe we'll find a hammer, so we can take the boards off a window or two."

He led the way across the murky living room into the room beyond it. It seemed to have been a dining room, but Mary Ward had clearly used it for other things. The heavy-legged table was covered with dried-out harness and ancient tools, and the sideboard was heaped with sewing baskets, pattern books and scraps of material. Across the room, the wall was lined with shelving stuffed with medicine bottles, horse liniment, farmer's almanacs, Sears catalogues, and a tattered phone book that lay under a phone with no dial. She stared, so intrigued that she was barely aware that he had picked up a hammer from amongst the stuff on the shelving and was starting back on the far side of the table—until he tripped over something and nearly fell.

"You okay?" she said, hurrying forward.

"Of course," he said. Then, with all the irritation gone from his voice, "So that's what the hooks in the porch ceiling are for."

Peering into the dark corner beyond him, she saw an old porch swing, its chains carefully arranged so they wouldn't tangle. "Oh! Totally cool! All Eleanor's stories about Mary Ward begin or end in that swing—she sat on it every summer day."

She turned to him, which was fortunate, because one glance made her realize what a disaster it would be to ask if they could put it up. There was absolutely no room for pushiness here. *She* might be excited about exploring Mary Ward's house after all these years, but it didn't take a genius to see that *he* was upset. Not so much about the place itself as something else...wait. She thought back to Mather College and the post-trustee-meeting gathering at which David had led the college lawyer to the place Helena was sitting...and the shock in their faces when they found out where the Ward Trust land was. Like, Letty Hendrickson had owned property near theirs for *all these years*, and she'd *never told them*. Was it possible that she also hadn't told...? before she dared finish the thought, Joel pursed his lips and walked out to the porch. A moment later she heard the squawk of releasing nails—good God! Cocoa would have a fit! She dashed out onto the porch, but she stopped before she reached the steps. Cocoa was dozing in the shade, resting one hind leg and swishing his tail occasionally. A $250,000 three-day eventer, her mind whispered subversively, perfectly at home as a farm horse.

She thought of passing that little irony on to Joel, but—sport coat shed and sleeves rolled up—he was yanking the plywood off the windows with such efficient ferocity that she hesitated even to offer help. Better to leave him to his mood and do a little exploring. The way things looked, she might never get another chance.

She paused on the door sill, thinking of the years she and Hattie had sat on the porch, sensing—or at least imagining—the presence of silent generations of Wards moving from room to room without recognizing each other, their wispy lives playing over and over like a black and white video. This was just as weird in its way. She walked back into the dining room, feeling Mary Ward's continuing presence swirl around her. The workaday atmosphere was so...immediate. No dirt. No spiders. Everything patiently awaiting its owner's return. There was probably some rational reason for its neatness—but was it really rational to keep up a deserted house for thirty-two years? It made no more sense than believing the careful spirit who had set out the mending had spent all those dark days anxiously, silently tidying the house.

Another scream of nails from outside and a sudden flood of light rescued her from silly speculations, and she pushed open the door on the far side of the cluttered table. A kitchen, but not one of those old farm kitchens with a wood stove, pump, and bucket. Mary Ward had updated it, which in the Fifties meant installing green linoleum, a shallow enamel sink under hot and cold water taps that came out of the wall quite a distance above it, a coal and electric hybrid stove, and a period-piece 'fridge with rounded corners. Beyond that, where there had probably been a pantry, there was now a tiny bathroom with very basic fixtures—but you could bet they'd seemed pretty luxurious after a privy in the back shed.

She walked back through the museum-still furniture to the hall off the living room. There was a bedroom on its far side, its curtains carefully drawn. Beyond them, a squawk and a thump let in enough light to reveal another room awaiting its occupant: dark headboard, dark dresser, Bible, worn hooked rug, and stove. Shivering, she stepped back into the hall and climbed the narrow steps.

Up here, the atmosphere was different—and not just the stuffy upstairs air. Everything was still unnaturally clean, but obviously no one had lived here for years. The end of the hall was filled by a huge wardrobe. On the wall to its right, two narrow doors opened into bedrooms so small that each was practically filled by its stripped bed and dresser. The room on its left had been turned into a morgue for old furniture, but it had obviously been the master bedroom before Mary Ward had moved downstairs because of the climb and the cold. She raised its yellowed shades, then wrestled open a window and looked through the old maples at the mowing that sloped down to the lake and its protective mountains. Wow. If she'd been Mary Ward, she'd have braved both the stairs and the cold to live up here, no matter how old she'd been.

Below her, Joel suddenly appeared, carrying a piece of plywood down the front steps. He rested it against the others leaning on the porch railing, then walked a few paces out into the yard and looked back at the house. She couldn't quite see his expression, but he was no longer standing the terrible, tight way he had been downstairs, which had to be a good sign.

She leaned out the window. "Hey, come up here and take a look at your view!"

He waved and came quickly, his footsteps hurrying up the stairs. His enthusiasm, after he had ducked through the door and stooped to look out the window, was so genuine that she decided she could risk a positive comment. "Couldn't this be nice?"

"Lovely," he said, looking around. "But there has to be more."

"There is—across the hall."

He shook his head. "No, the other way. This room just covers the living room. There has to be one above the dining room." He surveyed the back wall, then stepped out into the hall. "Oh, I see. Back here."

She hurried out into the hall just in time to see him ease himself between the wardrobe and the wall. "Wait a sec," he said as she made to follow. "There's no room until I get the door open...there. Ugh!"

She slipped through the passage and found him standing near the door, clearing cobwebs out of his hair. "Oh, gross!"

He laughed. "This room's inhabitant isn't as meticulous as the others."

So it wasn't just her imagination. There really _were_ presences... well, if he could accept their existence in that matter-of-fact way, so could she. She followed him forward into the dusty gloom, stopping only when he reached the curtained windows.

"Mind if I do the honors?" he asked over his shoulder. "This will be messy."

"Be my guest," she said—and was instantly glad she'd said it. Because after he had opened the drapes with a practiced swoop that included jumping back, two thick mats of cobwebs tumbled out of the windows and subsided onto the floor in a mass of hysterical spiders.

She was about to make some crack about preferring her ghosts meticulous when a look around the room stopped her. Its walls were painted white, instead of being covered with the sentimental wallpaper in the rest of the house, and there was an interesting little desk in one corner. The bed had a brass frame, and it was covered with a dusty crocheted spread. And on the other side of the room, a beautiful rocking chair was stationed between a stenciled chest and a bookcase. Books. In _this_ house?

Looking up, she found that Joel was smiling at her quizzically. "You know the Wards better than I do," he said. "Whose room was this?"

"Well," she said, sorting the dates on the tombstones quickly in her mind, "it certainly wasn't Mary Ward's." He nodded. "And it couldn't *possibly* have been a man's—could it?"

"Oh, no."

"Then it must have been Clara's." Seeing him frown, she added, "The one with the roses."

"Ah." He drew his handkerchief from his pocket and dusted off the desk and chest in a kind of benediction, then squatted down in front of the bookcase. She looked over his shoulder as he ran his finger along the faded titles: *Essays of Emerson, Whittier's Poems, The Lady of the Lake*—very old copies, those—*Ivanhoe, The Mill on the Floss, Pride and Prejudice, The Complete Plays of William Shakespeare, David Copperfield...* His finger reached the end of the shelf, and he stood up, looking around the room. For a moment neither of them said anything, then he asked quietly, "How old did you say she was when she died?"

The presence was so active in the room that it took her a minute to think. "Let's see—1912 to 1943 made her..."

"...Thirty-one, " he muttered. "Christ." Then in a very different tone, "Can that possibly be a car?"

She listened. "Yeah, but it's going too slowly to be a local. Sometimes tourists get confused when the road dead ends at the lake, and they turn up here." She glanced at his face, which was going thoughtful again. "Want me to go redirect them? I should check on Cocoa anyway."

"Sure," he said—and added as she slipped past the wardrobe, "I'll be right there."

She hurried downstairs and emerged on the porch just as an elderly blue Mercedes stopped opposite the house and someone shut off its engine. It was a visitor, then, not somebody who was lost. "Eleanor?" called a voice.

Oh! It was Helena. "No, it's me, Charlie," she said, running down the steps. "Joel and I came over to look at the house."

Helena rolled down her window with the smile that reminded you how awesomely beautiful her aristocratic face had been. "I thought that might be where he'd gone when I found nobody home at Eleanor's. I'm glad you had time to show it to him." She looked at the house. "David said it was a sweet old place," she said, nodding slowly. "Is Joel pleased?"

"I'm not sure. He doesn't—he isn't—" She drew a shaky breath. "Actually, it's a bit odd."

The silver eyebrows rose slightly. "Odd? How, odd?"

"Well, the house has been kept up for years and years, just the way it used to be...but not for any particular reason. And even more peculiar, Joel didn't know."

"Well, we knew he'd never been here."

"Yes, but—"

"Helena!" Joel hurried down the steps and strode across the yard. He helped Helena out of the car, and as usual the two of them greeted each other with an old-world kiss on each cheek. But as was definitely *not* usual, there was a little silence between them as she took his arm and walked to the house. If you hadn't been in the house with all those wisping presences, it probably wouldn't have been noticeable, but as it was...well, the air just *hummed* with something unsaid.

By the time the two of them negotiated the steps and turned back to look at the view, the moment was gone. "Lovely," said Helena. Then, glancing quickly to her right, she added, "Charlotte, is that your horse that's getting so restive?"

"Restive" was hardly the word for it. Cocoa had backed as far from the tree as he possibly could, and he was beginning to tug on his rope. Charlie darted across the lawn and pulled the release knot, cursing herself for trying his patience as long as she had. But apparently he was more than impatient—he danced around her, snorting and shying until she finally lost sympathy with his fears and tapped his chest with her whip. That stopped him, but only just. His head was high, his nostrils flared wide open, and he looked three times his normal size.

"Need help, Charlie?" called Joel.

Thank heavens he'd had the sense not to come running across the lawn. "No thanks," she called back, "unless you can tell me what's scaring him."

"Well, those cows you said he didn't like are all crowding around the gate."

The heifers. Of course, the heifers. Mr. Wolfington had conditioned them to come to the gate for salt when he drove up, so Helena's arrival had gotten their hopes up. She coaxed the sweating horse five steps forward and halted him across from the porch. "Thanks," she said. "And I'm afraid I'll have to say goodbye from here. I need to teach this city slicker that Holsteins are part of country life, and it's going to take some time."

It did. By the time Cocoa had learned to walk up and down the fence unperturbed by the mooing, shoving and slobbering of fifteen hopeful heifers, the Mercedes had disappeared down the driveway with the Joel at the wheel, and the Ward Place, except for its liberated windows, looked just as it had for thirty-two years.

3. Interiors

Eleanor closed the front door on Timberline Condominium 106G, reactivated the security system, and carried her vacuum cleaner down to the car. The job had gone faster than she'd thought; all there was left was the unpleasant business ahead, and then she could get home in time to show Joel the Ward Place. She owed him a lot more than reduced rent, after the way she'd deserted him last night and slipped out this morning to get the car.

She inched the Honda down the driveway and along Route 100, glancing into her rear-view mirror at the lengthening line of cars behind her. No, there was no escaping the business ahead unless she planned to hold up traffic forever—assuming, of course, that nobody rear-ended her. She turned off at the Victorian building that housed Hume and Rickerts Realtors. This was it. Faced with the necessity of bankrolling new struts immediately and a new steering rack presently, she could no longer afford a vendetta with realtors. Six years of resistance had done nothing to slow down the despoiling of Vermont, and continued stubbornness promised to have as little effect, unless her inability to support herself forced her to follow brother Peter's example and sell her land.

And that inability, it had finally dawned on her as she cleaned this morning's condo, was a real possibility. *Disability* was a buzz-word that provoked social consciousness. But its attendant *inability* provoked only irritation, especially the inability to handle phone calls. How many jobs had she lost to scheduling mixups since March, when Hattie had left? Three? No, four—two of them long-standing and substantial. That was $500 a month and a diminished word-of-mouth reputation. Placing another ad would simply spread word of her inability further. No, she needed a central office to handle her schedule as badly as she needed the volume of work Hume and Rickerts offered.

She wiped her boots on the welcome mat and conjured up a smile for the young man at the desk as she stepped in. "Is Colleen Rickerts free? I'm Eleanor Klimowski. She wrote me a note last week about cleaning jobs."

He spoke into his phone, and she walked to the chairs across the room before he could turn back to her. When it came to avoiding social chitchat, she'd become an expert.

Before she had even sat down, an office door opened and Colleen stepped out. "Oh, Eleanor! *Mxmx* delighted *mxmx!* Won't *mxmx* in?"

She held the door open, and Eleanor stepped through, hoping her smile betrayed no reluctance. "I'd like to look into the cleaning jobs you mentioned, if I may."

"Wonderful!" said Colleen. **"I was hoping you would. And I've thought of a way we can work together without all this shouting. Come sit over here."** She moved a small chair next to her leather desk chair and turned her monitor to the right. **"There,"** she said, sitting down. **"Just a second, and I'll have everything together."**

Eleanor sat down and looked at the diplomas on the walls of the office as Colleen clicked through a series of files. B.A., Simmons College, 1968. So Colleen was her age. She shot a glance at the face studying the screen. There had been dozens of such faces in her undergraduate days— attractive, girlish faces, behind which lay the unquestioned assumption that a woman's way forward in the world depended on her ability to understand the system and make it work for her. Twenty-odd years later, the face was no longer girlish but still attractive, and its ability to work with the system had given it an aura of professional competence. Now as then, it was hard to argue with the success that went with such faces.

"**There we go**," said Colleen, pushing the 'print' button. "**In a minute, you'll have everything written down.**" She looked up earnestly. "**I know you're overqualified, of course. But I know it's hard for people with, um, difficulties to find work up here, and** *everybody* **says you do a wonderful job. So I thought it would be worth asking.**"

She was sincere. No doubt she'd justified buying Peter's property in the same way: helping the unfortunate. Again, it was hard to argue. "You were very kind to think of me. How many houses are there?"

Colleen held up six fingers and looked expressively at the printer. When it finished, she handed the pages across the desk.

Stovepipe Hill: Schmidt, Piranian, Zinsser (see map)
Vacuum. Change all beds. Scrub sinks, mop kitchens. Clean all baths, Jacuzzis/hot tubs/saunas, whether used or not. Empty garbage. Clean stoves, refrigerators, ovens as needed. Leave heat at 55. Report any damage immediately. Clean weekly, pref. Monday. Price per house: $40.00

Timberline Condominiums: Powarski, Darlington (see map)
Same as above. Clean weekly. Price per condo: $35.00

Rickerts residence: Change master bed and others as necessary. Vacuum downstairs weekly, unused upstairs rooms every other week. Clean baths and Jacuzzi weekly. Iron clothes on hangers in laundry room. Empty dishwasher and do whatever dishes are in the sink. Clean refrigerator, stove and oven as necessary. Empty garbage. Price per week: $50.00

Eleanor read it twice, adding in her head. It was good money:
$960 a month would double her present income, and if all went well,
there would be more in the winter. There was no place for pride here.
"Monday and Tuesday are good days for me," she said judiciously, "so
I can do those second homes."

"**Wonderful!**" said Colleen. "**You have no idea what a load
that is off my mind! We open at eight—you can come in for the
keys, and return them when you're through.**" She hesitated a moment. "**And my house...?**"

"It'll be a pleasure. When would you like me to start?"

Colleen swiveled towards her computer, brought up Word Pad,
and switched the font to 20.

'Well, if you have time this afternoon, I just made special plans for
this evening, and my house is a mess.'

Her eyes flickered to Eleanor's face in what was close to an en-
treaty.

It was a shame, but fifty bucks was fifty bucks, and showing the
Ward Place to Joel Hendrickson didn't pay. "I can do it right now, if
you'd like."

Colleen beamed silent gratitude and turned back to her machine.

'Wonderful!!! I'll give you the keys to the back entrance. Unlock
the deadbolt on the mud room door, cross it, then punch in the
security number (05377) to the left of the kitchen door.'

It wasn't a delightful means of conversation, but having things
in print certainly spared the pain of asking for repetition. "Fine. Shall
I return the key when I'm done?"

'No, no. Keep it.'

The well-manicured hands hovered indecisively over the keyboard, then added,

> 'I know it's difficult when land is sold out of the family. I've been wanting to tell you that I've developed the parcel we bought from your brother so that it interferes only minimally with your view. There's only one driveway, and none of the three homes on the property will be visible from yours. We'll put in a pond across from your house, and everything around it will be tastefully landscaped.'

She looked up from the screen, and their eyes met.

"Thank you," said Eleanor quietly. "I appreciate your thoughtfulness."

In the silence that followed, Colleen took a fifty dollar bill out of her purse, wrapped it around the deadbolt keys and extended it across the little gap between them. Eleanor took it, forced herself to smile, and escaped.

In the car once more, she inched up the hill through the vacation estates whose immaculate lawns replaced the rock and buttercup-filled pastures that had once surrounded the Carpenter Place, and turned between the stone pillars that marked Colleen's driveway. The house dominated the mowing in which it had been built, its clapboard walls towering over the bulldozed hillside and its Palladian windows staring over a tastefully landscaped pond. Eleanor scrutinized it for a minute, then walked to the side entrance and performed the spell that let her into the kitchen.

As she pushed the door open, dustballs scuttled across the hard-wood floor and settled below the corner of the counter in a pool of something that smelled like citrus. She stepped forward to investigate. The blender top must have come off in the middle of a batch of daiquiris, and everything in sight—the marble counters, the copper stove hood, the revolving-door cabinets, and even the unwashed enameled pans in the sink—was encrusted with lime and sugar. Altogether, a graphic representation of the New Vermont: a developer's playground covered with homogenized stickiness that local residents were paid to clean up—no, that was grossly unfair. God, what was happening to her, that she should think thoughts like that? Business, business. The kitchen was going to take some time. She'd better see what else needed doing so she could pace herself.

She strolled through the dining area to the living room, taking in the carefully casual arrangement of the rugs and furniture, then climbed the curved staircase. Upstairs, all the doors were closed except the door to the master suite, so she started there. Not too time-consuming; it just needed some tidying. She started at the door and moved slowly towards the bathroom, collecting g-string panties, lace bodysuits, and uplift bras as she went. Interesting. Did Colleen wear such things to make her feel 'feminine' under those tailored suits, or did she live in hope of finding herself in a situation that would be enhanced by enticing underwear? Perhaps neither: one thing you learned as a cleaning lady was how many women long past modeling age habitually thought of femininity as the ability to arouse the pre-fab passion that filled the supermarket romances next to their beds. And how deeply their expectations let them down.

Lately, in fact—she threw the silken mass into the bathroom hamper and found a clean set of satin sheets to replace the ones currently drifting off the bed—lately, in fact, she'd begun to understand what her father had called Helena Woodhouse's genteel chastity. It was more than a question of sex *qua* sex; it was that the conditions under which sex happened to a single woman in her forties—other people's husbands, post-prandial drunks, second-home owners to whom the cleaning lady was fair game—negated the purpose of the act, which was to become less lonely.

What loneliness consisted of, of course, was a matter of opinion. If you thought of intimacy as something that extended no further than the edges of a Sealy Posturpedic, then it probably didn't bother you that the ratio of men with whom you could screw to men with whom you could talk was 1000:1. If you wanted more than that, you were in a far less enviable position—well, maybe not. She looked around the room with sudden sympathy for the longing that pulsed from every corner. "Special plans." Perhaps they would come to fruition—who could say? She festooned the quilts over the bed, arranging the silky pillows in what she hoped was a properly exotic way, then trooped down to the kitchen and started scrubbing.

⊱ ⊱ ⊱

Helena looked back as Joel eased the Mercedes down the driveway. "Charlotte is being remarkably patient and tactful with that horse."

"Her patience and tact extend beyond horses," he said dryly. "I haven't been much company the last couple of days, and she has circumnavigated my moods very generously. Can I look forward to dozens of Mather coeds like her, or is she exceptional?

"Oh, she's exceptional—in every sense of the word. She's what Nathaniel used to call 'a grown-up's child.' She's been home-schooled by a feminist mother, and drilled in the riding ring by an East German Olympic defector. Between those oddities and the Vermont summers that uproot her every year, she's never joined the circles most young people move in these days. I find the results attractive, myself, but I'm afraid it makes her an outcast among her peers. Not that David would allow her to mingle with hip teenagers on the Mountain even if she were interested."

"He wouldn't?" Joel glanced at her as they turned onto the road by the lake.

"Oh no," she said, laughing. "David's worldly knowledge makes him very protective."

Joel laughed too, but as the woods gave place to the handsome old houses on the outskirts of Draper, she felt a renewal of the distressing restraint that had developed between them in the wake of Letty's death. She had felt it throughout the tour he had given her of the house, for his manner had had none of the warmth that usually characterized the way he shared interesting things. He didn't seem to be angry; but he seemed to harbor some suspicion that she knew something he did not. She'd encountered that suspicion in others at Letty's funeral—the shock of the legacy and the recent date of the will had made speculation inevitable. Could he possibly think that she, Helena, had negotiated for the College's interests without telling him? Surely he must know she would never be so duplicitous.

"Straight?" asked Joel, as they pulled up at the stoplight in the center of town.

"Yes," she said. As she glanced to her right at the Draper Universalist church, its tiny porch was suddenly alive with a vision of Nathaniel, so excited by the nineteenth-century eloquence of its ancient preacher that the two of them had discussed theology for over an hour. She blinked away the vision, but its implication could not be banished so easily. It was not exactly duplicity, but she had never revealed to Joel—she had never revealed to anyone—that Nathaniel had spent two weeks of every summer since the War in Westover. Her discretion had been necessary to avoid scandal, though there had been nothing scandalous to hide; he had stayed at the Westover Inn, and he had never appeared at her house until late afternoon. Yet there it was: she and Nathaniel had known Joel intimately for decades and yet kept from him the central secret of their lives. She had denied to him the trust she wished for herself.

She *must* set things straight in the next hour or two. There could be no room for misunderstanding between them. She glanced at his profile—handsome still, and in a way augmented, not diminished, by its graying hair. There were few faces like it, as Nathaniel had remarked on the summer evening he had first told her about him.

"We've hired a twenty-four-year-old prodigy in English."

"A prodigy? That might be something of a risk."

"Ah, but this one, unlike other prodigies at Mather, will be more than a flash in the pan. It's in his face." He looked down into his sherry glass. "An extraordinary face. An Old Master."

"And so, like Adam Verver, you've added him to your collection?"

*"Of course," he said, smiling. "The museum lacked a potentially eminent Renaissance critic." But suddenly, with the bitterness one always felt in Nathaniel but rarely saw— "Adam Verver! Is that what I've come to? By God, when I was Hendrickson's age, I never **dreamed***

I'd fall that far."

"Hendrickson?"

"The prodigy—or the Old Master, if you will," he said. "Depending on whether you collect interiors or exteriors."

She shook her head, wondering once again if the intellectual career Nathaniel had abandoned had been as prodigious in fact as it was in memory. To her (and to many others) his ability to collect extraordinary scholarly talent was equally prodigious, and his gift for infusing the depth and spirit of his intellect into his College had been little short of miraculous. But he had always dismissed these as mere skills; it had been Joel's intellectual achievement he admired, and Joel's suffering in the squalid world of academic politics that had grieved him most deeply— But she must stop the past from impinging so immediately on her consciousness; there were sorrows enough in the present.

"Go right just past the church," she said. "Now left at the fork and up the hill—I do apologize for the ruts. And here we are. Come sit on the porch, and I'll find us some bread and cheese." She led him inside and pointed his way through the living room, noting with pleasure the warmth in his voice as he admired the Saraband rug and the Regency table that served as her desk. But when she joined him on the porch with the modest lunch she had assembled, his pensive mood had returned. He was sitting in the largest of the white wicker chairs, looking at the lifts and shaved trails that scarred the Mountain. "You're surrounded, aren't you?" he said.

She poured his tea, putting his usual dollop of milk in the bottom of the cup first. "I have two hundred fifty acres. It's enough to protect me."

"It must be...amazingly valuable."

It was unlike Joel to speak of value, not beauty, but she concealed her surprise. "It is indeed, if one thinks in terms of investments. My father bought it for $1000 in the Twenties."

"And now, I suppose, every acre is worth that?"

"So a reasonable man would think, but the world of the Mountain is as unreasonable as the world of Sotheby's. Its worth to a developer is twenty times your estimate."

He stared at her, his face a study in incredulity. "Twenty thousand an acre!"

"Surely, Letty's appraisal of your pretty place and its lake frontage should have prepared you for figures in that vicinity."

His gaze drifted off the porch to the red and yellow flowers in her mowing. "There was no appraisal."

His expression made her pass him the cheese instead of pursuing the subject immediately, but she felt a surge of irritation at the delay. Reticence in business matters always made her impatient. At last she said, "I assumed you agreed to the will because of the value of the farm."

"You assumed incorrectly." He put down his cup with excessive care. "After Letty inherited Nathaniel's property, she had Smith and Sons draw up a will that left the books and a few pieces of furniture to me, and the rest of her estate to the College. In spite of occasional threats" —he smiled wanly— "that will sat in the armoire, unchanged, for fourteen years. Until Andrew asked me to come talk to him, I had no idea that it had been superseded." He looked out over the mowing again. "And until I read it, I had no idea why it should have been."

"And why was that?"

"The old will didn't mention the Ward Trust. If it had, I would have learned it existed."

"You can't seriously mean you didn't know she owned the farm until—"

"—until the Friday after she died." His eyes finally met hers. "Apparently, I couldn't be trusted with the knowledge."

She absorbed the statement in silence, trying to think of a way to provide comfort in a situation that seemed to allow for none.

"She must have had some valid reason for not telling you. "

"So I told myself," he said bitterly. "I knew there was some sort of disagreement in her family. I suppose I was grasping at straws, but I thought maybe the farm had come from a faction she'd hated so much that she decided to let it go to forest out of revenge. Which, as she must have known, I would have tried to convince her not to do. Heaven knows, I'd argued enough about other subjects, and not always kindly."

"That's not grasping at straws. It's reason itself."

"It would be, if the place were the total ruin I was expecting when I came. But you saw it. The barn is lost, but the house, the lawn and the family graveyard up the hill are immaculately kept. According to Charlie, the hay is mowed every year—and as you saw, a local farmer puts his cows in the pasture. There it was, right in front of me: she *cared* for the place."

"Not necessarily," she said. "Minimal upkeep doesn't require personal affection; it merely requires distinguishing between hating a place and losing a valuable investment."

"I'd agree instantly, if she'd been you, Helena," he said, smiling grimly. "But Letty was the last person in the world to pass up the opportunity for a good hate just because it was financially unsound."

That was all too true, as Letty had proved from the moment Andrew Crawford had put her on the Board. But it was disturbing to hear Joel speak unhappily of Letty. The remarkable thing about their marriage had been his ability to temper her weaknesses without bitterness and accentuate the generosity of which she'd been capable. And she, in return—

Nathaniel was unusually quiet when he arrived that summer. Knowing better than to interrupt his thoughts, she sipped her tea silently.

"Joel and Letty are courting," he said finally.

"Good heavens! Are you sure?"

"Of course I'm sure. She and I live in the same house, don't we?"

"You don't sound pleased," she ventured.

"Oh, I'm pleased enough. She'd be smart to take him: he has a fine career ahead of him, and it's probably the last chance she'll have. She's thirty-two."

"Then why are you concerned?"

His eyes rested on the devil's paintbrushes in the mowing. "He could do a lot better—and probably would, if there were any selection."

"Nathaniel!"

"Spare me your reproaches, my dear. You don't know what it's like hunting for a wife in the wilds of Yale and Mather. The only circumstances in which Joel has met women have been repellently artificial. So when he sees her at my house instead of at a tea dance, he thinks she's domestic. When he talks to her in my company, he thinks she has literary interests. But as you know, the only time she's domestic is when there's a party to be given. And as for literary interests, if he and I were engineers, she'd listen to talk about suspension bridges with the same enthusiasm as she listens to talk about Spenser and Ovid."

"Intellectual depth isn't everything," she said gently. "You've forgotten beauty. And gaiety and charm."

"Not so," he said, tapping his fingers, "In fact, that's what I'm most concerned about. Ten or eleven reasonably eligible young men have been attracted to that beauty, gaiety and charm—and vanished once they got beyond its surface. They can't all have been wrong."

"That's hardly a kind thing to say about a lovely woman who has served you devotedly."

"Whoever accused me of being kind? Yes, she has earned her keep, and of course I'm fond of her." He looked up anxiously. "You do know that, don't you?"

"That you're fond of her? I've never doubted it."

"Wise woman that you are. But she doesn't turn on me the way she turns on them."

"Them?"

"The men who court her. Charm itself up to a point, and then suddenly—" He shook his head. "I've never seen anything like it. I even thought of a psychiatrist at one point."

"You? The arch-enemy of Freud and Jung?"

"That was what stopped me. At least, one of the things. The other was her absolute refusal to see one." He held out his cup for more tea. "But I think my concern had some effect. A couple of years ago, after a blow-up with the last of her suitors, she told me some people simply weren't made to be married, and she was one of them. I confess I was relieved."

"So it's Joel's happiness you fear for now, not hers?"

He nodded. "But what can I say: 'Don't marry her, m'boy—she'll eat you alive'?"

"You wouldn't have to say it in those terms."

"All the terminology in the world wouldn't change the fact I would be undercutting her when I had no right to," he said. "And besides—"

She gave him a prompting look.

"I think she may love him."

"That surprises you?"

She'd asked the question lightly, but he didn't smile when he looked at her. "Yes," he said. "Yes, it does."

When she had thought of it later, she'd been surprised herself. Letty had a large circle of friends, and she went out practically every night of the week, but it was attention that attracted her, not affection. Yet, at the party Nathaniel had thrown the following September to celebrate Joel and Letty's engagement, she'd been struck not by Letty's radiance—that was to be expected—but by a softening that rendered her beauty complete. And the softness had never entirely dissipated, in spite of the passage of years.

That, however, only made the will more inexplicable; surely, Letty must have known how deeply the revelation of a long kept secret would hurt him.

"Helena, may I ask you a question?"

She looked up, ashamed of how far her thoughts had taken her from the point at issue. "Of course."

"How long ago did Letty—or Nathaniel—tell you about the farm?"

Good heavens. For the past three weeks he'd assumed that she, Letty, and Nathaniel had conspired to keep him ignorant? No wonder he'd been so distant! She leaned forward and put her hand on his. "I knew nothing about the Ward Trust until Andrew told the Board about the will. And nothing about the land's location until David and I wormed the knowledge out of Jed Smith."

He looked down at the gray porch floor. "Forgive me," he murmured. "I never should have thought it."

"I should never have let you think it," she said. "I was upset myself when I learned the farm was in Draper. Nathaniel—" She caught herself. "Actually, Jed thinks Nathaniel knew as little about the property as you or I."

His head came up. "Really?"

"That's what he said, and though he's too young to remember the details of the Trust, when I thought about it, I realized he was probably right. Nathaniel knew surprisingly little about the life Letty led before she was sent to him; she simply refused to discuss it. I can remember how that irritated him when she was a teenager."

"I'm sure it did," he said. "It irritated me, long after she was a teenager. All she'd ever say was that her family didn't understand her, and who knows what that may mean?" He frowned. "On the other hand, I did come to feel that there had been some kind of damage."

"Well, of course."

"Was it that obvious? I must confess, I hadn't even thought of it until after we married."

"I only meant," she said mildly, "that it's impossible to live without sustaining damage."

"That's a pretty bleak view of the human condition, Helena."

"Only if you share the ridiculous modern assumption that pain—mental and physical—is a remediable exception, not a norm. But my point is, it's possible that whatever pain Letty endured made her decide not to tell Nathaniel—or you—about the farm. That should at least relieve you of the notion that her lack of candor implied a lack of love."

He looked out at the Mountain with an expression that told her she had said the right thing. If it also revealed a continuing shadow of undeserved betrayal, well, she shared his sentiments. But she had offered him the only consolation she could. She placed one hand on each arm of her chair and rose stiffly to her feet. "Would you like to see the garden?"

He stood up without a word, offering her his arm at exactly the right height, and they started down the steps. "It's over there," she said. "Inside the old barn cellars."

"What a lovely idea," he said, looking at the hand-laid foundations with an interest she hadn't anticipated. "Perhaps after I've demolished my barn, I'll take up gardening."

She looked at him with pleased surprise. "You're thinking of keeping the place?"

"I have no idea," he said. "But the barn is a death-trap to any child who might wander up from the lake, and I feel obliged to get rid of it. As for the house—I think I'll paint it, at least. Both it and I will be better for the work." He sighed. "And whatever I decide to do with it, its history deserves to be preserved. Quite apart from the wonderful artifacts in the dining room, there are books and papers. Just after Charlie left to find you, I opened a chest in the back room upstairs. It's full of farm accounts and some sort of journal. It's a treasure trove for a local historian, and I just happen to know one."

"Oh, that's right—Eleanor." Like her father, she'd always been interested in the Vermont that was slipping away from them all.

"I was thinking of Charlie, actually," he said. "She introduced me to the Ward family this morning—at least, to the family in the graveyard. I take it Letty's mother was descended from the Ward son who escaped to the city some generations ago, and whose children buried elsewhere."

"Letty's mother?" she said, frowning.

"I assume so. If the place had belonged to her father's family, wouldn't Nathaniel have inherited it? He was her father's only living relative."

"I suppose you're right." The irony, of course, was that Letty would not have cared. To her, people like the woman who had lived and died in that old house simply did not exist. He knew that as well as she did, but both of them had loved Letty too well to say so.

As they reached the gate of the lower garden, she stopped, sensing the depth of his wish to be alone. "Perhaps I should drive you back to Eleanor's," she said.

She was surprised when he bent down and kissed her forehead. Kind as he was, he'd never been a demonstrative man.

4. A Beer

Joel paged impatiently through Robert Randall's unabridged Cassell's: Vomer-*eris—ploughshare.* He noted it and went on, but the next agricultural word stopped him within five lines. Damn. He exchanged Randall's beautiful Virgil for the Loeb dual language edition on the next shelf. He'd known his Latin had been slipping, but every time he'd sat down to review, there'd been teaching, committees, politics, hospitals, chemotherapy—in short, every possible justification. And now he couldn't even read the *Georgics* without constant recourse to a dictionary. He opened the Loeb ruefully, remembering Nathaniel's scorn for readers whose flitting from text to translation kept them from appreciating the glory of the poetry.

Slowly, out of the book-filled silence around him, there emerged from the shade of Nathaniel, enthroned in his Renaissance chair and reading the Fourth Georgic aloud, rolling out the hexameters of Orpheus's tragedy with a voice that gained intensity as the couple struggled up through echoing caverns, that trembled with the anticipatory longing of the last few steps, then slowed as too eager, too loving, too young, Orpheus disobeyed the gods, and turned— The voice broke. The ringless hands closed the book. And after a few silent minutes, the listener, a twenty-four-year-old embarrassed by the grief of the man he admired so deeply, slipped out of the President's house into the midnight snow.

If he'd been older, wiser...if he'd stayed... No. It would have made no difference. The citadel that shimmered so temptingly behind Nathaniel's aloofness had been inaccessible. To the world at large, he'd offered intelligence, charm, and the charismatic devotion to education that had made his name. To his colleagues, he'd offered intellectual companionship—and compared with his cornucopia of intellectual passions, conventional academic interest was sawdust. To his friends, he'd offered Talk—and with him, Talk had been not just conversation (that could be found anywhere), but sustained discussion in which learning crossed the boundaries of the intellect and touched the soul. Evening after evening, stroll after stroll. Yet despite what passed for intimacy, the citadel had remained unreachable.

Yes, but that intimacy—however circumscribed—had assumed mutual respect and trust. It was unjust to doubt. Even Helena hadn't known about the Ward Trust.

"Joel?" Eleanor stood in his doorway. "We're due at the Walkers' soon."

"Of course." He jumped up. "I was ready so long ago that I started to read—" Her straining face reminded him he couldn't speak to her at that speed. "I'm all set," he amended.

Outside, she whistled for Derri, and the three of them walked down the road in a silence which, while welcome at first, gradually made him edgy. It was difficult, communicating with someone this deaf. The small talk that surrounded casual acquaintance was impossible, for quick changes of subject bewildered her. Wit was out, too; she could turn a phrase neatly herself, but she couldn't process a reply in kind. That left face-to-face discussion of serious subjects, but no topic seemed important enough to merit such formality. To compound the problem, it was hard not to suspect that conversation would be easier if she'd concentrate instead of drifting off—but that was discriminatory, or at least unproductive.

Just as he braced himself to make (and repeat) some remark about the horses in the well-kept pasture on their right, she turned up the driveway at its side, and the silence was broken by a salvo of barking from two golden dogs that squeezed under the white board fence to exchange stiff-legged formalities with Derri. Joel patted them as they sniffed him, then followed Eleanor up the drive toward a cluster of outbuildings. Charlie stepped out of the largest one and waved.

"Hi! Connie said you should both go up to the house. Cocoa and I will be there soon."

Eleanor looked at him. "Go ahead—you can't miss the house. I'll give Charlie a hand."

As he paused, hesitating to correct her, she turned away; there was nothing he could do but go on. Two hundred yards of narrower driveway took him past a tool shed and an ancient pickup to a house that rose in unexpected modernity from the side of the hill, overlooking the distant lake. Ray emerged from the door, carrying an ice chest.

"Perfect timing," he said, leading the way along the deck to an assortment of chairs. "Eleanor down at the barn?"

It was more a statement than a question, and Joel nodded, relieved.

"We'll get a start on them, then." Ray pulled two dripping cans out of the ice, handed Joel one, and took possession of the chaise longue.

Joel sat next to him, patting the larger golden dog. "You've got a beautiful place."

"Don't say that when Eleanor's around," said Ray.

"She doesn't like it?"

"Sure she does—now. But it took her a long time to warm up to it. See, until '82 it was part of a big farm. Three hundred fifty acres. Then Hume and Rickerts bought it and divided it up. That's what she doesn't like."

"I can understand hating to see an old farm break up," said Joel, "but couldn't Eleanor take some comfort in knowing its farmer got to retire in comfort? "

Ray grinned. "I wouldn't say that. The farm belonged to a New York businessman who raised beef cattle for a tax loss, then unloaded the land for a small fortune. That's the kind of people who've sold land for the last thirty years in this part of the state. The hill farms shut down in the Fifties and got snapped up by summer people like Eleanor's family. Then in the Seventies, when skiing got big, investors like this New York guy got interested. So by now most of the folks who are selling out are pretty well off. And if they aren't—well, realtors can afford to be reeeeal patient, until somebody like Eleanor's brother gets desperate." Ray shrugged. "I don't go for that, but what can you do? Nobody's ever going to farm Vermont again."

Joel tapped his fingers on his can, thinking of Charlie pointing over the wall of the Ward's graveyard. *The stones you can hardly read belong to the first Wards, who cut down the trees and started the farm in the early 1800s.* Thousands of Indians had fought to prevent the change to the white man's landscape that later became a quintessential part of Vermont. The land that seemed so permanently itself was in fact a reflection of human history, with all its injustices, sorrows and losses. And with a single clause in a will, he'd suddenly become involved.

Ray turned his head as the back door opened and shut. "We're over here, Connie. Eleanor'll be up in a sec."

"Okay." A comfortable-faced woman in a sweatshirt that matched Ray's joined them on the deck, carrying a basket of potato chips and dip. Joel jumped to his feet and fetched her a plastic table as they exchanged greetings. "I've been admiring your place. Did you do most of the work yourselves?"

"All of it," said Connie proudly.

Joel's eyebrows rose. "Barn, sheds, riding ring?"

"House, too," said Ray. "Came in a kit, all the parts cut out—all we had to do was follow the instructions. Our sons helped out some, but mostly it was just Connie and me. Took four years of weekends, but I got no complaints. Our old place needed more work than it was worth."

"I'll say," said Connie. "Seemed like I cleaned it every day, but it never did any—" Both dogs leapt up, barking furiously, and she stood up, looking towards the driveway. "It's David."

"Great," said Ray, hoisting himself onto his feet. "Now we get to meet that lady he's asked up for the summer. From what Charlie says, she's something else." He winked at Joel, and they joined Connie at the top of the steps.

David leapt from the Jaguar, tanned and athletic in a polo shirt and khakis. "Good to see you, Ray, Connie—and Joel, too! Great." The slight awkwardness in his voice was surprising, until the door to the passenger seat opened and its occupant emerged—tall, slim, brown hair swept back attractively into a twist, low-cut tank top, perfectly cut jeans. Very lovely. And not a day over twenty-five. With a sudden jolt, Joel remembered Charlie's tale of an airport socked in on a perfect day in May. Was it possible that David Reynolds—the man who made fast-set ease with women somehow enviable—had nervously invented an excuse to keep this one to himself? Repressing a smile, he descended the flagstone steps, his hand outstretched.

David shook it warmly and turned to the girl. "This is Joel Hendrickson. Yes," —as her eyes widened— "*the* Joel Hendrickson. I told you the summer Vermont phone book read like *Who's Who in Academia* back in our generation. In any case, here's one of the entries: Tilden Professor of English at Mather College, author of—"

The girl stepped through the rest of the sentence, extending her hand. "Salome Rose," she said. "Graduate student, University of Michigan, author of three conference talks and half a dissertation."

Joel shook the hand and smiled at the defensive face. "Will it be a whole dissertation by the end of the summer?"

"It has to be," said David, "She's one of the seventy lucky grad students in the USA who got a real job this year, but it's contingent upon—"

"—These must be Ray and Connie," Salome said, turning to them as they walked across the drive. "It's wonderful to meet you after hearing Charlie talk about you." She shook their hands in the straightforward manner feminism had made possible for young women, then turned from Ray's appreciative gaze to Connie. "You must have a magic touch with plants. That Bleeding Heart by your steps is gorgeous."

Very smoothly done. David really had nothing to worry about—except, perhaps, the possibility that she'd have his head on a platter before the summer was over.

The sound of hoofbeats made them all turn around as Charlie and Cocoa rounded the corner of the drive, Eleanor walking next to the pair in silent companionship. As they passed, Joel saw Charlie's welcoming smile turn to a wink as she caught Ray's eye. She rode on, and the rest of them strolled to the hand-hewn bench at the side of the ring. Once they'd distributed beer and Cokes, Ray and David sat down at the far end of it, discussing the comparative merits of backhoe attachments for small tractors. Salome followed David, still chatting with Connie, which left Joel and Eleanor together at the end. He made a few remarks, but she replied with the neutral phrases he'd learned had allowed her to preserve the illusion of reply without identifying the subject; and when Charlie and Cocoa started to trot in circles of varying sizes, she abandoned all attempts at conversation and watched them. Much as he would have liked to update his knowledge of backhoes, getting up seemed uncivil, so he watched a little himself—and found it far more interesting than he had expected. As the horse warmed up, his neck arched, and his strides rose higher and higher, until his feet seemed barely to touch the ground. It really was a form of dance, just as Ray had said; and Charlie, rising and falling effortlessly in time to the rhythm of hoof-beats, combined the elegance and presence of a dancer with the larger control of a choreographer.

"Hey," said Salome. "She's really *good.*"

"She should be," said Connie, smiling. "Eleanor taught her to ride."

Salome turned to Eleanor. "*You* teach her? You must be very good, to do that."

Seeing that Eleanor had not responded, Joel touched her elbow lightly and pointed to Salome. Eleanor turned immediately. "I'm sorry?"

"I was just saying you must be a terrific rider, if you teach Charlie."

The confusion in Eleanor's face became a smile as Connie repeated Salome's remark slowly. "A talented student always makes her teacher look terrific," she said.

"**She's more than talented,**" said Salome, looking straight at Eleanor and speaking slowly herself, "**I hadn't realized…I mean, isn't she Olympic material?**"

"Don't even *think* of it, Sal," said David, coming to stand behind her. "The price of sending a kid to the Olympics makes financing four years at Yale look like chicken feed."

"**But surely,**" said Salome—still to Eleanor— "**if you can become an Olympic *anything* you should go for it.**"

"Only if you love competition as much as you love the sport," said Eleanor.

Joel smiled at the surprise in Salome's attractive face. At her age, with a first job that proved he had bested all competition so far, he would have been equally shocked by the remark.

Charlie halted Cocoa in front of them. "You're talking about me."

"You bet," said Connie. "We're saying what a great rider you are."

"Pretty flawed greatness, if you ask me," said Charlie. "Eleanor, I can't get him to collect on the left lead. Can you come in here and tell me what I'm doing wrong?"

There was an excruciating pause; then Eleanor said, "Did you say you wanted help?" When Charlie nodded, she got up and ducked between the bars. Joel watched with interest; in the center of the ring, her habitual tension became confident authority as she watched the pair canter around her. Her instructions something to do with dropping an inside seat bone and relaxing back muscles—were lost upon him, but their effect on the horse was electric. The unbalanced canter became rhythmic, and slowed almost to walking pace. Beautiful. Amazing.

"Jesus," said Salome. "She really knows what she's doing. It's a damn shame."

"You bet it is," said David.

In the confusing instant it took him to realize they were talking about Eleanor, not Charlie, Joel had a flash of insight into the world as

Eleanor experienced it. Every phrase to be untangled. Every assumption questionable. Every answer a potential source of embarrassment. It was more than a damn shame. It was isolation.

Charlie slowed the horse to a walk, gave him his head, and smiled at their applause as she halted opposite them. "That's all, folks. You got a drink that isn't beer?"

"Sure do," said Connie, opening a soda and handing it across the fence.

"Thanks." Charlie poured a little in her cupped hand and leaned forward. Cocoa, apparently accustomed to the ritual, slurped it up appreciatively; then the two of them walked off, Charlie sipping from the can.

Salome got up, and David, seeing her, drained his beer. "Right. We should go," he said. "Sal's promised to make dinner, but there's nothing in the house to eat."

"It's getting towards that time," said Connie, looking at her watch.

David joined Salome, throwing an arm across her bare shoulders. "Good work," he called as Charlie passed the next time. "Enchiladas at 8:30 sound good?"

"Sure," she said.

"Okay, then." The two of them said goodbye and walked off, hand in hand.

Ray picked up his unfinished beer. "David's a lucky man," he said as the Jag started up. "New back-hoe, new car, new girl— So, how's your place look?"

Your place. Somehow the phrase pleased him. "Not as bad as you'd think, at least so far as the house is concerned. But the barn's beyond one man and a wrecking bar. Can you think of anybody who would help me take it down in return for whatever's still usable? Charlie said that might be a reasonable offer."

"Charlie doesn't know as much as she thinks she does," said Ray. "It's so reasonable I'll take you up on it, and help you fix the sheds as part of the deal. That sound okay to you?"

Joel smiled. "It's so okay I'll take you up on it."

66

"Done." Ray drained his beer. "Want to start right up?"

"Not if you have to do it on top of what you're doing across from Eleanor's."

"Most of that's a young man's job—I just do little stuff on and off. If I'm not around for the next couple of days, nobody'll care, so long as I tell the boss. How much work you got in mind? You going to paint it? Because if you are—"

"—I can't let you do that. It's much more than the barn is worth."

"I wasn't offering to do it," said Ray. "I was recommending a friend of mine. Experienced—scraped and painted Eleanor's barn last summer—works hard, doesn't charge much, needs money for college..." He looked expressively at the ring.

"Charlie? She's got time?"

"She's got nothing *but* time," said Ray. "Works the horse, gives a few lessons, that's it. She's not in with the teen scene here—just as well, I say now, but I would've felt different at her age. Before this summer that was fine, because she and Eleanor's daughter were thick as thieves, but now Hattie's in London. Eleanor works, Connie works, I work. Who's she going to talk to—her dad?"

Joel looked at the kind face, wondering if Ray knew how little a man who had recently been a caregiver had to offer...but of course he didn't. Outside the privileged world where self-indulgence posed as self-actualization, you looked after your own without counting the cost. And certainly if the house were to be painted in the next few weeks, he needed to employ somebody. Ashamed of his hesitation, he turned to the ring. "Hey, Charlie—Ray says you're an experienced painter. Want to work for me?"

She stared at him in disbelief. "You mean, paint the *Ward house?*"

"You got it. And during break time, you can read the stuff I found in the back room. Part of it's a journal—Clara Ward's, I think."

"You're kidding!"

"Nope, but don't get your hopes up. The first couple of entries seem to be about darning socks. Anyway, are you on?"

"Am I *on!* You've got to know it! I'll be there tomorrow, first thing!"

"Make that second thing—I've got to get tools together. And look, come in the rust spot with wheels, not on horseback, okay? Ray and I are going to be taking the barn down."

"Awesome!"

"Well," said Ray, chuckling as they walked away, "that settles that." He opened the door to his toolshed, and Joel was swept back four decades by the smell of oil, lumber and sawdust. He looked around contentedly at the orderly chaos of Ray's equipment. Just what he needed; work with his hands, in good company.

"Let's see," muttered Ray. "Chain, sledge-hammer... What we're really gonna need is the tractor. You can drive a Fifties stick shift, can't you?"

Joel smiled at the decrepit pickup. "Sure, it'll feel like old times."

"Great." Ray grinned at the truck, then looked over it at Eleanor, Charlie, and Cocoa, who were coming down the drive. "Now, isn't that a pretty sight?"

Joel stepped to the door. Charlie and the horse were walking side by side like two cross-country teammates who were cooling themselves out after a run. The horse's head was lowered comfortably; next to him, Charlie swung her helmet by its strap, and her hair hung down past her waist, wisping gracefully around her hips as she walked.

"Beautiful," he said, smiling a little sadly.

Ray followed the direction of his gaze. "The kid? Well, sure—but they're all beautiful at that age."

He'd been looking at Eleanor? There was no accounting for taste—but as she passed him, absorbed in whatever she and Charlie were discussing, he saw Ray's point. What was beautiful, though, was not Eleanor but the animation that illuminated and softened her sharp face. There was something familiar about it, too. He loaded two chains into the pickup, watching her and trying to think of what it was. But it wasn't until they'd gotten all the tools squared away that he realized what he'd seen and what had caused it. Eleanor hadn't just been talking with Charlie: she'd been giving examples, eliciting responses, drawing out ideas. She'd been teaching.

5. Atonements

So he was going to fix it up. Ray and Charlie were going to help. Eleanor watched her phantom self bounce down the road in celebratory handsprings as she and Joel walked sedately home in the long light. The Ward Place preserved! It was a miracle—an act of redemption that promised no financial reward to the redeemer. She glanced at Joel as they turned into her driveway, and dropped her eyes as she met a thoughtful stare.

"Ray and Charlie *mxmx mxmx* out on me."

She looked up. "I'm sorry—Ray and Charlie what?"

"—say you've been holding out on me." His face contradicted his light tone.

"How so?"

"The Ward house should have fallen down," he said, framing each word carefully. " It hasn't. Charlie and Ray don't know why, but both of them assume—"

"—that I do. And you're wondering why I haven't said anything about it."

"Exactly. But I was trying to put it—"

"—Less accusingly." She smiled wryly as she let Derri into the house ahead of them. "Come sit down. It's a long story."

She led him to the living room, acutely conscious that she hadn't invited him into any part of the house but the kitchen. He sat in one of the two faded arm chairs; she scooped Fou-cat off the other and sat on its edge. "How much do you know about your place's history?"

"I know what Charlie *mxmx* Wards in the graveyard," he said, smiling. "*Mxmx* reasonably accurate?"

"Barring gothic touches here and there."

"*Mxmx* roses *mxmx* local Heathcliff?" he said, letting Fou settle in his lap.

"That's quite a tale, isn't it?" she said, smiling. "But alas, the recent facts are entirely pedestrian. When Mary Ward died, Clarence Wolfington, the farmer who had helped her during her last years, agreed to do minimal upkeep on the house and lawn in return for the hay in the mowing and the right to keep his heifers in the pasture from May to hunting season."

He held up a hand. "Who *mxmx mxmx* with Wolfington?"

"Who made the agreement? Probably some local agent, but you'd never find a record. In 1959, caretaking was a matter of oral deals, renewed in person once a year."

"How long *mxmx* Clarence *mxmx* care-taking?"

"Through the Seventies and a bit beyond. I don't know the details, I'm afraid. After the mid-sixties, I was involved with college and graduate school, not to mention my husband's concert tours—"

"Wait, wait." His eyes suddenly widened. "Your husband was—?"

"Stanislaw Klimowski."

"The pianist?"

She nodded.

"*Mxmx* extraordinary artist. *Mxmx* heard him play in *mxmx*. *Mxmx* great loss."

"Thank you," she said quietly. "But to get on with the story, except for the summer after Stanislaw's death, I was so busy with Hattie and with teaching that I only came up here one or two weekends a year in the Seventies—just enough to know Clarence was faithful. So when I came back here to live and walked nostalgically over the hill, I was shocked: the barn was done for, the sheds were sagging, the graveyard was overgrown. It was a real symbol of lost Vermont."

"When was that?"

" '85."

He pursed his lips.

"What had happened was that Clarence had aged in my absence (as people will do), and died in '81. His son Mike, who'd taken over his farm, knew about the agreement; but he also knew the agent who'd renewed it every year had stopped showing up well before Clarence's death. Clarence and Mike figured the agent had passed on."

Joel looked up in surprise. "Died? *Mxmx* a little extreme?"

"No. In the old days, local agents didn't like paper work, so they didn't send bills very often. And since it was hard to tell a bill that didn't come because an agent didn't like paper work from a bill that didn't come because that agent had died, absentee landlords sometimes went for years without knowing they were unrepresented. Clarence figured that's what had happened, so he kept up his share of the bargain, waiting for whoever owned the Ward Place to catch up. But Mike, being a new generation, knew there were folks around who'd *pay* him to take their hay and keep cows in their pastures, and he decided the old deal was costing him money. Out of 'respect' for his dad and Mary Ward, he used the free hay and pasture, but he let the rest go."

Joel looked out the window. "*Mxmx* hardly blame him."

"You're the soul of charity," she said dryly. "Which is lucky for me, because we've come to the part of the story that's kept me from telling it. Obviously, when I found out what the problem was, I should have used the tax records to find your wife's address, told her that her agent had died, and volunteered to oversee the place for her. But instead, I—I just did it."

He stared at her. "Oversaw it? You?"

"Well, sort of," she said uncomfortably. "I was afraid that Mike would feel that my interest in the place let him off the hook, and there was no way I could have kept up the land without cows and mowing machinery. So I said I'd keep up the fence between the Ward Place and my brother's land and check on the heifers now and then. I helped with the haying a couple of years, until Ray took that over. As for the rest—well, after I'd mowed the lawn, I got to thinking about the graveyard; after I'd tidied that up, I started feeling bad about the roof. Then I worried about rot, so I aired the house and cleaned it a few times. Nothing extensive. Just enough to slow the process of decay."

She glanced at him, wishing she could see his face. "I didn't tell Charlie and Hattie; they could *never* have kept it quiet. I didn't even tell Ray, there being a fine line between neighborliness and illegal entry, unauthorized agency—whatever. There really was no excuse, except that when I was a kid, I spent hours and hours in that house, listening to Mary Ward's stories about old times and old folk, and seeing a Vermont most summer people never dreamed was there. It seemed a shame to let all that go."

"*Mxmx* apologize," he said, shaking his head. "The only apology necessary *mxmx* neglect *mxmx* lack of *mxmx.*"

She didn't dare ask him to repeat what he'd said.

He stroked Fou one last time, then looked up. "One thing. I've checked *mxmx* carefully, *mxmx* no sign of illegal entry. May I ask, just out of curiosity, how you got in?"

"Oh, of course." She opened the slant-top desk next to her and pulled a key from one of its interior drawers. "Mary Ward gave me this when I was seven. It's to the back door. That's the one she used, except when she went out to sit on the porch swing."

She handed him the key, but as he took it, she saw not it, not him, but an old woman in a flowered dress, swinging gently as she looked out over the mowing and the lake. The peas her arthritic hands were shelling rattled as they fell into the dish on her lap, and the soft "plunk" of the green pods that landed in a bag at her feet mingled occasionally with the sound of a single cow-bell.

He said something, and she returned to the room. "I'm sorry?"

"I said, 'thank you.' *Mxmx* somebody cared enough for Mary Ward to keep her house up."

"I don't want to imply that your wife—I mean, the place was beautifully kept for twenty years. That suggests that your wife cared for it, too, in some sort of way."

"Possibly," he said. "*Mxmx* doubt it. Letty never *mxmx* by halves. When she cared for something, all the world knew."

"And when she didn't?"

He smiled wanly. "It didn't exist."

There wasn't much she could say; the observation fit the Ward Place's history too well. She looked at him; he was gazing at the slant-topped desk with the expression that had shocked her the evening he had come. No wonder. Charlie hadn't just been being gothic again; it seemed that his wife really *hadn't* told him she owned the Ward Place. And her motive seemed to be not hate, not secrecy, but utter lack of interest. The implication of his legacy was all too obvious.

He lifted Fou gently off his lap. "However, *mxmx* does exist *mxmx* needs work." He stood up with what was probably meant to be a smile. "Ray said *mxmx* two *mxmx* posts. Do you?"

"Do I have two—? Oh, jack-posts. Sure; they're in the barn. They're pretty old, though; you'll probably have to put WD-40 on the screws. It's in the parlor; the pedal was squeaking."

He looked at her the way she imagined she looked at people whose words were incomprehensible. "The pedal?"

She laughed. "On the piano. I play it occasionally, when nobody's around, and the last time I felt the need of a morose prelude, the pedal was a continual distraction."

"A piano," he said, almost reverently. "Could I—?"

"Good God, yes! If I'd known you played, I would have introduced you to it right away. It was Stanislaw's—a real beauty." She crossed the hall and opened the door. "There you go."

He played a few chords, a scale, and stopped. "*Mxmx* won't disturb you?"

"Oh no! This is the first time since Hattie was ten that it hasn't been going six hours a day. The house feels like a tomb."

A faint look of sadness crossed his face, but as he began to play, she could feel everything other than the sound vanish from his life. Smiling, she went out to the barn to put WD-40 on the jack-post screws.

He was still playing when she came back through the gathering dusk—proficiently, so far as she could still judge. But the way he stopped when he came to difficult passages and shifted to another piece reminded her of the beautiful stride he'd settled into when he'd chased Derri the night he'd come, and his exhaustion after two hundred yards. Some time along the line, he'd given up things that had meant a great deal to him. She hoped he'd sacrificed his pleasures to scholarship, not to the demands of the wife whose legacy suggested she cared for him as little as she'd cared for the Ward Place.

If, of course, that was what the legacy suggested. Her mind drifted past the Wards' cemetery and down the hill to the silent house, untouched since Mary's death. It was so familiar she'd almost forgotten how strange it was.

A Steinway B; the prince of pianos. Joel gazed at the instrument in the fading light while he flexed his fingers. Too big for an old farmhouse—it looked crowded even though there was nothing else in the room but a music bookcase—but what a treasure! Like the Chippendale desk out of which Eleanor had so casually extracted the key to the Ward Place. In the days of Robert Randall and Stanislaw Klimowski, it had been possible for laymen, so to speak, to leave their heirs beautiful things, with thoughts only of their craftsmanship. But now, almost twenty years later, the pressures of investment had changed the face of inheritance. Nathaniel's possessions had become one of the largest collegiate legacies in Massachusetts history. The Wards' hill farm had become property with a view and lake frontage worth ten to twenty thousand an acre. How could one hope to preserve the past in such an atmosphere?

That was romanticism, of course. Helena, for all her sorrow at the sale of Nathaniel's things, would be the first to laugh at him, pointing out that "value" had *always* had a double meaning, that indeed, there would have been no Renaissance chests, no *Golden Legends,* no Picasso paintings if there had been nobody wealthy enough to pay for them. Granted. But now, the inflated "value" of past beauty defiled the very act of loving it. Even he, the romantic, couldn't look at Eleanor's Chippendale desk without thinking that selling it would enable her to give up cleaning houses and renting rooms for years. Twenty years ago, the thought would never have crossed his mind.

He plunged into a Chopin prelude he had no hope of finishing without the music—God, how much his fingers had forgotten! His technique had slid as far as his Latin, all for his devotion to... No. Bitterness was self-pity with a different name. There was no point in dwelling on his sorrows. And if Eleanor had revealed their source so clearly, she was unlikely to share her revelation (and her obvious perception of its implications) with others. To whom, after all, did she talk?

His fingers stumbled as if in horror at the unjust thought. Eleanor Randall Klimowski had not kept up the Ward Place secretly for six years simply because deafness cut her off from gossip. She'd done it out of the same desire to preserve a shared past that caused her to keep the Chippendale desk—and in her situation, how could she *not* have thought of the security the sale of that desk could buy? Or for that matter, the sale of the house and land around it? But here they stood: the desk, the house, the land, the Ward Place. *It seemed a shame to let all that go.*

Oh, Letty, Letty, Letty. How was it possible to care so little...?

He pursed his lips—and suddenly became aware of the tempting smell of some Italianate dish. Chicken, garlic, tomatoes, basil. Mmm. He walked to the door and looked down the hall towards the kitchen, where Eleanor was slicing something saladish. There was quite a bit on the board. Was it possible that she was at last going to join him for a meal? He should damn well make certain that she would, by joining her now. It would be easy. Praise the piano. Set the table for two. Talk more about Stanislaw Klimowski, all of whose brilliant recordings he owned.

No, no! If he set the table while he talked, she'd be totally cut off from what he said, and he'd get the hunted, apologetic look she'd given Salome at the ring.

All right. So he'd go in, wait until she looked up, praise the piano, talk about Klimowski. *Then* he'd set the table for two.

Would that be an intrusion? Or, worse, would it seem—? He retreated to the piano and marched his fingers up and down the keyboard in a Hannon exercise they badly needed, hating his lack of discipline. How could he have the gall to ask her if he could stay for the extra weeks it would take to fix up the house when he knew that she was wolfing down a snack before he ate and finishing what he left for her? The man he once had been would never have allowed the situation to evolve, let alone continue. But it seemed he was not the man he once had been. Forced to deal with the difficulty of assuring his landlady he wouldn't dream of using a woman to comfort himself, a delicate task at best, now rendered excruciatingly embarrassing by the repetition it would necessarily involve—

A thump drifted down the hall to his ear, and with it an inspiration worthy of the man he had once been. He brought Hannon back to the tonic, rose, and walked to the kitchen—quickly, so no second thoughts would pursue him. "Eleanor?"

She startled at the sound of his voice, but she turned with a smile. That was promising.

"Eleanor, let me help you. May I set the table?"

She hesitated, then took two dinner plates from the cupboard and handed them to him. "The silverware and napkins are over there," she said, pointing to the drawer.

So far so good, but he could feel her reluctance as he performed his task. "Tell me something," he said as she brought the pungent casserole to the table and sat down.

"Tell you something?" she said, watching his lips carefully.

He sat down at the place he had set for himself, praying that his smile looked conspiratorial, not threatening. "Yesterday morning, I got into the Ward house unceremoniously by kicking the front door in the place I figured it was bolted." Her expression allowed him to continue with more confidence. "The screws in the hasp were so loose that they did no damage to the jamb when they came out. Is it possible that someone cleverly—"

"—loosened those screws?" she finished, laughing. "It certainly is. Having skittered away from you Wednesday night and disappeared Thursday morning without giving you the key, I was felt the need of atonement—so on my way to work I stopped by the house to offer what welcome I could. It was only later that I considered how eerie that welcome must have been to someone who had never seen the house before."

He nodded as she filled his plate. "*Welcome! This vacant chair is thine,/ Dear guest and ghost.*"

"Dear guest and what?" she said, looking up apologetically.

"Ghost."

"Oh, of course, of course. How perfect! Who is it?"

"Longfellow. I spent part of this morning with his Complete Works, a fine old volume stashed in—oh! Did Charlie tell you about the room upstairs that belonged to Clara Ward?"

He had changed subjects too quickly; she looked confused. He repeated the first statement, then urged her to tell him about Charlie's enthusiastic account of the room. But it took him the entire meal to explain that he had found the Longfellow and the journal in Clara's chest, under heaps of accounts and old folders, for no amount of interest on her part could enable him to talk while he ate or her to eat while she listened. When he finally rose with an offer to do the dishes, she blanked, and he had to repeat that, too.

A damn shame. He listened pensively as Derri's toenails clicked up the stairs behind her. The problem was that deafness formed a barrier to the one aspect of conversation everyone took for granted: its pace. The demands that placed on the speaker made it hard not to give up. He dried his hands and wandered back to the piano, drawn to it as if by a magnet.

The light next to it shone softly off its mahogany surface. A well-thumbed edition of the Chopin Preludes sat temptingly on the music rack.

A damn shame indeed! What sort of jerk had he become to dismiss her pityingly? If he couldn't communicate with an intelligent woman, the shame was *his*. He slid onto the bench and thundered out the C minor prelude with sudden fury at all he had lost and all she could not hear, the glory of the instrument reproaching his inadequacies with every chord.

6. Discoveries

Charlie lay in bed, watching the gray drops collect on the twelve panes of her window and spill off in infant waterfalls. No riding lessons today, and from the looks of things, no painting either, at least outside. Fortunately, Joel and Ray had helped her get primer on the west side last night as the clouds rolled in, and some serious rain was certainly due after three weeks of nothing but showers. Well, there was plenty to do inside. Scrape that wallpaper off the living room, for example. It would be a nice companionable day, the three of them working together. And if it cleared by late afternoon, she and Cocoa could do some conditioning work.

She dressed quickly and started downstairs, so she could get out of the house before David and Salome...shit. Already? She glanced at her watch, trying to ignore the grunts and moans that issued from behind the closed master bedroom door. Christ Almighty, it was only six-thirty, and they had come in pretty late last night. She went back to her room, found her Walkman, and plugged herself into it. That took care of it—except the chance that David would stroll in as she ate breakfast, looking triumphant or fulfilled or whatever, and whistle as he made Salome a latté to drink in bed.

Funny it should bother her more this summer than it had before. She'd been onto what was happening since she was nine or ten, and she'd never been jealous or any of that Freudian stuff. In fact, she hadn't really given it much thought. But it had only taken a couple of days working with Joel to make her realize how unutterably cool her Vermont summers would have been if David had been…well, different. Not that she had any complaints, really. David cared about her in his funny sort of way, and he didn't mess with her life—which was a blessing, when you thought of the disgusting way parents hovered over their kids at the barn. Still, it had occurred to her yesterday, as David had padded back to the bedroom, that it would be nice to have a leisurely breakfast talking to your father about books, or politics, or even what was going to happen that day. Especially this summer, when there was no Hattie around to chat with over an early morning breakfast of Eleanor's fantastic muffins.

But there was the Ward Place. Hey, what about an early morning breakfast with the ghosts? The electricity was on now, and one of the things Ray had used to make sure all the plugs in the kitchen worked was the pre-sputnik toaster with the sides that opened out. There was a coffeepot, too. Plates. Sure. And while she ate, she could *finally* get a good look at that journal. "During break time," Joel had promised—what a laugh. The only break they took was lunch, and that was when they talked, and the talk was awesome. Yesterday, she'd explained that everyone called her Charlie because when she was six or so, she'd been upset about being named after a spider. Joel had said when she read *The Golden Bowl*, she'd find a Charlotte she liked better. No hurry, he'd added. Difficult style, but wonderful, subtle psychology—James understood that while sexual fulfillment was gratifying, the most *interesting* relationships between people were those that were not overtly sexual. Ray's guffaw had echoed all the way down to the lake, but when Joel dared him to think of one book or movie in which happy sexual union took center stage, he couldn't do it. Neither could she. What people wrote about was the stuff *around* sex—desire, or near misses, or jealousy, or desertions—or, as Joel had pointed out, relationships like the ones in *My Antonia* or *Portrait of a Lady* that might have been sexual but weren't. Later, Ray had remarked that after you'd talked to Joel, things looked a bit different.

Anyway, she hadn't gotten to the journal, and this was the perfect time. She should have thought of it days ago. In two minutes, she filled her backpack with breakfast and lunch stuff, shoved her feet into her sock-stuffed Wellingtons, and slipped out to her car. Not a moment too soon, either. As she'd taken off her Walkman, she'd heard someone open a door upstairs.

She eased the poor old Toyota up the Ward Place driveway and squinted at the house through the rain. It was beginning to look less shabby, but if you ignored the bare walls where the barn had been, it wasn't much different. And that was good. It would be a shame to displace the Wards. She stepped over the threshold, listening. Except for the patter of rain on the porch roof, there was nothing to hear but silence; not that there ever was. She walked to the kitchen feeling it waft around her and hoping that making breakfast wouldn't cause offense. Apparently it didn't. In a few minutes the stove-top percolator was blipping along in its primitive way, two slices of bread were undergoing uneven metamorphosis in the toaster, and the silence had receded to a respectful distance.

The journal was lying on the dining room table, where Joel had put it. There were other things, too—an ancient volume of Longfellow's collected poetry, a pile of yellowed papers that looked like accounts, and a folder of old pictures and clippings—but the journal was obviously the place to start. She rescued the toast in the nick of time, poured herself a cup of coffee, and opened the old-fashioned notebook to its first page. "Diary. Clara B. Ward. May 15, 1929–"

May 15, 1929. Heavy rain. Late for school, mud. After, Mr. Clark asked how Ma would feel about me going on. Told him I'd ask, but Ma and Asa too tired this evening. Darned 4 socks.

May 16. Sun but cold. Asa planned to start planting but took Ned and Tom to be shod instead. Gid not here, had to help with milking, couldn't finish lessons.

Ma. Asa. Gid. They had to be Mary Ward and her two brothers. And since 'Ma and Asa' sounded sort of like a corporation, presumably Asa was the 'good' brother, and Gid, who ran out on the milking, was the one old-timers still spoke of as a ne'er-do-well.

May 17. Still cold. Started <u>Ivanhoe</u> in school. Mr. Clark's favorite book. Bonnie had her calf at night, it died. Gid still not back.

May 18. Rain. Gid back early morning. Asa gave him whatfor, but Ma said it was all right, it hadn't been fit weather for planting. Rebecca has met the Black Knight. I like her better than Rowena. Ma's hands sore, I did the milking.

May 19. Very windy. Mr. Clark visited. Ma said I could go on, Grandpa Ward would have liked that, but I'd have to get a scholarship, was that possible for girls? After, Gid told me he could get the money easy, but I said there was no point to riling Asa again, where would he live if he didn't live with us?

So what Mr. Clark wanted Clara to 'go on' in was school—college, probably. That was really interesting. Joel shouldn't have quit after the first couple of entries. But then, he wasn't into the Wards the way she was. She made herself two more pieces of toast and read on as she ate them.

May 27, 1929. She looked back to the last entry. That was over a week's gap. Was Clara just too busy to write, or had Gid not followed her advice and 'riled' Asa, turning the atmosphere of the house into one she'd rather not write about? There was no way of telling.

Sunny and warm. Planted potatoes all day, missed class on the Tournament, the most exciting chapter. Hate to disappoint Mr. Clark.

May 28. Sunny. More planting. Asa got a letter from his old army sergeant, hasn't seen him since Legion meeting in 1923. Never seen Asa so excited.

May 29. Raining. Mr. Clark gave me his notes at dinner hour, so I didn't miss much. After milking, Asa had me write a letter inviting his sergeant to visit when he comes to Newfane in June. Had to copy it five times, he didn't want any mistakes.

Asa couldn't write? Charlie munched the last piece of toast reflectively. That was strange, because Mary Ward certainly could; Joel said a lot of the records in the folders were hers. Maybe their dear, alcoholic father had thought education was women's work.

May 30. Sun. Planted 17 rows beans, 20 rows peas, corn, winter squash, summer squash. Will be canning all August.

May 31. Sun. Asa in Memorial Day Parade, looks much handsomer than most of the others. Saw Mrs. Taylor, she asked would I like to work for her. Picnic by the lake with Wheelers. Joe Howe there with Susan. Gid not home, afraid he's gone again.

June 1. Sun. Gid not back. Told Ma about Mrs. Taylor, it would be good money for college. She said Newfane is too far off, and Pa would turn over in his grave if he knew a Ward hired out to fancy summer folks like the Taylors.

June 2. Rain. Gid back, he and Asa shouting very late in the kitchen.

June 7—another gap. It seemed her instincts had been right; those breaks were associated with arguments over Gid. She was going to have to find someone who could tell her what Gid had been up to. No good, you could be sure, if he thought it could make enough money to send Clara to college.

Rain for last two days. Finished Ivanhoe, he should have married

Rebecca, Susan thinks so, too. Mr. Clark asked if I could read books for college in the summer. Told him I'd try, but can't think when I'll find the time. Gid and Asa still not speaking.

June 8. Rain. Asa got a letter from his sergeant. He will come June 12! Ma and I scrubbed the parlor floor and blacked the stove. Asa so particular.

June 9. Hot. Scrubbed kitchen and dining room floors. Ma finished slip cover.

June 10. Hot morning, storm later. Susan very pretty at graduation. She and Joe Howe will have the Howes' little house, near the Wheeler place. Should be ready for them by the end of summer. After, Mr. Clark drove me home. Beautiful horse, but he says he wants a Ford. Asked me if I planned to get married after graduation, like Susan. Asked him to let me out at the bottom of the drive, so got very wet when storm started.

June 11. Clearing. Cooked all day.

June 12. Sunny and clear. Beautiful dinner with Sergeant Brent. Younger than Asa, I hadn't realized. Gid says he has an English accent, but can't see how Gid would know. Stayed until milking time, got chores done very late.

That was sort of an anti-climax, after all that cleaning and cooking. It would have been nice to hear a little more about Sergeant Brent. But maybe... She looked up suddenly—there were footsteps creaking across the front porch. Pushing her chair back, she hurried guiltily into the living room. Joel hadn't told her she shouldn't eat anything but lunch here, but maybe she should have asked.

It wasn't Joel who stood dripping in the doorway, though; it was Eleanor, smiling an odd smile. "You made them coffee," she said, sniffing. "How kind of you."

"Them—?"

"The Wards." Eleanor laughed and pushed back her hood. "I came to give you a day off. Joel and Ray left for Keene half an hour ago, and they won't be back until late afternoon."

"Gee, they might have told me."

"They tried. They got the answering machine, then a few minutes later David called back, saying you had already left. By that time, they were eager to get going, so I said I would come over here and give you the message."

"Well, thanks. And look—come on in. There's toast, there's coffee, and there's this great journal."

"Great…?"

"Journal," she said carefully, pointing over her shoulder to the dining room. "It's in there. Want to see?"

"Oh, the journal, the journal," said Eleanor, looking longingly at the table. "Joel told me about it over a week ago, and I've been trying to find time to come over and look at it and the other stuff."

"So come in! We can read it together, and you can tell me about Gid—"

"—who? No, look, never mind. I would love to spend the morning with you, but unfortunately I have a doctor's appointment in less than an hour, and it's in Greenfield."

"In Greenfield! What's wrong?"

Eleanor made a wry face. "Nothing that hasn't been wrong for some time. I'm going to check in with my audiologist. I knew Hattie had been doing more and more for me, but I hadn't realized how much I've lost until the last couple of weeks. Joel has been absolutely noble—every supper, he patiently talks to me about the progress you all have been making. I can just *see* his need to talk about other things, but there's nothing I can do. There's something about constant repetition that reduces emotional distress and intellectual insight alike to one-syllable words. And so rather than be a burden—"

"—you're *not* a burden!"

"If I'm not now, I will be soon. At the very least, I need to find what technology can do for me. My aids are five years old. I'm sure the new ones are better."

Five years old. Suddenly she was twelve, sitting frozen in the back seat with Hattie as Eleanor drove home from Greenfield with silent tears pouring down her face. "Hey, would you like company? I haven't been to Greenfield for a long time, and my car is running great."

Eleanor's face softened as she slowly processed the offer. "You're a sweetheart. I'd take you up on that, except that there is a second part to my mission here, which is to suggest you spend your unexpected vacation at home."

"At home!"

Eleanor nodded. "David and Salome dropped by the house yesterday evening, looking for you. They said you haven't been around much."

"There's nothing to *be* around. I mean, both of them write all morning and part of the afternoon—which is of course when I'm gone—and when I get home, well, even if they haven't gone out, we're not an everyone-eats-together family."

"I didn't get most of that," said Eleanor, "but I don't really need to."

"No. It's nothing new."

"It might be. Salome is—well, different from the others."

"I'll say!"

Eleanor smiled quizzically. "She's tough as nails. I rather like that."

"So does he, apparently." Somehow it came out more bitterly than she'd intended.

"Okay, okay," said Eleanor. "But having talked to them, I really can't let you drive me to Greenfield. Enjoy the journal. I promise I'll get to it soon, and then we can talk." She smiled and put her hood up. "Here I go."

Suddenly, it was just unbearable watching her cross the porch. "Eleanor—" She was going to add *I love you*, but Eleanor ran down the stairs and out to her car without hearing her call, so all she could do was wave.

Inside, she put her plate in the sink and went back to Clara. Let's see, Sergeant Brent had left June 12th, and predictably, Gid left the 13th, which meant that Asa, Mary and Clara had to do the hoeing on the 14th and—and look at that! Brent came back the 15th. And the 18th, after the thunderstorm. Something was definitely up, even though all Clara said about it was 'Brent visited' at the end of a few entries. Because 'Brent visited' an awful lot of times: June 20, 21, 23, 25. You wouldn't expect him to come back that much just to see Asa. If only Clara would say a little more! Her eyes wandered down the page, stopping on an entry in which the even hand turned to a scrawl and made no note on the weather.

> *July 3. Brent said he would take us to Brattleboro fireworks in his Ford. Asa said Ma and I were going to the Wheelers' picnic at noon. Ma said there would be plenty of time after, Gid said there would be lots of other girls in autos at the fireworks. But Asa said, not nice girls.*

> *July 4. Sun. Beautiful day for Wheelers' picnic. Susan asked was I feeling poorly. I said no. Nothing left of my pies, everybody liked them. Asa and Brent gone to fireworks when Ma and I got back. Gid gone too, left milking for us.*

So much for that. It seemed Asa was glad to see Brent at the farm and liked him well enough to enjoy a drive to Brattleboro, but when it came to his niece—well, it was the same thing that made it necessary for Mr. Clark to leave her at the bottom of the driveway in the rain. She was, by God, going to remain a 'nice girl.'

The penalty for which, of course, was the end of what might have been a courtship—but wait! It wasn't! It rained every day after the 4th; Gid didn't return the night of the 4th, or any thereafter; but Brent 'visited' July 6, 7, 9, 10, 12,—over the page—13. And then, on the 14th, the entry changed: 'went walking with Brent.' Wonderful—a romance. She tucked one foot under herself in the chair and prepared to enjoy it.

Somebody knocked on the front door. God, could it possibly be…? She tip-toed across the creaking living room floor and peeked out the window that overlooked the porch. It wasn't David; it was

Salome. And there wasn't any chance of ignoring her either, because she'd seen the curtains move.

Charlie opened the door. "Hello. What brings you— Shit, what have you been doing, swimming?"

"I might as well have been," said Salome, dropping her Gore-Tex jacket on the porch and looking down at her soaked jeans. "When we stopped by last week, David said he would never attempt that driveway in the Jag again, and since I told him I was going to go downtown to get the mail, I had to be extra careful, so I left it at the bottom of the hill and cut across the pasture. And all these huge creatures charged up, drooling and licking their chops—I thought cows were herbivores, for Godsake!"

"They are," said Charlie, laughing. "But these cows are a little spoiled; Joel likes them, and he's been giving them salt every day. Even so, it's not necessary to roll under the fence and run through the mowing. You can just say 'shoo.' Come on in. There's coffee."

She led the way to the kitchen and warmed up the pot while Salome sat at the table, shivering. Neither of them said anything until Charlie moved the journal and plunked down two heavy white mugs next to Longfellow. "Milk or sugar?"

"Both, if you've got them. Look, Charlie, there's no reason to live like this."

"Like what?"

"Like I've run you out of David's."

"No way have you run me out of David's. It's always like this. I've got three jobs—Cocoa, the riding lessons, and now painting this house. That means I'm just not around much."

"You can't tell me you have to leave at 6:30 on a rainy morning."

Charlie looked back across the living room. "Well, no. But it's nice and private here—and, well, I mean, sometimes you guys could be a little quieter."

"Was *that* it? God, I'm sorry—I guess we got kind of carried away. You'll see, when the time comes." She looked up from her mug. "I take it, it hasn't?"

Charlie felt her face turning red. "That's for me to know and you to find out."

"Hey, there's no shame in being a bit behind-hand. Sometimes I wish I'd waited myself—adolescent guys are such animals."

The rain pounded on the roof, and the presences whispered reproachfully.

Salome looked around. "This place is something else. Are those the old papers Eleanor and Joel were telling us about last night?"

"Yes, I suppose so."

"Cool. I've never really been into local history, but I hear it's a real way forward these days, if you get serious about it. And boy, talk about the perfect venue—wow. But look, I'll tell David what you said, and I totally, absolutely promise things will be different."

"Thank you. I'll try to be around more. But like I say, I'm very busy, and I'm used to living here and there. After all, there've been other—shoot, I'm sorry."

"Don't apologize. Of course there have been."

"You *know?*" Charlie stared at her. "You *came* here, knowing...?"

"How else could I have come here? A man's reputation travels before him, and the MLA is a very small world."

"You didn't think it was pretty fucking pathetic that he should do that to himself?"

"Charlie, he doesn't do anything other attractive men don't do. It's no crime for a single man to date, so long as he keeps his hands off his students and his colleagues. And he does." She looked up. "Believe me, I wouldn't be here if he didn't."

"Because then it wouldn't do you any good?"

"Jesus Christ!" said Salome. "So you think I'm—"

"Cool it! I just listened to what you said. You knew about him. You're too bright to be co-dependent. You're too classy-looking to have to turn to an old man for sex. So logically, there has to be something in it for you."

"Okay, okay." Salome stared down into her cup. "Um—how old are you?"

"Seventeen."

"Right. Let me tell you where I was when I was seventeen. It's

1983. There's a slump. My dad is laid off from the Ford factory, my mom has no skills. I luck into a waitressing job, but they want me forty hours a week, on top of high school. What happens to my grades?"

"They go down, I suppose."

"Fucking right they do. Only to B's, but that's enough to lose me college scholarships. So I wait tables all through college, all through grad school. I go to the MLA convention. I get offered a job which will become tenure track if my dissertation is done by the end of the summer, which it can't possibly be, because summer means waiting tables ten hours a day, six days a week. I'm sitting in a bar, crying about this, and up comes a good-looking guy who bucks me up, buys me a drink, and asks me to spend the summer in his house in Vermont, so I'll have time to finish. What would you do if you were me?"

"I'd wait tables until my teeth dropped out."

"No, you wouldn't. Not if you'd been doing it every year for nine years, one day after another, so tired you could hardly see straight, getting your ass pinched by drunks who don't tip. Not if you imagined sitting on a hill, working eight hours a day at your computer, and spending the other part of the day with a man who really knew your field, *plus* being a good dancer and good company and…well, vulnerable. Call me a cynic if you want, but I was too weak to resist."

"So you're just doing it to keep the job?"

"God, I hope not. I like David. He's got enough faults for four different people, but he's really, truly generous. And bright. You've got to know this is the first time in my whole life I've had somebody to talk to about what I'm interested in. It's so amazing I can't help being grateful."

"I think he wants more than gratitude," said Charlie sadly.

"I know. I've been doing my best for him. Look, I'm not trying to say I'm some sort of winner, Charlie. I just want you to know that I do care about what happens to your father—" Salome rubbed her eyes. "And I wish you'd come back to the house, because I don't feel too good about the whole thing, if you need to know, and driving you out makes me feel even worse. Especially since I talked to your friend Eleanor. See, David introduced her as Eleanor Klimowski. It wasn't until last night that I found she was also Eleanor Randall, the woman John Adams College fired because she went deaf."

"*You* knew that? I mean, it was six years ago."

"Every feminist in America knows that! The whole thing was discrimination made worse by dirty politics—like, *unthinkable*! If she had been a man, they never could've gotten rid of her—never would have even *tried*. And not a single man in academia protested, including David. He has the good grace to be ashamed of that, but she— she's *cleaning houses* for Chrissake, and she's brought up this brilliant new woman pianist without being able to hear, and been a second mother to you on the side—see, I made David tell me all this stuff, and I— Well, hell, what can you say about somebody who's somehow managed to stay true to herself through all that, when you've let yourself believe what you've done is the only way to get ahead?"

Charlie put down the mug and looked at her. It was hard to believe that girls like Salome cried, but there she was shivering in her wet jeans, sobbing her eyes out with her head on Mary Ward's table. The poor kid. Charlie put one hand on her shoulder. "There's no reason to run yourself down. You've had a tough time, and you've done really well with what you've got. Just let me get my stuff together here, and I'll drive you down to the Jag and follow you home."

Leaving Salome to her tears, she washed the mugs, tidied the kitchen, and gathered the stuff into her backpack. As they left, she closed the journal gently, hoping that Clara and Brent hadn't been listening somewhere in the shadows. Imagine what they would have thought.

7. Calls

Derri paused expectantly by the phone as Eleanor walked down the upstairs hall. She could hear its insistent ringing, but she didn't pick it up. Not now. Not right now. She waited six more rings; when it finally stopped, she said a few words to the dial tone to confirm Derri's conditioned reaction, then hung up. There. That should do it. She patted the dog, walked into her bedroom, and slowly slipped off her skirt, watching the sun break through the scattering rain clouds and illuminate the ruins across the road.

She should have known. She *had* known—at least, she'd known that her hearing was getting worse. But if she had realized how much worse, she would have spared her poor car the trip to Greenfield and herself the cost of a day's work. A hundred bucks, plus the price of the testing, not that she begrudged Susan her fee. Very few audiologists, watching the pattern of unheard beeps emerge on their charts, would have had the kindness to curtail the test. Very few, recognizing her inability to distinguish her old friends *popcorn, hot dog, sidewalk* from each other, would have stopped and let her out of that dreadful, soundproof cell. Or let her look at the charts. Diagnosis: sensorineural degeneration. Word comprehension: nil. Level of loss: profound.

"But that's impossible! I'm managing!"
"Of course you are. Your speech-reading is amazing."
"It's a hell of a lot less amazing when I'm talking with somebody who hasn't been trained to talk to the deaf. One of those new hearing aids wouldn't help?"
"You can try, but frankly, at your level technology has very little to offer except expense. At least at present. There's a new procedure called the cochlear implant—very promising, as computer chips get smaller—that would be perfect for you eventually. Right now, it wouldn't give you more than you have, but in ten or fifteen years..."

Ten or fifteen years. When she was fifty-five. Sixty.

Derri jumped up and trotted to the hall, looking back. Again? On impulse, she put her aids on the bureau and walked slowly towards the phone. She couldn't hear it. Not even standing right next to it. Maybe it had stopped. She put her hand on the receiver, and the sound leapt into her mind. Again. Again. Again. Again. Again.

Strange that somebody would call her so persistently. It couldn't be Hattie; she knew better than to call herself, and Goldsmith had David's and the Walkers' numbers for emergencies. Could it be for Joel? Possibly—but not likely. He'd hardly used the phone at all. And even if this were for him, answering it without an aid was absurd. In fact, as those four lost jobs had proved in the last few months, answering it at all was absurd.

The last few months. That fast.

She patted the baffled dog. "Don't worry, fella. You did fine. I just can't manage it right now."

She wandered back to the bedroom and put on her jeans, jogging shoes, and a work shirt. It could be worse. Hattie was on her own, now. It had been tough enough, becoming a pianist up here with a mother whose loss of music cut her off from her father's circles. If

Hattie were younger, still dependent on the byzantine telephone arrangements that accompanied lessons and the attendant commutes to Boston and New York, it would be next to impossible.

No, if it had to happen, it was good that it had happened now. All she had to worry about was the threat of dependency—and that, by God, could be overcome. Colleen was finding more work for her. The TDD Susan had suggested would allow her some access to the phone. She'd figure out what Salome would call "a way forward." Of course she would. But not right now. Right now, she'd—

Derri's nose nudged her hand. What, again? She stepped to her bureau and shoved her aids into her ears, but instead of the telephone, she heard a welcoming bark and the scramble of toenails down the stairs. Joel must be back. She hurried down the stairs herself, but as she reached the door, the telephone began again.

"Hi," she said as he stumbled into the kitchen, his arms filled with bags and boxes, "can you get that?"

"Sure," he said—then, looking at her more carefully, "Is something wrong?"

Ring. Ring. Ring.

"Not that I know of, but it's been doing that for the past half-hour at least."

He gave her an odd look, but he strode down the hall and answered it. It *was* for him. She heard his voice rise in surprised greeting, then continue in some sort of discussion. She waited a minute or two, but at last she scribbled "gone for a walk" on a piece of paper and stuck it on his packages with a clothespin.

Outside, Derri started up the mowing, but she directed him across the road. The maple grove was still unspoiled, and at the top of the hill it still looked over the Ward Place and the lake. She'd walked there when Mary Ward died. With her father, after her mother died. By herself, after her father died. With toddler Hattie, when Stanislaw died. It was a comforting spot, with its uninvolved, timeless perspective. Yes, she'd go there.

Helena looked up from her yellow lupines, sighing as the phone began again. In past days, she would have scrambled to her feet and run in to get it, but as two failed attempts had already proved, her present speed did not even allow her to reach the porch before the ringing stopped. Maybe she should go in; it had been ringing quite persistently. And yet...she looked past the lupines to the poppies, bowed but fortunately not destroyed by the morning's rain. At a distance, in this light, their incandescent splendor was magnificent, but a closer look revealed grass and fading bluets starting at their feet and spreading into the astilbe and the foxgloves. There was much to do, and it seemed a shame to interrupt it—especially since the caller could easily be just another realtor who had heard she'd had her place appraised. No, she would not go in; she would work further from the house.

She walked slowly through the barn cellars, pausing here and there to pull up a weed or snip a faded blossom, until she stopped in satisfaction at the irises. Replanting them in rich compost had had marvelous results: they'd doubled their size, and the exotic black "Midnight Clears" were in full flower. She pulled a few impertinent violets from between them, and was suddenly catapulted back twenty years to the darkened Mather College gardens from which she'd stolen them.

Nathaniel leaned on his cane, his hair shining silver under the lamp-post. "For heaven's sake, Helena! Dig them up! It's not as if it were a felony."

She plunged her trowel deep into the ground; within a few minutes she'd secured ten small "Midnight Clears" and more grass than should have been entangled in their roots. "Are finances really so bad that you can't afford to have somebody tend the gardens?" she asked as she stood up. "It seems a shame to let the grounds go."

"You were at the Board meeting," he said. "Alumni gifts down 50%. Enrollment shrinking yearly. Inevitable rise in tuition despite

lowering of academic standards—"

"Of course," she acknowledged hastily. "The grounds are low priority."

"Exactly. But I assure you, I'm not insensitive to symbolism. Prospective students who visit Mather can see its degeneration before their very eyes, and be forewarned."

She slipped the irises into a paper bag. "Perhaps they'd ignore 'degeneration' here just as they do everywhere else if you'd present the current slump in other terms."

"Perhaps. But rhetoric can only achieve so much in the face of truth. Observe." He limped ten stiff steps away—then turned, lifted his cane, and strode towards her as he had when they'd first known each other, smiling, with his ringless hand outstretched. She had just long enough to feel shocked by the passage of time before his right knee buckled under him, and he fell sideways.

"You take my point?" he panted.

"Only as a false analogy," she said, helping him up. "Rhetoric or no rhetoric, colleges, unlike uncompromising idealists, aren't mortal. Degeneration doesn't inevitably lead to their demise."

"Well done," he said lightly. "I should know better than to stage arguments for you." But he walked back to the president's house in evident pain, and when she gave him her arm, it was he who leaned on her.

Degeneration. Helena steadied herself on the white gate as she stepped down to the next garden. It was inevitable, of course, but its specific forms always took one by surprise. Who would have believed, thirty years ago, that Mather College, half of whose students had been brought to the campus by Nathaniel's tireless recruitment in farm and factory towns, would be condemned as a bastion of discrimination because all those students were male? Who could have anticipated that Mather College, which had offered classical education to men of every conceivable race, would be criticized because the Greeks and Romans were thought to have been white? The aged should not judge, of course. Yet so far as she could see, the present world had become Edwardian again, with a few powerful, wealthy people dependent on the labors of a working class bundled off to the third world and the services of a home-bred class of hirelings. How peculiar that such a society could condemn Nathaniel's elitism while remaining oblivious to its own.

She knelt awkwardly on the damp grass and began to weed the columbines and thrift. Before she was half finished, a car roared up her driveway and stopped in a storm of flying gravel. She looked up, not to find who it was—for it could be nobody but David—but to determine why he should have come at this hour. As he vaulted over the gate, his face solved the mystery; some crisis was evidently at hand. She struggled to her feet, wondering what it could be.

"Thank God!" he said, taking both her dirt-encrusted hands, "Nobody has been able to reach you—I was expecting to find you keeled over amongst your delphiniums!"

"It will be a few weeks before there's any danger of that," she said, laughing. But she was touched; she had never imagined that her failure to answer the phone would cause such concern. "I'm sorry to have worried you. How long have you been calling?"

"Only a few times before I jumped in the car—but the president's office has been trying to get you ever since lunch. Andrew finally called me himself and asked if you were all right."

"Andrew! Good heavens, has the college burned to the ground?"

"Don't smile like that," he said reproachfully. "A big pooh-bah—Warden, or Principal, or Chairman, whatever—of Literature at Trinity College, Cambridge called Andrew this morning, because he hasn't been able to get hold of Joel."

"I see," said Helena dryly. "And this is a matter of such deep concern that Andrew called me right after he gave out Eleanor's number?"

"Damn right! It's *got* to be a job offer—with a label, no doubt, at his level."

"Oh come. It could just as easily be an invitation to speak at a conference."

"Nonsense! When a lady pops off and leaves an historic legacy to Mather College, and when that lady's husband is a major Renaissance critic, warning bells go off in department offices all over the globe! Face it, *everybody* makes offers to big-shots after their wives die. The first thing I told Andrew when he called about Letty was that the college was going to have a hell of a time holding onto Joel, now."

Helena hid a smile. "Still, there's no hard fact behind your conjecture, is there?"

"No," he admitted. "But Andrew wants to put together a counter-offer, just in case. Which is why he wants to talk to you. There's bound to be money involved, not to mention—"

He went on, but while she forced herself to look attentive, she wondered how long Joel had been at Mather. End of the Fifties? No, Nathaniel had first spoken of him during the summer Kennedy got the nomination. But that was a long time ago. And later—

"Hold onto the faculty!" Nathaniel poured them each a double shot of cognac. "My dear, to see the academic vultures hovering over Mather's bones, you have only to look up. They've been wheeling over the campus since the first whiff of financial trouble." He handed her a snifter with his usual ironic bow, but to her sorrow, he put his own on the table and sat down stiffly before he picked it up. "I'm going to announce two resignations at the board meeting tomorrow: O'Brian and Rosenthal."

"You're joking!"

"I assure you, I'm not. The vultures offered them more money and less art. One graduate course a semester, every third year off for research. Remember, higher education these days is no longer concerned with teaching the young; it's concerned with grants, research, government projects. In a world that buys and sells intellect, what's surprising is not that O'Brian and Rosenthal yielded to temptation, but that it took them almost the whole semester to do so. That's Joel's influence, I think. He convinced Standish not to leave last year, you know."

"Joel will be getting offers himself, pretty soon, if they're starting to be made," she said thoughtfully. "His book made something of a splash, didn't it?"

*"A big splash. Nobody will ever be able to read Renaissance po-
etry the same way again. And as for offers—Yale called him a while
ago and suggested that he apply for the endowed chair they had open."*

*"You two are certainly souls of discretion. Here I've been in bliss-
ful ignorance—"*

*" —The discretion was all Joel's. The offer was made last fall; I
found out about it last week, through one of my Yale friends. Apparently, the job would have been his if he'd applied, but he refused—politely, of course (when is Joel **not** polite?), but immediately, absolutely,
over the phone. He said his wife wouldn't be as happy in New Haven
as she was in Whitby."*

"I...see," she said slowly.

*He shook his head. "I couldn't say anything to him, of course,
since he wanted to keep it to himself. But, God! To stay at a college
that's fighting for its life, when the Mellon Center is going to make Yale
the Mecca of Renaissance scholars—!"*

*"Well," she said, "Joel's consideration for Letty's professional hap-
piness sounds strange to our generation, but it's becoming more and
more common. And certainly, the entertaining Letty does for you gives
her more status in the academic world than she'd have as a Yale wife."*

*"You're forgetting that Letty's 'profession,' as you so kindly call it,
is completely dependent the continuation of my presidency. Neither
Joel nor Letty seem to have thought of that." He looked down at his
knotted hands as they swirled the cognac in his snifter. "I should be
touched at their belief in my tenacity."*

*"Not to mention, immortality" she said, smiling. But when he
smiled back at her, the weariness in his face made her realize, for the
first time, that it had been more than pride and stubbornness that kept
him from yielding to the pressure to retire.*

"—And there you have it," said David. "Complex, no?

"Indeed," she said, struggling back to the present. "No matter
what we propose, Yale—"

"Cambridge, Cambridge!" he said, laughing. "Which is just
as well, because we have a handle on him for Cambridge that we

wouldn't have for Yale—the Ward Place."

"The Ward Place! I thought he still hadn't decided what to do with it."

"Don't you be too sure," he said. "The other day, Sal and I stopped by to see if we could find Charlie—she's painting for him, and between that and the horse we never see her—and there he was, on the roof, whistling away and fixing the slates. Not bad, for a guy whose arm you had to twist to get here for two weeks, huh? It's been more than three now, and he shows no signs of leaving. Looks like he's hooked on the place. If he is, and if we can think up a deal that makes it easy for him to keep it—" He broke off, frowning. "You look skeptical. What do you know about the Ward Place that I don't?"

"Nothing. I was merely thinking that, as Joel has been at Mather so long, it might not be a bad thing for him to move on."

"How can you even *think* such a thing! Christ, thanks to Letty (may she rest in peace), Mather has lost so much prestige that Joel's reputation is the *only* thing that entices first rate Literature people to apply for jobs there. The place'd be belly-up without him!"

"And what has it cost his work to keep the place afloat in the proper position?"

"His work's fine! His last book came out in— Well, it has been a while, come to think of it, but he must have something in the hopper. He got that Guggie in '87—"

"—And couldn't do the research he needed because Letty couldn't leave Whitby."

"Christ! The woman was really pernicious!"

"The woman was really ill," she said gently.

"Okay, okay. But that's all in the past. There's nothing to keep Joel from his work if he stays at Mather now."

"Nothing but the past."

David tore his immaculately coifed hair. "I can't believe this! You're seriously advocatin—"

"—All I'm advocating at the moment is that we determine whether Trinity College, Cambridge has made Joel an offer or not. Andrew should know by now."

"Then you'll call him?"

She glanced at her watch. "Right now, if you'd like to be involved."

"No, no," he said in relief. "I'll leave it entirely to you. Besides—" starting towards the gate— "I've got to get home. We're supposed to be at the Zimmermans' at seven for dinner, and Salome doesn't like to be late."

"Of course not," she said.

He spun out of the driveway, waving cheerfully, and she went inside, wondering who Salome might be, that her likes and dislikes affected his actions.

Trinity College, Cambridge. It would be very interesting finding what Andrew had to say. Her gardening jeans were so muddy that she felt obliged to change them, a process which, like everything else, took longer than it used to. By the time she sat down by the phone, it was well after six, and Andrew was unavailable even at his private number. She left a message, imagining her canned voice speaking into the empty study that had once been so familiar.

8. Offers

King's College Chapel from a Cam lined with daffodils. Conversational punting journeys to the pubs in Grantchester. The sound of change-ringing, drifting like mist around the edges of leaded windows. It would, to say the least, be a far cry from this. Joel inched forward on his back and set up the final jack post under the Ward house porch. Bracing one foot against the foundation, he sat up as far as he could and tightened the screw, grunting as the effort increased. The beams creaked, and the post dug itself into the two-by-eight he'd set it on. That was probably enough.

He lay back, hearing again John Ferguson's clipped, sensible voice offering him—perfunctorily, almost casually—Trinity's new Queen Elizabeth Professorship of Renaissance Studies. "That's Elizabeth I, in case you're concerned about a retinue of corgis." And then, after the details, "I realize there are many things you have to think over, Joel, but the financing is contingent upon our hiring somebody this year, and as your reputation for unavailability is legion— No, no,

I assure you, you're the only man with a whole-hearted, unanimous vote. It's just a matter of timing. Would a month be long enough for you to decide?"

He rolled out into the late afternoon sunshine, feeling sweat trickle down the sides of his face. It wouldn't be the sleepy fenland Cambridge of his Junior year abroad, of course. Now it was becoming England's Silicon Valley, hi-tech, upscale, paralyzed by traffic. Inside the college walls, the Olympians at whom he'd stared in circumspect awe were long dead, replaced by younger men hustling their scholarly wares and dreaming of the greenback pastures of the States. But a Renaissance Professorship would give him a base from which he could work to unite a Balkanized field. He and John Ferguson, whose literary passions had raised him to Olympian heights even in this fallen age, and with whom, on the two memorable occasions they had met, he had talked the night through in a way he had talked with no one but Nathaniel. It was such an exciting prospect that he'd agreed to take the month. Temporizing fool that he was.

What could he possibly have been thinking of? He couldn't leave the country now. There was the will, with all the duties of executorship. There was the Ward Place and its needs. And there was Mather College, where a host of obligations awaited—demanded—his attention.

A few yards away, Ray shoved a couple of barn boards into the pickup. "Quittin' time—hey, that looks better!"

Joel wiped his face. "Think it'll last if I don't do more than that?"

Ray bent over and examined the work judiciously. "It'll last as long as you do."

And who was Joel Hendrickson, that he should ask his work to last longer than he did?

"You look like you could use a beer," said Ray. "Want to stop by?"

"Thanks, but I think I'll get on home."

"Okay." Ray heaved himself into the truck, his foot automatically avoiding the hole in its floor. Joel crept back under the porch, gathering tools. After a little silence, the truck started and drove off.

He ducked out onto the lawn and slouched past the straightened, freshly painted sheds to the back of the house. Charlie was perched on the top step of Ray's six-foot folding ladder, steadying her half backbend by clinging to the roof with one hand while she painted under the eaves with the other. The position no longer alarmed him; he'd learned she was unaffected by the laws of physics.

"Charlie? Quitting time."

"Okay." She gave the eaves one last swipe and straightened up. "Hey, listen. I brought my suit. How about a swim?"

He considered it as she climbed down. It might be just the thing; he was dirty and depressed, and the lake was beautiful. On the other hand...his mind floated back to the sporting-goods store where he'd bought running clothes a couple of weeks ago, and to the full-length mirror in which he'd taken a good look at himself for the first time in years. He shouldn't have been shocked, of course. Only fanatics like David aged gracefully, and for that matter, David was aging ungracefully in his own way. He glanced at Charlie as she tapped the top back on the paint can. If he'd had a daughter, he would have given her the attention she deserved.

But he didn't have a daughter. Never would. No, his life was confined to things that would last as long as he did. "A swim sounds nice, but I think I'll pass."

"Oh, come on," she said. "Just a quick dip."

Just a quick dip—but there she'd be, heartbreakingly young, completely at ease with her beautiful body in the tank suit that had been hanging on one of the dining room chairs all day, while he, fish-white, unfit—"It's out of the question," he said firmly, not looking at her.

"Okay," she said. Then, after a short pause, "I wish you'd tell me what's wrong."

He started back to the front yard. "What makes you think *any-thing* is wrong?"

She said nothing, but her startled face told him he had snapped. "I'm sorry," he said, trying to smile. "There really isn't anything wrong—just a decision I wish I didn't have to make."

"A decision!" She looked at him in alarm. "About the Ward Place?"

And here he thought he'd been so circumspect. "No. At least, not directly."

She put the paint can on the porch and began to rinse out the brush. "Sometimes," she ventured, "talking about things helps people make decisions."

"Not when they're too grouchy to discuss things rationally."

She looked up wryly from the can of paint thinner. "Rationality isn't everything. My mom says it was invented by 18th-century men and inflicted on women and children ever since." She stood up and pulled a nickel out of the pocket of her cut-offs. "Try flipping a coin."

"You're going to replace rationality with probability?"

"Nope. I'm going to replace rationality with a way of finding out what you really want." Leaving the brush, she came and sat down next to him on the steps. "Watch. Heads is one of your options, tails the other. And the rule is this: once the coin lands, you've got to give up the losing option entirely and adopt the winner—no negotiating. Okay? Here we go."

Unwillingly, he watched the coin flash in the air. Heads, Cambridge. Tails, Mather.

"Tails it is," said Charlie, extending the nickel on the back of her hand. "Now, quick, before you have time to think—are you glad or sorry?"

He gazed morosely at the tiny, circumscribed Monticello. Well, that's what he got for not turning down the offer over the phone in his usual manner. *Your reputation for unavailability is legion.* You bet. A temptation firmly squelched didn't haunt one the way—

A hand laid itself gently on his knee. He jumped up, every muscle tensed.

"Hey, I'm sorry." Charlie's voice mixed with the clank of his tools as he tossed them into their box. "You just looked so miserable."

Oh, to be instantly transported to a desert island, where he was the only human being present! Except—ah, the irony of it!—this *was* his desert island. Joel Hendrickson's haven of refuge, safe from all obligations, temptations, interruptions. Delusion, delusion! One of hundreds! The fond idea that given time, he could do work of lasting value. The absurd assumption that he *had* such time. The dream that he could start anew.

Nearby, a door creaked open. Turning, he found that one of his wishes, at least, had been granted. He was alone.

"Charlie?"

No answer.

He walked up the steps and peered through the screen. "Charlie?"

"Over here," she said, shoving the shed door closed. "I'm off for that swim. See you tomorrow, second thing." She jumped into the Toyota and took off, waving out the window.

He watched her disappear, then stashed his own tools in the shed and started up the pasture hill. Had he hurt her feelings? All he'd done was stand up too quickly because she'd irritated him—*try flipping a coin*. Christ! Turning by the graveyard, he strode along the path he'd worn to Eleanor's, shooing Mike Wolfington's cows out of his way. *Rationality was invented by 18th-century men and inflicted on women and children ever since.* Oh, sure.

He ducked under the wire gate and strode up the hill to the newly graveled driveway that had replaced the hemlock grove. As it turned, he looked up the clear-cut hill to his right—and remembered with a shock that he'd seen Eleanor sitting up there yesterday, with her back against the trunk of the last felled maple and her head on her knees. And he—he'd gone on to the Ward Place, savoring the temptations of Ferguson's call. Done nothing. Appalling. The man he once had been would never—

And who was to blame, if he was no longer the man he once had been? Who had so willingly refused advancement to save his wife from change? Who had put aside Virgil and Chopin in order to have time to save his college from his wife? Who had sacrificed scholarship itself in order to protect and support his wife as she struggled with cancer? Joel Hendrickson, the Galahad of his generation, pathetically sure that chivalric loyalty and self-abnegation were their own rewards. That was the greatest of his delusions—except the unexamined, unthinking confidence that despite the hidden sorrow marriage had brought upon them both, his wife had loved him.

He kicked a rock off the driveway and marched on to the East Wing. Eleanor wasn't home, which was a blessing, because in his present mood he couldn't possibly say anything comforting. As he changed into his running clothes, in fact, his unwilling thoughts of talking to her tomorrow slowly resolved into a determination to tell her he was winding up his stay. The Ward Place would be all painted by the end of next week, Helena's tea would be held on the Saturday of the Fourth of July weekend; he could call Andrew in a day or two and say he'd be back the 9th. The 9th—that meant he'd have spent nearly five weeks in Vermont. Yes, it was time he got back to his stripped house. Bought a car. Went back to his work—or what had been his work, back in the days in which he could have taken an offer from Cambridge seriously.

Queen Elizabeth Professorship of Renaissance Studies. A copyright library. Time. Talk.

Quick, before you have time to think—are you glad or sorry?

What the hell difference did it make? He'd bound himself hand and foot to Mather College over a quarter-century ago. And Nathaniel had let him, even though he must have known, must have at least suspected...

He banged out the door and started down the road, not at the geriatric jog he'd gradually worked up to, but at a pace his body recognized instinctively from his cross-country days. One-two-one-two... the Walkers' white fence passed on his right, then two old houses left over from the age in which Vermont had been farming country. One-two-one-two...the descending road and gently moving trees gradually became generic cross-country scenery; except for the pain in his knees and thighs, he could have been running down the back road in East Rock Park, innocent of the very existence of any college but Yale, devoid of any ambition but getting straight A's and winning the next meet. One-two-one-two...he turned left at the fork, since the right led to the lake, and started up the hill, shortening his stride to keep the rhythm. How could he possibly have given up this privacy, this euphoria?

The stitch that shot through his side almost bent him double, but he pressed his hand against it, feeling the hateful flab heave in and out beneath his fingers. It wasn't all that far to the top, and he'd run through pain countless times before. Two hundred yards to the big maple. Two hundred more to the logging road. Over the top, down the gravelly descent on the far side—

He tripped on an out-jutting rock and fell forward at full length.

For several minutes, he lay still, breathing in gasps that drove his wildly thudding chest into the stones. Eventually, however, he summoned oxygen enough to roll into the ditch, thus enabling himself to pant and sweat undisturbed by any car that might crest the hill. But when he finally persuaded his legs to hold him again, he rather regretted that no cars were in evidence. He would have welcomed a lift home, even though it would have been embarrassing to explain his skinned knees, elbows, and palms.

He sighed and began to hobble up the rise and back down the long hill. The reality of running one's heart out was certainly less attractive than the prospect of it—especially when no coronary materialized to end the pain. It was such torture to walk. It was such agony to breathe. It was such a long way home.

It was such a God damn stupid thing to do.

Helena sat at her desk, looking over the document before her and waiting for Andrew to call, which his secretary had assured her he would do promptly at five. When the phone rang, she glanced at her watch with mingled amusement and admiration.

"Andrew? You come most closely upon your hour."

"I do my best," said Andrew's voice. They engaged in a few pleasantries, but he soon got to the point. "I take it David told you everything."

"Well, he told me there's a rumor about Joel."

"I've confirmed that rumor. 'Confidential,' at Cambridge as at Mather, means only that one must wait twenty-four hours before leaking information to interested parties. It's a newly endowed position, with a salary in the fifties (pounds, that is), a suite of rooms, high table, National Health. Plus a select handful of grad students, an occasional undergraduate tutorial—in short, practically nothing to do but putter around the library."

That stood to reason; vultures ran true to form. "And what did Joel say?"

" 'Thank you,' I'd imagine."

Her smile quickly became a frown. "You imagine! You mean you don't know?"

"Of course I don't. Joel, in the usual way of men who've been made a tempting offer, has not called. But when he does, I want to be ready for him. If you'll approve investing some of Letty's money in the fund for his Chair, that's a start."

"Of course. But if you really want him to stay, you'll have to think of other things. A couple of bright young people in Literature for him to talk to, for instance."

"Helena, if this were the old days, I'd hire six of them, just to thank Joel for all he's done. But it's simply out of the question. Only a fraction of our students—or anybody else's, for that matter—major in Literature now. To rebuild Mather, we have to construct a curriculum that attracts customers: that means offering the digital thinking and global knowledge that sells after graduation. We're training students for professions that don't even exist yet—"

"—Doesn't shooting in the dark disturb you?"

"Shooting in the—? Oh, I see. Well, all colleges are doing that, given the pace technology's changing. And it's about all Mather can do, besides convince people we turn out a better product than our competitors. —Look, Margaret is beckoning at my door. I confess I was punctual because we're due at a function in Boston at 5:30, and we can't be more than five or ten minutes late. Think about things that'll keep Joel here, okay? I'll get back to you tomorrow morning."

She rang off and went out to sit on the side porch. From there, one couldn't see the scarred resort, only the steeple that rose against a backdrop of wooded mountains, a view unchanged since she and Nathaniel had last sat here, basking in an unexpected late April sun. Customers. Products. Ignorant armies striving by night. Had that been the degeneration he'd foreseen, or had it been his own? Even now, she had no idea.

She poured him a glass of sherry and left the decanter within his reach. "I'm afraid it's last year's," she said. "I've only just opened the house, and—"

"—and visitors rarely intrude upon you without notice at this time of year."

"Or any other."

He sipped his sherry, ignoring the question that hovered between them. "It's all right," he said. "Very nice, in fact. The taste of the Old World." He leaned back in the wicker chair. "How was the Old World?"

"Italy? As it always is. Beautiful. Impoverished. Politically impossible. But I doubt you drove up here from Whitby just to inquire after its health."

"No." He looked down at the steeple through the budding branches. "I drove up here to tell you about my impending resignation. Or retirement, if you prefer the word."

She had half expected the announcement from the moment his Dodge had pulled up by the house. But when she finally brought herself to look at him, the *lines of his face blurred under her gaze.*

"Come, now—there's no reason to look like the Tragic Muse," he said shortly.

"You want me to rejoice, then?"

He shrugged. "There will be a lot of rejoicing when the word gets out."

"And a lot of mourning. Many people still believe in what you stand for."

"I'd never have continued if I'd been unaware of that."

She nodded. "And Joel—does he know?"

"Not yet. When I left Whitby this morning, I had simply thought

of discussing the matter with you. But there it is: even old age isn't immune to sudden revelation."

"And what was revealed to you?"

"That by posing as the defender of Liberal Education against the forces of money and ideological muddle, I'd accidentally killed the soul of the beautiful maiden I'd set out to rescue. It's not that I defended her weakly; it's that during the years I've been fighting for her, she's been trapped in a castle, unable to change. As she stands now, she has very little to offer the world as it has become. That's why bright, forward-looking students no longer apply to Mather College, and why the liberal alumni feel I've betrayed it." He gave her a sorrowing smile. "That may be no revelation to you, but it was to me."

He seemed to expect no response, which was perhaps fortunate, since she wasn't sure she could trust her voice. They sat in silence for a long time.

"Letty will be very upset," she said finally.

"She will indeed. I'm not looking forward to telling her."

"Be gentle. The college means a great deal to her."

"The college means entirely too much to her," he said. "It's my fault, I suppose. I should have insisted that she strike out on her own. But there it is—I'd come to depend on her graciousness, and it was easy to continue in the old way. And then, when she married Joel, I thought she'd give it up as soon as she had children."

"I doubt it. Letty doesn't like children."

He smiled sardonically. "A trait she shares with you. But children would have made a tremendous difference to the marriage. You've seen Joel with children?"

She nodded. It was impossible not to see Joel with children when both were present. "I've never heard him complain, though."

"No," he said. "Except in matters of intellect, Joel is a giver, not a demander. He could be trained to receive, I dare say, but not by Letty. Or by me." He tapped his fingers on his glass. "When I look back, I feel like a reverse Midas. I was given a world full of gold, but because of things I've done—and things I haven't—everything I've cared for most has turned to iron at my touch: the college, Letty's life, Joel's—"

"—Surely, you won't spend the rest of your life wallowing in self-pity and regret!"

His look made her realize she'd spoken more sharply than she'd intended, but the words had the desired effect. His face changed, and he reached for his cane. "Show me your garden," he said. "I've never seen it at this time of year."

So they walked through the narcissus and hyacinths, she snipping faded flowers and he reciting Ovid's tragic tales as only he could, until, circling back they reached the iris beds, and he stopped. "Are these the ones you stole from Mather?"

"Some of them are. I can't tell which, until they bloom."

He looked at them reflectively. "Perhaps I'll come up and see them this year," he said. "That would involve coming sooner than I usually do, but I was thinking I might stay a week longer than I have in the past, if you'll have me. After all, I'm fast becoming a gentleman of leisure."

"You may stay as long as you want," she said. "And once you've dispensed with your business in Whitby, you might find Italy a pleasant place to spend the winter." He gazed over the wall without replying, but his hand left his cane, found hers, and raised it to his lips.

Helena blinked once or twice and watched the long sunlight and shadows play across the mountains. It was very different, this intimate, understated green, from the darker green of Fiesole's unsecretive hills. Nathaniel would never have grown to love Tuscany the way he'd loved Vermont. After all, in spite of his appreciation of *l'Inferno* and *Il Purgatorio*, it was *The Prelude* he'd habitually turned to when they read aloud. It had less to do, she'd always thought, with language or period than with sensibility. The lush, uneven beauty of Wordsworth was, like the landscape that inspired it, essentially private, a reflection of mist, long twilights, and early darkness—not at all like the intensely political vistas of Dante's imagination, where fire-lit circles gave way to uncompromising Italian sunlight on the cliffs of penance, and at last to the impersonal light of airless, substanceless glory.

No, he would not have loved Fiesole; and for that matter, he would have been a stranger to her there, where her Paolo and Francesca memories still, after seventy years, haunted every vista. That he had possessed (or at least revisited) a landscape in which she would be similarly an alien, she had no doubt; but the unspoken condition of their intimacy had been that each of them was to know, not nothing, but nothing of importance, about the other's youth—except that what had been of importance had ended in unutterable pain.

Yet, in spite of all the complications that would have attended his coming to Italy, she was glad she'd asked him, and glad he'd recognized the offer for what it was. Their understanding relieved her of much of her grief a week or so after Commencement, when Joel called and told her, as gently as only Joel could, of Nathaniel's death. The two of them could so easily have parted without acknowledging the one golden fragment that had survived their fatal touches. How kind of fate—how kind of them—that it had not been so.

9. A Romance

When Charlie pulled into the driveway, Eleanor was loading the vacuum cleaner into her car. She didn't look around, even when Derri barked from inside the barn. In fact, she slammed the trunk and opened the door on the driver's side.

"Hey, Eleanor!" Charlie jumped out of the Toyota and dashed forward. "Wait!"

Eleanor turned, her surprise melting into a smile of welcome. "Charlie! What brings you here?"

"A question. I have a theory, and I want—"

"—hold on, hold on. I missed all of that except 'question.' "

"Sorry." Charlie moved so that the sun was in her face, not Eleanor's. "It's about Joel."

"Joel? No need to worry. He's fine, just a little stiff. Skinned knees really hurt for a day or two—"

"— skinned knees?! What happened?"

"He fell when he was out running last night—pushed himself

too far, he said. Not exactly what he needed on top of all the other things he's had on his mind, but he'll mend."

"That's my question. Do you know what's on his mind?"

"What's…oh, on his mind." Eleanor shook her head. "No. And I've tried not to speculate. There's no point in adding gossip to his other burdens."

Gossip. Ouch. And here she'd been feeling proud of her detective work. At the Ward Place, Joel, obviously upset about some decision; at home, David, obsessed with phone calls to Helena and President Crawford. Everything was hush-hush, of course, but Salome said Joel's name was coming up all the time, and the two of them had speculated that it was almost certainly a job offer, as Eleanor might be able to confirm… What was it about the thrill of the chase that made you forget the mystery you wanted to solve was none of your damn business?

"Point taken," she said, lowering her eyes. Then, glancing at the East Wing, "If he's stiff, would he like a ride over to the Ward Place?"

"Would he—? No, no, I got it. Ray gave him a lift. They were going someplace first, but I'm afraid I can't say where. They told me, but…"

"Hey, you promised Hattie that when you missed things you'd ask for repetition."

" That…? Oh, sorry. I did ask. But after people have repeated things twice, it's hard to ask again."

"Well, when you get those new aids you were talking about—**new aids**," she repeated as Eleanor's face became a mask.

"New aids won't do me any good," said Eleanor, buckling her hair into a switch behind her head. "The official word is that I've reached the end of the line."

Oh my gosh. And here she'd been speculating, gossiping…doing everything but dropping by to see how the audiologist appointment had gone. She moved forward to give Eleanor a hug, but Eleanor stepped away, so all she dared say was, "I'm…I'm sorry."

"So am I," said Eleanor. "And sorrier I can't talk about it. Soon, maybe."

"Sure," she said helplessly. "Any time." But you couldn't just leave when somebody looked like this. You had to find something cheerful—oh, right. "Look, I have been reading Clara's journal." She paused to be sure Eleanor had changed subjects with her. "I haven't finished it yet, but it's in with a bunch of old pictures of the Wards, and I told Joel he should bring them here for you to identify—did he?"

"Did you say pictures of the Wards?" Eleanor's face changed entirely. Good.

"Yes. I'll bring them by this afternoon on my way to work Co-coa—**this afternoon.**"

"Great," said Eleanor. "And I'd love to see the journal, when you get done."

"You bet!— Well, I'd better get going...oh. I knew there was something else. Helena. David is worried about her."

"David is worried about...oh, Helena." Eleanor frowned. "Anything specific?"

"Just that she's up there alone."

"Alone? She's always lived up there alone, except when she's in Fiesole alone."

"Do you know why? David doesn't."

Eleanor shook her head. "My father said he heard second or third hand that Helena's father bought her the place up by the Mountain—it was absolutely remote in the 1920s, of course—in the wake of some emotional trauma, which, since she was in her late teens, everyone assumed had to do with an affair of the heart." She smiled. "Of course, that falls into the category of speculation—as did the rumor that Nathaniel Brantford would have married her if she had been willing. The truth of the matter is, when a beautiful woman chooses to remain solitary, _everybody_ speculates, so both those stories are probably just romances."

Charlie gazed at the valley. "Is there something wrong with being solitary?"

To her surprise, she felt an arm slip around her shoulders. "Absolutely not," said Eleanor. "It implies a kind of self-sufficiency that even people who are social tend to respect. And sometimes solitary people find each other and live very happily together, each granting the other the necessary huge amounts of space."

"Oh! Do you think Hattie has met somebody, then?"

"Do I think…? Actually, I wasn't thinking of Hattie. I was thinking of her father." Eleanor smiled and opened the door all the way. "Look, I have to go. If you remember those pictures, leave them on the kitchen table."

"Sure thing."

She followed Eleanor's car down the road, feeling…well, chastened. Eleanor didn't talk about her husband very often, but when she did, it reminded you how many people's lives didn't turn out the way they had hoped. Such awful things happened, for no reason you could put a finger on. And here she was, reading the stuff Yale was sending her about orientation, writing to the girls she was going to room with…she waved as they turned in opposite directions at the T. …looking forward to meeting people she fit in with, to *not* being solitary, to actually living the life she had spent all this time preparing for—it all sounded too wonderful to be true. Then one look around, at people like Helena or Eleanor or Mary Ward, suggested that maybe it was.

As she pulled into the dooryard of the Ward Place, Ray and Joel had just finished unloading lumber and hardware from Ray's truck, and Ray was getting into it.

"Hey," she said. "You welching out on us?"

"Yup," he said. "Gotta take Connie into Brattleboro. Big sale. So I won't be back until after the excitement's over." He winked at Joel, started his cranky engine, and left.

Charlie turned to Joel, who was picking up a 2 x 4 as if he were a hundred years old. Thank God Eleanor had told her about those skinned knees, or she would have asked if he was all right—*not* the way to make up for upsetting him yesterday afternoon or speculating with Salome last night. "Would you like me to finish painting the back today?" she asked cautiously.

He leaned the 2 x 4 against the shed in evident relief. It seemed he had skinned his elbows as well as his knees, which would explain the Oxford shirt. "Actually," he said, "I was thinking of doing something more sedentary, like looking at the papers in the dining room."

Ah, so he was feeling a little cautious too, and not just about the scrapes. She smiled tentatively. "That sounds good. I started Clara's journal day before yesterday. I only got half way through—David and Salome *insisted* that I go to Manchester with them—but just as I stopped, I came across the beginnings of a romance. We could start there, if you'd like."

"The beginnings of a romance," he said, smiling back. "Very promising."

"Do you want to go in, or shall I bring it out here?"

"Out here sounds fine."

By the time she got back to the porch with the journal, he had settled himself stiffly on the steps. She sat next to him, opened the journal and paged through it, filling him in on Clara's family situation and the beginning of Brent's courtship. "And here it is," she said, pointing. "The Great Breakthrough."

He pulled his reading glasses from his shirt pocket and peered through them at the entry. " 'Went walking with Brent'—that's all?"

"No, it's not all. What you find, reading the earlier parts, is that there's a lot more going on than you see on the page." But seeing the page involved sitting shoulder to shoulder, which was a little uncomfortable. "Maybe it would help if I read it aloud."

"Good idea." He moved a couple of inches away and settled himself against the railing.

"Okay, here we go, then:

July 15, 1929. Sun all day. Asa says we'll start haying tomorrow if it holds, will try to get Tom Wheeler. Ma said Gid will come back because of sun. Asa said what made her think so. Walked with Brent again, he asked where was Gid. I said here, of course.

"Just a minute," he said. "Where *was* Gid?"

"Good question," she said. "He always seems to disappear just when he's needed, but there's no pattern to it, so far as I can see."

"I take it the family suspects he's up to something, if Clara keeps it from Brent."

She nodded. She'd known he'd be good at this. "Shall I go on?"

"By all means."

"July 16. Sun. Asa hitched up before daylight. Tom Wheeler haying for Fullers, Jed Stevens haying for Smiths. Ma and I put up two bushels of beans, wonder what we'll do with the rest. Walked with Brent. Told him about college, he says many women go now, I should too.

"July 17. Sun, hot. Four loads. Asa mowed until almost dark. Walked with Brent, he asked why was I so quiet.

"July 18. Sun, hot. Four loads in, just Asa and I. Ma put up beans. Tired.

"July 19. Sun v. hot. Five loads.

"July 20. Sun. 90 degrees. Five loads. Walked with Brent. Brent angry—says if only I hadn't fibbed to him, he would have helped with haying all week."

"That's interesting," said Joel. "Brent's willing to give up gentility and help on the farm."

She frowned. "What makes you think Brent's a gentleman?"

"Everything you told me. He hasn't seen Asa since they were both in the army. He's younger than Asa, but he's a sergeant. He has an English accent, which at the very least suggests he doesn't speak the Vermont vernacular. He thinks nothing of driving a great deal. And he is evidently acquainted with educated women."

"He could have all those things and not be a gentleman."

Joel shook his head. "Not in 1929. And besides, he was staying in Newfane instead of working, which makes him summer gentry."

She grinned. "Like David?"

"No, no" he said. "Like Helena."

Her eyes widened. "You're kidding. And he's courting Clara

119

Ward?"

"Well, I can't be sure, after only reading this much, but that's how it looks to me."

He was probably right, come to think of it. She'd realized herself that Brent wasn't just a local yokel; she just hadn't given enough thought to the WASP aristocracy scene, and how the aristocracy related to the natives. "Well, maybe we'll find out more as we read on." She bent over the page again, but the purr of an engine made them both look up. "We seem to have company," she said.

He struggled to his feet, and she joined him, hoping it was Helena, who could shed some light on the class situation. But it wasn't Helena's old Mercedes in the driveway. It was a gray Cadillac, one she'd seen around town quite a bit, and it belonged to—to—oh no! Colleen Rickerts. She stepped forward with Joel, repressing the urge to stand in front of him. As the two of them shook hands, Ray's parting comment flashed across her mind: *won't be back until after the excitement's over.* So that's where Joel and Ray had told Eleanor they were going—the Hume and Rickerts office.

"This is Charlotte Reynolds," Joe was saying. "She's been painting the house."

Colleen's eyes opened wide. "Charlie Reynolds! Good heavens, you're so grown up I hardly recognized you. And how's your dad doing?"

"Fine, thanks," she said, forcing a smile. Then, to Joel, "Is there anything you'd like me to do while you're working on—this?"

"Not now. Go ahead with the journal if you want. Ms. Rickerts is appraising the Ward Place, so I'll be tied up the rest of the morning."

It was a dismissal, and there wasn't much she could do about it, even though it went against the grain to leave him unchaperoned with Colleen. She'd been kind enough during the summer David had dated her, but there were things Joel probably should have been told before he did business with her. "Okay if I finish the journal out on the porch?"

Joel nodded. She went back to the house as the others progressed to the barn cellar. As she mounted the steps, Colleen's voice floated towards her: "...very clever...substantial tax benefit...such a pleasure to deal with a good businessman."

Good businessman, ha! He was putty in her claws. Charlie sat disconsolately in the porch swing they'd re-hung after she'd painted the porch, but then smiled as she read the first entry. Talk about being on location.

> *July 21. Sun. 95 degrees, must be going to break soon. Asa, Brent hayed, six loads. Picked 2 bushels peas, never thought I'd like shelling peas so well.*

> *July 22. Hot, then storms. Gid home, brought radio. Asa said he should have been where we needed him, folks beginning to talk. But listened to news and music all evening. Gid looks poorly, wish he'd say where he went.*

> *July 23. Sun, cooler. Gid mowing, but feeling poorly. Asa, Brent turning wet hay. Not too much lost, no thanks to Gid, Asa says. Put up rest of beans. Walked with Brent. He has to drive to New York with Amy and Elsie Taylor, but will come back as soon as he can.*

So Brent had connections in New York, and he knew the people Mary Ward called "fancy summer folks." Joel was probably right, then. Out of the corner of her eye, she saw him make a gesture towards the house. Colleen nodded, and they walked towards it.

"I jacked up the porch last week," he said as they came up the steps. "It's structurally sound, just needed a little bracing. And as you can see, the ceiling holds a swing and an occupant."

"Goodness!" Colleen's voice came back through the door. "And it was just like this when you first saw it? How romantic!"

Romantic schmomantic. Charlie gave the swing a push.

> *July 24. Stormy. Gid has fever. Saw Mr. Clark down street. He went clear to his house to get the list of books for me. Told him Brent thought I should go to college, had talked with Asa. Thought*

he'd be pleased, but he didn't look so. Feeling poorly this evening.

July 25. Rain. In bed all day, fever.

July 26. Rain. Still fever. Ma poorly.

July 27. Sun, very hot. Asa very poorly. I did the milking, it took 3 hours. Terrible headache, but none of the others can stand.

The rest of the page was empty. Poor Clara. Charlie listened a moment as what could only be called cries of horror echoed out of the kitchen. That should lower the price a little. But as Joel ushered Colleen back through the living room and up the stairs, he seemed unperturbed.

Sighing, she turned the page. Brent had apparently returned to Vermont during the break in entries.

August 5. Sun, cooler. Took dinner to Brent in upper mowing. He says he'd much rather be a farmer than a banker, which is what his father is. Told him he wouldn't think that if he farmed all year.

August 6. Sun. Brent brought in four loads, I helped fork it into loft. Talked about <u>Ivanhoe</u>, he said nobody in college reads Scott anymore. Asked would Ma let us go see a college in Northampton, Mass., a friend of his teaches there and could tell me what it was like. I said no point asking until Asa and Gid well.

August 7. Sun, windy. Asa up, still can't do milking. Picked blueberries behind upper mowing. Brent read me some of Shakespeare's sonnets when horses resting. Showed him Mr. Clark's list. He asked why I didn't start reading some of the women writers. Asked him how could I read <u>anything</u> when Gid gone, or everybody sick.

August 8. Rain. Ma let me take Ned down street. Went to the library, took out books by George Eliot and Jane Austen. Mrs. Jenkins said they didn't have the book by Virginia Woolf. Started a shirt for Asa.

August 9. Rain. Put up 15 quarts of peas, hands hurt from shelling. Sewed collar on Asa's shirt, Gid says he needs one too.

August 10. Sun. Brent haying. Said he was sorry he had made me cry about the books, but we couldn't talk, had to pick raspberries with Ma. Made 5 quarts jam and a pie. Gid well enough to do milking. Finished Asa's shirt.

August 11. Sun. Gid, Brent haying. Picked blueberries again, but Gid stayed in upper mowing at dinner time. Read two chapters of <u>Pride and Prejudice</u>, but Ma asked why was I burning the lamp so late. Will blow it out, Ma still feeling poorly,but won't go to bed until dark.

August 12. Rain. Went down street. Mrs. Jenkins said books not due yet, but no point to keeping them out. Can't even find time to answer Brent's letters.

Letters. They were writing to each other letters. What had happened to them? She hurried into the dining room and searched quickly through the clippings, pictures and accounts, but there were no letters. Maybe someplace upstairs... Damn. Colleen was up there, so she couldn't look. Because of course Clara would have hidden them—and both of them would have had to find secret places to leave them for each other. She went back to the swing, trying to imagine what it must have been like to love somebody with all your family around, watching to be sure the young folks didn't have free time together. Not that free time seemed to be common.

"And this was the master suite?" Colleen's voice drifted out the window. "Of course, no one likes the master bedroom without a bath, but you could put one across the hall." Her footsteps clicked across the living room ceiling, then stopped. "Or, better yet, you could put a door in the wall and make this back room into a master bath and walk-in closet."

A master bath. The picture of a fiberglass tub and rhinestone faucets loomed between Charlie and the next few entries. She was so busy reading around it that she didn't pay full attention until she realized Brent had taken Clara to see Smith College. She went back a couple of entries and tried again.

August 16. Sun. Asa not happy about Northampton, but Ma said, so long as Brent had friends down there to stay with, there was no point to fussing. Brent says we will go day after tomorrow.

August 19. Sun. Got back just before milking. Such a beautiful college, just for women. So many stores, ready made dresses <u>very expensive</u> but the students look so fashionable. Fancy restaurants with French food, very elegant. Brent gave me beautiful, illustrated copy of <u>The Mill on the Floss</u>. I can take as long to read it as I need, now.

August 20. Sun, cool. Brent, Asa sawed. Started digging potatoes with Gid, but he left after dinner. Pickled cucumbers with Ma, thought she'd want to talk about Northampton, but she was very quiet. Wrote all evening, but none of it sounded right.

August 21. Sun, windy. Picked the last blueberries, five quarts. Told Brent why no letter, not because I was upset, but because I couldn't write out how happy I was. What about college, though? Told me he has to get established, so I will have time to finish at Smith before we get married, would that be all right. I said it would. His parents are coming up next week to visit Taylors. Asked did I think Ma would agree for me to spend a week in Newfane, if I told her. But tonight I couldn't bring myself to ask.

Footsteps came down the stairs inside and stopped in the living room. "It would be easier," said Colleen's voice, "to take care of all these details at the office."

"I'm sorry," said Joel's voice, "but I don't have a car."

"No problem. I'll be happy to drive you back after we're done."

"That's very kind of you," he said, "but I don't want to interrupt your lunch hour."

"Oh, we can just stop off at the Alphof Inn—one of my friends runs it, such a wonderful chef—and finish our business after that."

Oh, no no no no! Charlie jumped off the swing, but as they came through the door, she could see no action was possible.

"Ms. Rickerts and I are going to wrap up business over lunch," said Joel. "So I won't be back until three or so." He turned to Colleen. "That will give us enough time, don't you think?"

Colleen reached into her purse for her keys. "Plenty, if we get going right away."

"Okay," said Charlie. "I'll finish up the back wall. If I get done before three, I'll take off. I have to give a lesson at four, and there's Cocoa to work."

He nodded, and the two of them walked out to the listing Cadillac. Joel opened the door for Colleen, then walked around to the other side. He waved to her as the car started down the driveway, but that wasn't much consolation. There was nothing she could do, either for him or for the Ward Place, if he willingly put himself into Colleen's hands. She blinked a couple of times, then climbed slowly up to Clara's room and sat in the rocking chair. She might as well finish the journal; there were only a few pages left.

August 22. Sun, then rain. Made blueberry jam. Ma said, was I sure, it would be different than I was accustomed to. She'll speak with Asa about Newfane, not sure he'll like it. Gid back tonight after milking, brought a Kodak. Went upstairs early but heard them anyway.

August 23. Sun. Brent, Gid, Asa split wood out back. Ma, Asa had words during milking. After, Asa told me I could go to Newfane, but if he'd known how it would work out, he would never have had me write to Brent.

August 24. Rain. Went down street, bought six yards silk, very expensive, but potato crop good this year, Ma said it would be all right. Sewed all afternoon. Very slow, not accustomed to cloth this nice, but Ma knew how. Didn't know Grandma Bartlett was

125

a dressmaker.

August 25. Rain. Ma and I sewed all day. Finished one dress, very stylish, and only five yards material. Wish I could buy hat, but don't dare ask. Brent said not to take on so, his parents didn't expect a lady. Asked him was he ashamed of me, then, to tell them that. After, Asa said, what did I expect, fancy folks bound to look down on me. I said they better not.

August 26. Sun. Ma did all the pickling so I could sew. Brent to come by tomorrow morning after milking.

Then the next morning, Prince Charming whisked the beautiful maiden off to Newfane to visit King and Queen—she turned over the leaf. There was nothing except blank pages. She stared at them. What could have happened?

But she knew what had happened—actually, she'd known all along, if she'd thought of it. Because the grave in the cemetery was marked Clara Ward, not Clara anything else. Maybe his parents didn't approve of her. Maybe when she met them, she got scared. Maybe— but it didn't really matter what had happened or why it had. What mattered was…she looked around the room, at the white painted walls, the stenciled chest, and the books. Slowly she took *The Mill on the Floss* off the shelf, but before she could even leaf through it for the illustrations, she saw the bold incription on its fly-leaf. "From Northampton, with all my love. Brent."

And here it was, over sixty years later, in the deserted, silent room that Colleen Rickerts was going to make into a master bath and closet after Joel sold the farm.

She put the old book gently back on its shelf and went outside to paint, wiping her eyes with her sleeve.

Joel swept into the C Minor Prelude, reveling in the sound. It was certainly going to be difficult to adjust to his little spinet after playing Eleanor's Steinway for a month. And he should certainly stop putting off the details of his departure. Skinned knees—a misery he'd forgotten since childhood—barely excused him from working on the Ward place today; they were no excuse for his failure to call Andrew Crawford. Or for not telling Eleanor that he was going.

As he reached the pianissimo passage, he heard the click of Derri's toenails on the hall floor, and the noise of the screen door opening and shutting. He should tell her now; except for their largely silent dinners together, this was the only time of day he was likely to find her. When the sun set, she'd go upstairs—and write, presumably. He always heard the sound of her computer keys when he left the piano for his room. All right. He finished the final bars distractedly, then walked to the screen door and looked out.

She was sitting sideways on the doorstep, looking out over the land that was no longer hers with an expression he'd never been able to fathom, though he'd stood here, studying it, several times before. Extraordinary: that was the only word he'd ever found to describe her face. Not beautiful, certainly; she had none of the outgoing dynamism he had always so enjoyed watching in Letty. Nor was it just intelligence; he'd met bright women at conventions, and their faces had had none of whatever he saw in hers. Which was—he shook his head, but it was a recognizable quality. He'd seen it in Nathaniel's face, and, less frequently, in Helena's.

As his hand touched the doorknob, Derri looked up and Eleanor turned around. The expression he'd been studying instantly disappeared; before him was the Eleanor he always encountered when he walked into the room: tense, defensive, straining to hear.

"May I join you?" he asked.

"I'm sorry?" she said, standing up so he could open the door.

One glance told him that he didn't need to humiliate her by repeating what he'd said, but it gave him no help at all finding a topic for conversation. He finally fell back, in Henry Higgins fashion, on the weather and everybody's health. "Nice evening."

"Yes, it is." But as she spoke, he could feel her waiting for him to explain his presence. There was something about her silence that was more pressing than the barrage of questions he was used to. Not that it was indirectly accusatory. No, what was pressing was the sense that she was listening to *his* silence, sharing it, considering its possible meaning. There were apparently as many shades of silence as there were of speech.

He watched, musing, as she got up and began to weed the columbines in front of the house, looking over her shoulder occasionally as the red sun drew nearer the mountains. As the light lengthened, even he could feel the pressing wordlessness dissolve into a companionable mode, then into a communion with the graying landscape and brilliant reflective clouds.

At last, Eleanor stood up and dusted the dirt off her knees. "Would you like to see some Wardiana?" she said. "Charlie stopped by this afternoon with some portraits she hoped I could identify for you. She obviously hadn't looked at them closely enough to see that the identification had already been done, but no matter. They're quite wonderful."

"I'd be delighted to look at them." And as he followed her into the living room, he was delighted. In the first place, the man he once had been would have looked at the Wardiana weeks ago, instead of resisting it. In the second place, it had been difficult, this parallel living. It was too bad that only now—

"Here we are," she said, pulling an old portrait out of a ragged portfolio.

He took his reading glasses out of his pocket and sat down in the chair facing hers, studying it. On the right side sat a man with a heroic gray mustache and a beard that half hid his high white collar and tie. His rounded shoulders threatened to burst through the seams of his suit, and the hands that rested on his thighs were enormous, but his eyes were thoughtful and unexpectedly soft. Behind him and slightly to the side stood a stocky young woman uncomfortably corseted into a ruffled black dress. She might have been attractive if she had worn her hair differently, but the severity of her bun accentuated her square jowls and uncompromising forehead rather than the cheek bones and interesting dark eyebrows.

"They're superb," he said. "Who are they?"

"Turn it over."

He looked at the rounded hand on the back. " 'Grandma and Grandpa Ward, 1885,' " he said reflectively. "That means they are—"

"Henry Ward Senior and Alice," said Eleanor. "And the writer must be Clara. She's the only one of the grandchildren that survived. At least, the only one that lived here that survived."

He looked back at Henry Ward's unsmiling face. "He's not what I think of as a typical Vermont farmer. There's a little too much poetry."

"A little too much—? Oh, poetry. Exactly! That's what's interesting about him. I looked him up in *Draper Worthies* this afternoon, and it occurred to me he'd be pleased his house had come to you." She opened an old book and flipped through its pages. "Here we go: the Draper historian says that after Henry Ward 'received the common education of most boys in Draper,' he went on to study at Springfield Academy and then taught for a while to pay for his tuition. All of which seems to have turned him into a scholar. Listen to this: *'In his imagination Lyell was revered and glorified. Bryant, Longfellow, and Whittier were his heroes; he could repeat them by the hour without so much as a glance at the page from which he'd taken them. In 1870 he returned to his father's land, and has for the rest of his life been a farmer—perhaps because it gratified his inherent love of home, and brought him into a more intimate touch with nature. For the solitude of field and forest induced study and meditation as the noise and bustle of town life could not.'* " Eleanor raised her head. "So there he is—a romantic, a pastoralist. Also, I might add, a man much respected in the town, and very active in the Grange. But I suspect that had something to do with the woman our historian records as 'loyal wife and mother'—the one Charlie calls a matriarch." She pointed to the stalwart young woman at Henry's side.

"You may very well be right," he said, looking up from the young woman's determined face. "Are there any portraits of the children?"

"Only snapshots, but they're quite revealing."

She pulled four faded photos out of the portfolio; he looked at them and smiled. The older son—Henry, according to Clara Ward's inscription—had been one of those boys who grew all at once. In 1892, he towered over his mother and brother, though he was so thin their square bodies all but hid his as he stood behind them. Two years later, his shoulders had broadened, but he still looked unfinished as he stood on the front porch, dressed in a suit which (unlike the one in the earlier picture) covered his forearms and ankles. Joel placed both snapshots on the table between his chair and Eleanor's, turning towards her so she could see his lips. "I think Charlie was wrong about Henry's being a rebel," he said slowly. "It looks more like he followed his father's footsteps to Springfield Academy. Do you know what happened to him later?"

"I'm afraid not. My only informant, other than *Draper Worthies*, was Mary Ward—Robert's wife and Clara's mother. And she was not very communicative."

"That's too bad," he said. "The house has come to me through Henry's descendants, so far as I can figure. But my wife, like Mary Ward, wasn't very communicative." He paused to make sure she'd understood, then added, "I gather there were—differences."

"Oh, yes. Starting with Henry and Robert, I think. Look at the other two pictures."

He did, and found himself studying the stocky son from the group picture, accompanied by prize animals: a calf with a ribbon fluttering from its halter in 1894, and much later (1911, according to Clara), a team of well-groomed horses built on the same general principles as himself. "No scholar there, certainly," he said, "but not a man an educated brother should look down on."

"Look—? No, I got it. And no, nobody could look down on Robert. For starters, he and those Morgans were still a legend in horse-drawing circles when I was a kid. No matter how much weight a winning team pulled at the county fair some old timer was sure to say, 'Yeah, but Rob Ward's team would've licked 'em, easy.'"

Joel looked from the beautifully muscled horses to the responsible, pragmatic face of the man who held them. "He kept them very well."

"He kept everything well; you can still see his work if you look. The stone walls on your property, for instance. According to Mary, he re-laid every one of them. Took him five years, section by section, each rock shaped and set just so—this, in a countryside of odd-sized rocks heaped on top of each other, finished off by rusty barbed wire that holds up the posts."

"A craftsman," he said, thinking of the graceful wall around the graveyard. "The kind of man who likes to see things done right."

"Done—? Oh, done right. Exactly. Which brings us, as it brought him, to the Bartletts, and to what I think was the reason for the Ward family 'differences.' "

"Were the Bartletts—" He sat forward as he saw the strain in her face. "Were the Bartletts really off-limits? Enough to cause family differences? Charlie told me about the drunken father and the Irish girl that died in childbirth, but I thought people helped the kids out."

"Sure they did. But doling out food and clothes here and there was one thing. Taking on one of the kids as a hired man, which is what Robert did when Mary's brother Asa turned fourteen, was a bit different. To be fair, after Asa turned out to be so steady, other farm families took on the younger Bartlett boys. But marrying Mary Bartlett—well, only a man with Robert's determination to see things done right would have risked it. And only a man as greatly respected as he was could have pulled it off."

He stared at her, dumfounded. "But Charlie said Mary was beautiful!"

"Beautiful? Oh, yes. But she was the only daughter of the widowed town drunk—which meant that in addition to cooking, cleaning, and sewing, she was forced to perform certain other duties for her father."

"My God," he murmured.

"Even during my childhood, a background like that made a girl unmarriageable, no matter how deeply charitable people pitied her. In 1911—!" She shook her head. "But there it is. Robert Ward, whose team and farm made him one of the most eligible bachelors in the county, quietly took Mary Bartlett to a J.P., and then to Niagara Falls, where they bought the picture that's in the living room."

The picture. To him, it had recalled the industrial wasteland surrounding a once-noble river. To a woman lifted from the shame of her father's household to the beautifully-kept prosperity of the Ward place, how different its connotations must have been. "Is Charlie right in assuming that the marriage took place after Alice Ward died?"

"Is Charlie right about—? Oh, Alice. She may not have been as matriarchal as Charlie thinks, but no loyal Vermont son would have inflicted an "unworthy" daughter-in-law on his mother, especially since they would have all lived together. So she was spared. But Henry, junior, who we may assume had finished his education and gone on to some respectable profession—well, if you're looking for an occasion for family difference, that's it."

He looked again at the raw young face in Henry's photo. It didn't seem judgmental, but God knew what he'd picked up along with his education. "Draper, you say, was wiser?"

There was a silence; looking up, he realized she'd missed the question entirely. And no wonder; he'd spoken to his lap. "Was Draper more charitable than Henry?"

"Eventually. How long acceptance took, I don't know, but Mary was certainly a respected member of the town by the time I came here. People were protective about her, in fact. And still are." She smiled at him. "I can't think of any other house that could have stayed empty for as long as yours without being vandalized."

"I wondered about that. Even with your stewardship, it's little short of miraculous."

Eleanor pulled back the hair that had escaped from her long switch and buckled the clasp. "There's some story behind it, you may be sure. In fact, I _am_ sure. But I don't know what it is, and probably never will. There's still enough of a town here to close out non-natives when it's deemed necessary."

"I take it you're not a native?"

"Oh no," she laughed. "Summer folk are not natives, even when they come here to live full time. It's a funny kind of status: the guys in the gas station and the hardware store come up and help me sometimes, and last ice storm, somebody pulled me out of a ditch without charging—which is a real test. But there are some things I'll never know."

"Interesting," he said. In fact, it was all interesting. *She* was interesting. He studied the pictures once more, trying to think of a way of prolonging this unexpected conversation without talking too much himself. Surely, all the years he'd spent listening to Nathaniel would— He looked up suddenly. "Do you like to read aloud?"

"Do I—? Oh, read aloud? Why, yes, though I haven't done it for a while."

"I was wondering if you'd like to."

There was obvious pleasure in her smile. "I'd like it very much."

"Anything in particular?"

"Let me see—how long has it been since you read *Bleak House*?"

"Eons. There's a lovely copy on the north wall of my room. Shall I go get it?"

She nodded, and he hurried to his room as quickly as his stiffened knee-scabs would allow. When he returned, she was looking at *Draper Worthies,* stroking Derri's adoring head, which shared her lap with the sleeping cat. He paused in the doorway, looking at the peculiar domestic bliss with mingled amusement and sadness. He should have thought of this long ago.

"Here we go," he said, handing her the book and settling himself in his chair.

If he'd felt even a twinge of sorrow for the impossibility of exchanging readers, it was immediately dissipated, for she read beautifully. Sentence after sentence rolled off the page, and in a few minutes, they were both were immersed in the implacable fog of 19th century London. It was not until Esther and the two wards of Jarndyce had reached Bleak House itself and Eleanor had put down the book with a smile that he realized she had been reading for over three hours, and that her voice was almost gone.

⊷⊷⊷   ⊷⊷⊷   ⊷⊷⊷

Eleanor put down the Soft-Scrub and picked up the sponge, yawning as she stepped into Colleen Rickerts' sunken Jacuzzi. Only half awake, but she had no complaints. How long had it been since she'd stayed up the better part of a night talking? For that matter, how long had it been since she'd been able to maintain intellectual conversation at any hour? Not that she could now, of course, but between Joel's patient repetition and the pad of paper he'd brought into the living room after he'd made her tea— The floor beneath the Jacuzzi shook as if somebody had slammed the front door. She rinsed off her feet and climbed hurriedly back up to floor level. Who on earth would be coming into Colleen's house at this hour?

"Eleanor?"

She glanced at her watch. "Up here, Colleen. I'm afraid I'm running a bit late."

"No problem." Colleen appeared in the bathroom door. "_Mxmx_ hoping to catch you! _Mxmx_ new tenant and I _mxmx_ business yesterday." She looked in the mirror and smoothed her right eyebrow. "_Mxmx_ beautiful piece of property."

Eleanor met the eyes as they watched her carefully out of the mirror. Was she checking out the lay of the land _already?_ "His wife has only been dead for six weeks."

"Well, that's true," said Colleen. "But _mxmx_ good to get a bid in early _mxmx_ place like that—just so he knows there's someone interested." She turned around. "_Mxmx_ know how his wife _mxmx_ the property?"

"Inheritance—she was probably related to the Wards that left town in the 1890's, but there's not much evidence. The Wards were close-lipped about family matters."

"Their sort of Vermonter _mxmx_ close-lipped about everything," said Colleen, shrugging. "_Mxmx_ his wife _mxmx_ no sentimental attachment to it. What about him?"

"I'm not sure," said Eleanor. "He's spent a lot of time fixing it up."

"*Mxmx* pretty torn up about his wife. *Mxmx* happy marriage?"

No point in adding sorrow to Joel's attractions. "It lasted nearly thirty years."

"*Mxmx* have to see," said Colleen reflectively. " *Mxmx* pass probate *mxmx* does want it appraised. Just about done, are you?"

"Just this and the sink. Then I'm off."

She polished off the bathroom and walked out to the Honda, pocketing the wretched fifty bucks and wondering why Joel had settled upon Colleen to appraise his property. And what the sudden urge to have it appraised had to do with the five miles he'd run the day before yesterday. And above all, what he'd thought of Colleen. But though Joel met her in the driveway, insisting that she allow him to cook dinner while she took a nap so they could read *Bleak House* in the evening, he said nothing about the appraisal, much less the reason for it. It was enough to drive one to speculation.

10. A Tea

Joel stood in front of the mirror, knotting his tie. The familiar action collapsed the recent past into months and years of gatherings—receptions, conventions, fund-raisers—of men's public selves, shaking hands, sizing up opposition, forging contacts under the guise of pleasant conversation. How strange that public meetings, not private thought and shared ideas, should determine the fate of colleges, governments, economies. Or perhaps, like the discomforts of his tie, it merely seemed strange in contrast to the pastoral seclusion and quiet companionship of the past few weeks.

It would certainly be strange to attend a social occasion without Letty, who had somehow become complete during such occasions. Looking at his reflection, he saw not his face, but the image of himself drifting from group to group under the maples on Helena's lawn, a man bereft of his public self. For a moment he stood still, immobilized by a pang of longing. In the afternoon silence, he could almost hear Letty singing as she dressed. *"Goodnight, Irene, Irene—*

Goodnight, Irene..." He'd asked her, once, why she sang only that song, and only when she dressed for parties, but Letty-like, she'd had no idea. *"Irene Goodnight, goodnight Irene, I'll see you in my dreams"* ... he shook his head as he put on his jacket, hoping to clear the sound away. But the tune pursued him as he went out into the yard to wait for Eleanor.

⁂

Charlie squirmed into her new dress and looked dubiously at her reflection. It had seemed like the perfect tea-dress yesterday, but outside the world of rock music and solicitous sales girls, it looked a lot less appropriate. There she'd be, in a dress four inches shorter than everyone else's, obviously under twenty—not quite a child, but clearly not a full-fledged member of the community of intellectuals that flocked around Helena in the summer. As for Helena, she would be wearing the elegant white tea-dress she'd worn at all teas within living memory—which, come to think of it, said something about the grace with which Helena had aged as well as about tradition. When Hattie had been little, she'd been sure that if you touched the dress and made a wish, it would come true. Neither of them had ever dared to try.

She took out the studs in her earlobes and slipped in her silver earrings. Eye shadow, eyeliner... And which would look more sophisticated: hair up or down?

"Charlie?" David's voice bounced impatiently up the stairs.

"Right there."

Down, then. She brushed it hurriedly and ran down the stairs. There was David, resplendent in a light summer suit and dark silk shirt. And there was— Shit, Salome was wearing one of those chiffon ensembles you had to be over twenty-five to carry off, and she more than carried it off. The perfect figure, the perfect coloring, exactly the right earrings. Stunning. Enough to make a not-quite-freshman feel just as awkward as she looked. There was nothing she could do, though, but follow them to the car. Even if she had time to change, another dress would not supply what was wanting.

⁂

Eleanor slipped on her one decent dress, wishing that she had invented some reason to absent herself from the tea. The only reason she had not was pride: to the well-adjusted summer folk who graced Helena's teas, her excuse would have been instantly diagnosed as a symptom of withdrawal. 'Poor Eleanor,' they would say. 'If she'd only make an effort!' So she'd make the effort—the effort to return brief, slightly apologetic hellos from couples with whom she'd once been friends; the effort to understand their small talk, most of which she would have to ask them to repeat; and subsequently, the effort to participate in conversations by smiling when others smiled and laughing when they did. Sociability now was a triumph of form over content, in which what had once been only background became the whole experience. Haircuts. Dresses. Shoes. Expressions, gestures— and with them, the awareness of what people were thinking, so confusingly different from what they said.

She brushed her hair out and began to put it up, then stopped as she met the eyes in the mirror. She blinked one, then the other. Yes, they were hers. But the expression! It dissolved into thoughtfulness as she tried to place it, then into preoccupation as she put in the final hairpins. But when she gave herself the ritual parting glance, it reappeared. *Noli me tangere.*

The words followed her down the stairs, and with them, her father's pensive smile. *"No, no—it's fine for you to go there. I'm just amazed that she invited you. They say she hasn't talked to a soul for years, and you can see it in her eyes. Noli me tangere."*

She'd nodded, grateful for the explanation, because she'd wondered about the expression that made Mary Ward's face different from other people's. Who would have thought, thirty-odd years ago, that she'd see it in her own?

Helena straightened the lace on the cuffs of her white tea dress and hurried through the living-room. It was, thank heavens, a lovely day; there would be none of the awkwardness that invariably arose when the guests had to gather on the porches and wander into the dining room for food and drinks. And this year's caterers seemed to be much better trained than last: they'd adapted to the kitchen without a moment's hesitation, and they'd laid out the tea and drinks most attractively. They were hardly more than children, but perhaps that was the source of their—

"—Helena? Check out these canapés, could you?"

She tasted one. "Very good." And stunningly arranged. How odd that impeccable work should accompany the pro forma familiarity of the service generation.

"Glad you like them." The pony-tailed chef glanced over his shoulder. "That a car?"

"Three of them," said a voice from the kitchen.

"Looks like things are starting up," he said, smiling. "You better get out there." And as she turned obediently towards the door, he gave her a thumbs up.

The three arriving couples knew each other only slightly, and the fourth car that drew up held Eleanor and Joel. Potentially, that was a little difficult. Eleanor, once so wittily gracious and tactful, could no longer disperse initial awkwardness; and Joel, after years of dealing with the results of Letty's remorseless social political dealing, tended to withdraw into a shell of impeccably polite watchfulness at the least hint of tension. But as things evolved, there was no awkwardness to dispel; the moment Joel stepped out of the car, the Zimmermans' weekend guest rushed across the lawn to meet him.

"Dr. Hendrickson! I had no idea you'd be here—it's been so long— Of course, we've heard about your wife—terribly sorry."

Joel's smile was so vague that Helena went to his rescue. "This is Henry Stubbs," she said distinctly, laying one hand on Stubbs' s arm and turning him towards Eleanor. "He was just telling me that he studied with Joel in the Seventies."

Taking her cue, Eleanor extended a hand and murmured a generic greeting, and Joel gratefully followed suit.

Henry pumped Joel's hand vigorously. "Come meet Emmy and the kids," he said eagerly. "They've heard all about you—you're a mythical figure around our house."

Joel politely followed him to a spot where a young woman was holding two children far too young to appreciate myths. Helena joined Eleanor in his wake, but a klaxon horn announced the Reynolds' arrival, and she had to turn back before the two of them had time to exchange more than amused smiles. By the time she reached the driveway, Charlotte had extricated herself from the well behind the Jag's seats and was waiting while David opened the door for a young woman who in any other company would have been called beautiful. Salome, was it? Not an easy person, judging from the determined chin, but it was good to see David with a woman whose face promised intelligence as well as charm.

"Finishing your dissertation?" she said, echoing David's introduction. "That's wonderful. And where are you studying?"

David opened his mouth to reply, but Salome glanced at him and said that she was at the University of Michigan.

Helena suppressed a smile. "And your field?"

"Cultural studies—my thesis is on transvestitism in popular drama. There's a chapter on Shakespeare, of course, but it's mainly concerned with American vaudeville."

It was a shame that young people had to sink to such topics in order to receive attention; but of course the girl was not to be blamed for the growing absurdities of her profession. "Shakespeare—then I trust you've met Joel Hendrickson?"

"Of course," interjected David. "But not in the proper context for conversation."

"Well, come talk to him now," said Helena, and led them towards the spot where Joel was listening to Henry Stubbs.

Henry's attention, once diverted, turned to herself. "What a coincidence!" he said, grasping her elbow. "I was just going to write Dr. Hendrickson, and here he is!"

"Well, isn't that fortunate—"

"—You see, I've been wanting to write a biography of Nathaniel Brantford for some time, but Mrs. Hendrickson wouldn't allow any-body to examine his papers."

She raised her eyebrows. "And you've asked Joel to let you see them?"

"So far, I've just prepared a way—explained how re-publicizing Brantford's belief in classic liberal arts will help us in the struggle we're bound to have with the so-called progressive alumni who want to use the legacy to change the curriculum and force the college to go co-ed."

Ah, so he was one of Letty's devotees, was he? Poor Joel. Would he never be spared?

"And of course, I've promised him that the book will be dedi-cated to his wife's memory." Stubbs smiled. "So I think you'll agree I have every reason to hope."

"Perhaps so," she said, smiling in return. But as Stubbs rambled on, she earnestly hoped that he did not. The disadvantage of being dead was that one could not choose one's biographer, but Nathaniel would have been horrified by the thought of such a biographer's rum-maging through his life. Joel would know that, of course. But did Joel have control of Nathaniel's papers? Surely not, if all Nathaniel's estate had gone to the college. Ah. Perhaps it was time for her to dispose of Nathaniel's letters—and of her replies, which Joel and Letty had sent to her after finding them carefully boxed in the attic of the President's House. What a pity. It had been a wonderful correspondence, and it was occasionally pleasant to look at it. Still.

Stubbs looked at her reflectively. "I'd love to catch Dr. Hendrick-son's perspective on his wife's role in the post-Brantford College, but I think I should wait another month before interviewing him formally, don't you?"

"Yes, I think waiting would be wise," she said. And since experi-ence had taught her that the best way to restrain Letty's supporters was to divert them as tactfully as possible, she continued. "I'm sure the other research you're doing will keep you busy. Is it interesting?"

"Fascinating! Just the other day, I found out something that proves Brantford knew what he was talking about when he defended the liberal arts: he originally set out to be a scholar."

"You didn't know that? He made no secret of it."

"Oh, I sort of knew, I guess. But I hadn't known that when he was on his Rhodes, he was the Great White Hope of the Oxford critics, or that when he came back to Harvard, the big-wigs there expected the dissertation of the century. But then the stock market crashed, and he left Harvard and came to Mather with his dissertation undone." His eyes suddenly widened. "Say—you knew him back then, didn't you? Can you fill me in?"

"Nathaniel and I didn't meet until the Thirties," she said. "So I'm afraid I don't know much more about his Harvard period than you do. All he said was that when he got to Mather, he discovered his administrative talents and decided to give up scholarship."

"But, see, he didn't! He promoted it vicariously in student after student, and that's why Mather became a great college."

There seemed no point in telling him that after the Crash, promoting scholarship vicariously had been as close as Nathaniel could come to engaging in it. Why that should have been, she had no idea. She suspected, having spent many evenings reading to him while he sat enveloped in black despair, that the Crash had triggered a major resurgence of the depression that had followed him home from the trenches and plagued him for the rest of his life. But it would be disloyal to make her suspicions public. Turning to the driveway, she was relieved to see the Howells' car pull up near the barn. "I'm afraid I'll have to excuse myself."

He seemed to accept the dismissal, for he turned away; but she had hurried across only half the distance between herself and the Howells when David appeared at her side.

"Has Joel said anything about Cambridge? Andrew's going nuts, and so am I."

"Not a word, and he's called several times since I talked to you."

"Damn. Then he's really holding his cards close to his chest. Do you think you could—nothing overt, mind you—get him to—?"

"You should know better than to ask, David."

"I do," he said, sighing. "But sometimes I just can't help myself." He offered her a penitential arm. "Let's go say hello to the Howells."

E leanor accepted a canapé off an artistically arranged plate and returned the smile of the modishly-dressed catering girl who had offered it. "These are delicious," she said. "Are they putting you through college?"

"*Mxmx* already," said the girl. "Two years ago—*mxmx* loans, now. But this *mxmx* I want to do. Amherst *mxmx* great parties, but *mxmx* intellectual stuff *mxmx* so arcane!" She smiled again and wove her way through the growing crowd.

And for this, feminists of the Sixties had fought for equal educational rights. But academia had asked for it, in its way. Deprived of its money by the Right; deprived of common sense by the Left—she looked around as somebody touched her elbow. "Oh, hi, Charlie! I was just going to look for you, so I could tell you how much Joel and I enjoyed the Ward pictures. Have you turned up any papers to go with them? Joel's wife seems to have been descended from Henry Ward Jr., but I know nothing about that branch of the family. So it's up to you."

"It is?" Charlie brightened. "I'll look, then. *Mxmx* still sorting *mxmx*. Listen! *Mxmx* Clara Ward *mxmx* romance! *Mxmx* really sad *mxmx*. I'll bring it over *mxmx* tomorrow."

"That would be great," said Eleanor. And no doubt, when whatever it was appeared, its nature would become clear.

Charlie's eyes wandered to the spot where Salome and Abe Lefkowicz were talking excitedly with Joel, while the Zimmermans and David looked on. "*Mxmx* looks interesting. *Mxmx* join them? *Mxmx* write for you."

"You don't have to do that."

Charlie lifted one eyebrow. "All right, be that way. But *mxmx* can't follow any longer, *mxmx* notebook. You brought it, didn't you?"

"Of course." She followed Charlie into the circle and watched carefully, struggling to ascertain the topic of conversation, but after two or three minutes, she'd learned only that the ideas being discussed were exciting. Reluctantly, she pulled her notebook out of her purse, but before she could hand it to Charlie, the erstwhile student— what was his name?—appeared at Joel's side with an expectant look that strangled discussion. Joel acknowledged his presence with some kind of announcement.

"*Mxmx* fascinating subject," said Abe. "*Mxmx* tragic hero of education."

Charlie glanced at her and reached out automatically for the notebook. *Henry Stubbs*—she scrawled. *Writing biography of Great Nathaniel.*

How interesting. She watched his lips carefully as he answered Abe, but she could get almost nothing, and when she turned to the notebook, she found Charlie was speaking.

"Democratic! *Mxmx* there for commencement—*mxmx* totally upper crust, and *mxmx* male bastion *mxmx!*"

Joel began to explain something; Abe, the Zimmermans, and David listened with respectful interest, but Henry Stubbs, confusingly enough, shook his head violently. Eleanor turned to the notebook in despair.

Joel saying Nathaniel's Mather far more liberal than current college, Charlie scribbled hastily. *Amazing recruitment policy, wanted coeds by end of presidency—only conservative aspect, his refusal to change classical curriculum. Stubbs disagreeing, such an ASS.*

Eleanor frowned, trying to recall the Brantford debates. They'd created quite a furor at the time, but she'd read about them long ago, in a life so different from her present one that—

Charlie jogged her elbow. *Abe asking if coeducation and modernized (i.e., 20th century) version of classical curriculum now a possibility at Mather—Joel, definitely, modification essential—Stubbs, no,*

alumni who Mrs. H. spoke for will not let her money be used to un-
dercut G.Nath's ideals— Abe: difference between reverence for a great
educational leader and making a college into a fossil—Christ, look at
Joel!!!

She looked, and saw pain far different from the raw sadness of
recent loss that had so appalled her when she'd first met him. In the
withdrawn glance and wearily frozen face, she saw the soul of the
marriage David's stories had caricatured: endless attempts to reason
with the unreasonable, hours of patiently concealed frustration, years
of quiet efforts to minimize damage. And the impossibility of escaping the conversation, the politics, the college without deserting the
woman to whose life they'd been essential.

This mustn't continue. She looked quickly around the lawn, and
her eye fell on Stubbs's wife, who was standing on the fringe of the
circle, disengaging a four-year-old boy from her skirt with one hand
and holding a baby in the other. Joel had been looking longingly at
those children not so long ago. What if—? She tapped Charlie's scrib-
bling arm, reclaimed the notebook, and wrote: *You up for asking a ca-*
terer to offer around canapés in this group, then, while I divert Stubbs,
spiriting Joel and those two kids away to the fish-pond?

Charlie read, grinned, and slipped away. A moment later, the caterer stepped discreetly into the center of the circle. Looking around
quickly to be sure nobody else was speaking, Eleanor reached for a
canapé and smiled at Stubbs. "I'm afraid I'm not up on Brantford's
educational theories," she said. "Could you give me a brief—?"

There was no need to complete the sentence; he plunged into
an explanation, and the group dispersed with what she knew were
muttered phrases about refilling drinks. Out of the corner of her eye,
she saw Joel's face light up at some quiet suggestion from Charlie.
Within minutes, the two of them had collected the Stubbs children
and started towards what Charlie and Hattie had, a decade of teas
ago, dubbed the Secret Garden; and Mrs. Stubbs, her face glowing
with unexpected freedom, tapped her husband's arm and made some
request. He listened amicably, then looked back. "Emmy and I *mxmx*
tea. *Mxmx* you something?"

"No, thank you," she said, and turned towards David, Abe and Salome, feeling rather good. Even without content, there was something to be said for form.

Joel smiled at Emeline Stubbs and her little boy as Charlie held out a finger to the baby. "Your children are wonderfully well-behaved," he said, "but this can't be very exciting for them. Charlotte and I were just thinking they'd enjoy exploring the gardens. Would you trust us with them for half an hour?"

"Oh, yes!" she said. Then, turning to the little boy, "Wouldn't you like that, Jimmy?"

The boy clung to her skirt and began to sob, so Joel stooped down. "Miss Woodhouse has a fish pond in her garden," he said. "And if you walk up to it very, very quietly, sometimes the fish come to the top of the water and look at you."

Jimmy let go of his mother. "Sharks?" he said hopefully.

"I've never seen any. But maybe that's just because I haven't walked quietly enough."

"We could try sneaking around the back of the barn," suggested Charlie. "That way, they can't possibly see us coming. That sound all right to you?"

Jimmy nodded, so she led the way around the back of the house and along a path of ferns that reached high above his head, entering the lower garden by the gate from the woods.

"Don't run," whispered Joel, seeing that Jimmy was about to. "If you want to see anything, you've got to sneak up on it."

"On my hands and knees?"

Joel nodded sagely. "That would probably be best."

Charlie watched anxiously as Jimmy dropped to his knees and crawled slowly forward. "What are you going to say when he sees there aren't any sharks after all this?"

Jimmy peered over the edge, then dashed back to them. "I saw one! I saw a shark!"

"Really?" said Joel, smiling at Charlie. "Miss Woodhouse will be delighted; she's been worried about them. There should be several. Think you can find the others?"

"Sure!" Jimmy started back. "But don't come any nearer—you might scare them away."

Joel sat down on one of the stone benches that flanked the pond; Charlie sat beside him, cuddling the baby. "This is great," she said contentedly. "How brilliant of Eleanor to think of it."

He looked at her in surprise. *"Eleanor* thought of this?"

" 'Engineered this' is more like it. Didn't you see her writing?"

"I saw *you* writing," he said. "But I thought you were helping her."

"I was. But then she took the notebook and wrote a plan for liberating you."

He thought back to the strain in Eleanor's face as she tried to understand what he and Abe had been saying about Salome's thesis, then to Stubbs's interruption and the quick change of subject. Without understanding a word, she'd seen—? He shook his head. "She's amazing."

Charlie gave him a funny look. "You just noticed?"

He jumped up as Jimmy teetered on the edge of the pond, but it was a false alarm. "No," he said, sitting down again. "But I'm afraid it took me a while. She keeps a lot to herself."

"She sure does," said Charlie more kindly. "A regular hermit. The hearing makes it worse, of course, but that's not all of it. How can you be that intellectual *without* being a hermit? I mean, it sets you outside the circle of most people right from the start, and then there's the problem of having all this brain power and what are you supposed to *do* with it?"

He glanced at her, sadly wishing Yale would help. It might, of course, but her kind of perceptiveness and originality was precisely the quality the Ivy League tended to pass over in favor of more pedestrian intelligence. "Yes," he said. "It is a problem."

"Right. It's really tough, unless you're like Hattie, where all the brilliance sort of congregates in one place, if you see what I mean."

"The piano?"

"I'll say. Absolutely *awesome!* Like, she started studying at the New England Conservatory when she was *seven*, and not just because her dad was a big cheese there, eith—"

"—Sharks! Sharks!" Jimmy raced up to them. "I saw *two!*"

"Wonderful!" said Joel. "Since you're so good at seeing them, maybe we should start keeping track. That'll be difficult. We'll need a little gravelly spot and a stick—"

"—Over there! Look!" The boy seized Joel's hand and pulled him to the gravel by the gate. In a minute or two, they'd found an appropriate stick and made two careful hatch marks.

"Okay," said Joel. "Now, every time you see a fish, you sneak over here and make a mark. But be *very careful* not to run or shout, because if you do, all the sharks will dive way deep in the pond, and all you'll see is goldfish."

"I could make marks for the goldfish, too," volunteered Jimmy. "Way over here, so they wouldn't get mixed up with the shark marks."

"Wonderful!" said Joel. "Wait!" —as the boy sprinted off— "Slowly, remember?"

Jimmy dropped obediently to his knees, and Joel walked back to Charlie. "I didn't know Klimowski was at the New England Conservatory."

"He wasn't there long. He took the job because Hattie was coming and he wanted to be around to watch her grow up, instead of on tour all the time. But then he died—an embolism or something—when Hattie was only eighteen months old. So *sad* for Eleanor—I mean, he was in his fifties, but she never *expected—!* And her family wasn't much help, because her brother had gone schizo on LSD, and her parents were just destroyed. I guess he was a very promising classicist." She looked across the garden, watching Jimmy tiptoe away from the pond and make a mark in the gravel. "He's a dishwasher in Boston. This, after *all* the Randalls' savings went to his psychiatric expenses. And now he's sold the property across the road. It just isn't *fair!*"

Before him, the happy little boy and the fishpond dissolved into the image of a clear-cut maple grove, and Eleanor, sitting next to the last felled tree, crying. "No, it's not fair."

"Anyway," said Charlie, "Eleanor got a doctorate and a job—the whole single mother bit, except her hearing got worse and worse, which gave the powerful men at her college an excuse not to give her tenure. I didn't know that was a big deal until Salome started laying into David about it the other day—like, how come he didn't talk to the chauvinists at John Adams? or get the AAUP to take a stand?!"

He pursed his lips, recalling that he'd heard of the case only some months after it was over, and given it little thought. God! How he'd let the gates of Mather College restrict his vision! But in his heart he knew that even if he'd seen and acted... "Cases like that are difficult. It's hard to separate discrimination from normal jealousy and politics."

"Yuck! Don't even mention politics! That's what Eleanor engineered us out of having to endure, remember?"

"I do, indeed. And I'll thank her profusely, within the hour."

"Of course, there are people who enjoy it, like David. You should hear him gossip!"

"Charlie," he said wearily, "there's always gossip. Professional scholars seem to be particularly adept at ferreting it out—no doubt it's their research training. You get used to it after a while."

Charlie rocked the baby back and forth. "You don't look as if you'd gotten used to it."

"I've gotten used to ignoring it," he said, trying to keep the bitterness out of his voice. "But never to retaliating in kind. Nathaniel used to berate me for it. *'Listen, Joel—academic politics is a form of guerilla warfare; you've got to learn the tactics.'* But then, there was a side of Nathaniel that relished a good fight."

"There's a side of most men that relishes a good fight," said Charlie disapprovingly.

"True. Which leaves mediators as full of arrows as Saint Sebastian."

She looked at him affectionately over the baby's shoulder. "And one foot in paradise."

What a lovely, kind girl she was. How sad that she couldn't stay always as she was now, here in the garden, with the sun shining down on her and the two children, untouched by the world. Brushing aside a lock that strayed across her face, he leaned forward and kissed her gently on the forehead.

⁂

The tea party had reached the point at which groups of people left the food, some drifting towards the driveway and others towards the garden. After saying goodbye to the Lefkowiczes and two other couples, Helena joined Eleanor and Salome as they strolled towards the barn cellar gardens. To her amusement, David, who in the past had left the garden to the women while he and the lingering men adjourned to wicker chairs and cigars, quickly joined them.

"You've got to see what Helena's done to her old barns," he said, taking Salome's arm. "It could be done with my barn cellar, if there were someone around who liked flowers."

Salome did seem to like flowers, but her enthusiastic comments conveyed no particular interest in becoming the permanent gardener in David's establishment. Too bad: they were a handsome couple, and he badly needed the solidity that lurked behind her sophisticated exterior.

Footsteps scurried behind them as they reached the roses; looking around, she saw Henry and Emeline Stubbs. "I'm afraid we have to leave this wonderful gathering," said Henry. "The Zimmermans have a dinner engagement. You wouldn't have seen where Charlotte and Dr. Hendrickson took our kids, would you?"

David edged forward, frowning. "Charlie's with Joel?"

"Joel and the kids—Emmy says they were going to look at some fish."

"In that case," said Helena, "they'll be in the next garden." She undid the catch to the white gate and started carefully down the stone stairs. When she was free to look up, she saw what could only be called a perfect tableau. Charlotte was sitting on the stone bench, her long hair back-lit by the late afternoon sun as she cradled the baby. Joel sat at her feet, his arm braced on the bench's seat, and his lap occupied by a slightly damp, soundly sleeping little boy. They were talking too softly to be heard from the gate, but something about Joel's face made Helena hesitate to interrupt them. She hadn't seen that kind of softness for a long, long time—not since, at Charlotte's age, she had inspired it, in a garden far from here.

"Oh, there they are!" Emeline ran down the steps, but David stopped at the gate.

"Charlie!" he called disapprovingly. "You should have brought the kids back sooner! The Stubbses have been worrying about them."

"It's my fault, not Charlie's," said Joel, jumping up as the little boy awoke. "We were going to come back long ago, but then Jimmy fell asleep, and I didn't want to wake him."

"No problem," said Henry, as Emeline collected the baby from Charlotte. "We weren't worried at all. I remembered all those Mather picnics, with Dr. Hendrickson as pied piper. It seems the magic still works." He pointed to the little boy, who was chattering excitedly to his mother. "He'll believe in the Hendrickson legends, now."

"He sure will," said Emeline, smiling at Joel. "Thank you very much."

The Zimmermans and the other remaining couples appeared at the top of the steps, then descended with the ease of the comparatively young, bearing David and Salome with them. The Zimmermans and Stubbses said a hurried farewell; the others admired the garden (which did look lovely), then drifted back up the steps in ones and twos. Soon they would wander towards the driveway and wait, talking a little awkwardly, until she appeared to say goodbye, so she started to the steps herself. As she neared them, Joel said something to Eleanor, and the two crossed the grass together.

"Helena, we've got to start back," he said. "But it has been perfectly wonderful. The tea, the company, the garden—what a lovely place." He smiled at her with a relaxed happiness she hadn't seen in his face for years, then, turning towards the steps, offered her his arm as a matter of course. She took it in the same spirit, but she noticed with a touch of irritation that she was making ample use of his support, not only on the stairs, but as they walked through the upper garden. "Tell me," she said, to distract them both, "who has custody of Nathaniel's papers?"

"You're worried about Stubbs?"

"Among other things."

"I promise you, the papers are safe. Letty gave them to the college last April, with the proviso that the gift was not to be announced until next fall, and that the papers themselves were not to be opened until fifty years after her death." He smiled down at her. "It lacked the melodrama of a bonfire, but after some consideration, Letty agreed that it had its advantages."

"I'm glad to hear it," she said. And wondered how long it had taken him to persuade Letty to consider those advantages.

His reply, if he had one, was forestalled by half an hour of thanks and protracted farewell conversations, through which his invaluable arm supported her until the Reynolds' departure left only Eleanor's car and the caterer's van in the driveway. By that time, she was so weary that her suggestion that they come sit down was merely an expression of appreciation—which, fortunately, they were acute enough to understand. It would be better, in any case, if she thought over the problem of the letters and their preservation by herself, before discussing it further. She returned their waves as they drove off, then made her way to the porch and sank gratefully into her accustomed chair.

Another tea past. As she closed her eyes, the murmuring voices of caterers and the clink of dishes merged with drifting memories of this peaceful, satisfied repose for—how long? She subtracted three times, arriving at seventy so consistently that she was forced to accept the figure. Seventy years. Three score and ten. And yet, thrushes were singing just as they always had as she'd sat on the porch after the teas. From the perspective of this blessed solitude, the child entranced by the goldfish today became Peter Randall; Salome Rose, with her sharp-tongued wit, became Eleanor. And Charlotte and Joel—

"Helena, we're going to take off, now—Helena? Helena? You okay?"

She opened her eyes and met the worried gazes of the pony-tailed chef and the girl who seemed to run the business with him. "Yes, yes," she said. "Of course I am. About the bill—"

"—That's all taken care of," said the chef. "You'll get a copy in the mail next week."

"Fine. And thank you very much. Everything was lovely."

"Glad you liked it," said the chef, turning to go.

But the girl looked at her, frowning a little. "You look pretty tired. Want me to make you a sandwich or something before we split?"

"That's very kind of you, but I'm fine."

"Okay, then," said the girl. "Have a good weekend. It's been great working for you. And listen, I've been wanting to tell you—your dress is just exquisite. I *love* period clothes."

She watched with some amusement as they left; then, as their van bounced down the driveway, she got up and walked through the house to the kitchen. It was immaculate, even unto the dishes and pans, which had all been put away in the right places. She hadn't encountered that kind of timeless professionalism in this country since her parents' last servants retired.

Timeless. Many things were, of course. And yet, and yet—she surveyed the living room, trying to envisage the house as it had been a lifetime ago, when she, only a little older than Charlotte was now, had given the first tea. The regency table had certainly been in its present place, and so had the Saraband rug. The rest had come later, the results of trips to Europe, occasional auctions, accidental finds. The two pieces apart, the only things in the room that remained from the era of that first tea were herself and her dress, both inevitably altered.

And despite the timelessness of the teas, they'd altered just as inevitably. It wasn't just that the first generation of guests had died; it was that their descendants had disappeared. With the sole exceptions of David and Eleanor, for one reason or another—division of inheritance, divorce, bankruptcy, fifty-week-a-year schedules—the children of all the early tea guests had sold the estates in which their parents had spent leisurely summers. And to the young professionals who had bought the truncated remnants of those estates and the farms that had surrounded them, leisure itself had become hectic, and the landscape that had reflected the old pastoral *otium* had changed accordingly. She strolled out to the porch, feeling the heavy material of her dress move lightly with her. Behind her, the song of hermit thrushes rose in poignant longing from the woods; before her, gentle waves of nodding timothy swept down the mowing. For a long moment she stood still, her eyes moving from the distant parking lots, inns, and 'country' shopping centers that straggled through the valley, up to the lifts and trails that disfigured the mountain.

No, she would not burn the letters. They were a part of the past, and as such, should be preserved. Not just for the edification of an age to which her life, Nathaniel's—to which letter-writing itself—would be a mystery. There were things worth preserving solely out of respect and love of what they had been. She sat down again in her chair, resting her head against its wicker back. In a few minutes, she would change, then bring down the earliest boxes from the attic, and start sorting. Next week, after a few calls to lawyers, she would send them off to Andrew Crawford. Would that the land could be so easily preserved.

The land. The land that had drawn her here at the end of her life, a lifetime ago, that had sustained her, become to her what no man—not even Nathaniel—had been since those days in the garden. In fifty years...

She pulled a lace handkerchief from her sleeve and applied it, with some annoyance, to her eyes. She certainly hoped she wasn't becoming one of those pathetic elderly women who wept when they thought of a past that could not be recovered.

11. A Reconsideration

Eleanor glanced at Joel as the Draper traffic light stopped them in the empty village. There was no reason to ask him if something were on his mind; the pressure of his unspoken thoughts was almost tangible. Perhaps that was a good sign. The prolonged silences into which he'd lapsed during the last week had permitted no intrusion, but almost from the moment they'd turned out of Helena's driveway, she'd realized that the peculiar combination of impersonality and intimacy that car-travel created would have led him to speak, if speech had been possible.

"Suppose we take Derri for a walk?" she asked. "The sun won't set for an hour or so."

The light changed, so the details of his acceptance were lost on her, but there was no mistaking the surprised gratitude of his tone. That promised well.

She changed back into her jeans as soon as they got home, and emerged from the house in Derri's blissful company to find Joel pacing up and down. It really did look as if he might finally bring himself to tell her what was disturbing him. Unfortunately, he was too gentlemanly to plunge in directly; her initial soundings, as they strolled up the mowing, produced only polite reflections on the tea. It wasn't until they reached the poorer light of the woods that he began. "Talking *mxmx* young scholars *mxmx* realize how quickly *mxmx* critical discourse *mxmx* changing."

She nodded. "Terrifying, isn't it? Last time I talked to Abe, I came home feeling so antiquated that I revised a whole chapter."

He tossed a stick for Derri. "*Mxmx* not that. *Mxmx* happier if it were *mxmx* Lately, I've had nothing to offer Abe's generation, let alone Salome's."

"That's sure not what they think! When you and Charlie were fish-viewing, Abe and Salome were both *raving* about your work. To you, sensitive readings and informed use of new theories may just be common sense, but to them, real scholarship like yours provides ballast in the Sargasso Sea of faddism."

He laughed and said something about her being no sailor, but as they reached the clearing at the top of the hill, he was pensive again. "*Mxmx* fact remains, *mxmx* years since I've had ballast—or anything else—*mxmx* young critics."

"Be patient with me," she said. "Are you saying—?"

He stopped and faced her. "I'm saying that I've written nothing for seven years."

"Really nothing, or 'just articles and reviews' nothing?"

"Really nothing. My last book *mxmx* '84. Then *mxmx* '87–'88 *mxmx* grant for research *mxmx* book on pastoral romance, but circumstances *mxmx*, and I put the writing aside. *Mxmx* never gotten back to it."

"That's hardly surprising, given the nature of the 'circumstances,'" she said gently. "Your wife was ill a long time—"

"—so I told myself, but *mxmx* really not it. Last summer, I persuaded Letty to spend two weeks *mxmx* Nantucket. *Mxmx* recent scholarship *mxmx* subject. But *mxmx* came back to the college *mxmx* immediately submerged—" His voice trailed off into the expression she'd seen fleetingly at the tea.

Seven years of eternal politics and an intellectual life foregone. The impossibility of expressing natural resentment to a spouse struggling for life. A will that suggested all his forbearance had been in vain. The wonder was not that he'd failed to write, but that he'd emerged from those years merely fragile, not shattered. Not that the danger was over yet.

She glanced at him, thinking of the tender way he'd held the sleeping child in Helena's garden, and wishing she were either old enough or young enough to offer him uncomplicated, unrestrained affection. It was probably the only thing that would help—but, alas, it was not a possibility. She led the way through the blueberry patches to a long-forgotten stone wall. In silence, they hoisted themselves up on the warm stones and looked out at the mountains.

"*Mxmx* very far away here," he said finally. "*Mxmx* wish I didn't have to leave."

Ah. Well, she should have expected it; he'd planned to stay for only two weeks. But it was sad to think of *Bleak House* lying on the coffee table with the marker half way through it. "*Do* you have to leave?"

"I should have left a week ago. *Mxmx* business to take care of."

"Surely, putting off college business for a week or two in the summer is no crime."

"*Mxmx* very persuasive," he said, smiling. "But *mxmx* not college business."

"Will it take long?"

"Oh, no. *Mxmx* matter of days."

"And when it's done? Will you be able to stop yourself from submerging?"

His silence was eloquence itself.

"Would it be possible," she ventured, "—don't laugh, I know money is money—but would it be possible for you to take a leave from Mather for long enough to draft the book?"

He looked at her thoughtfully. "It might be, at that. *Mxmx* bargaining power."

"I'm sorry—what could you use as bargaining power?"

"Oh, I got an offer last week. *Mxmx* can't consider seriously, but *mxmx.*"

Last week. The phone call. And the next day, he'd run himself into the ground. Poor Joel. "An interesting offer?"

"Queen Elizabeth Professorship in Renaissance Studies at Trinity College, Cambridge," he said, with bitter clarity.

Good heavens. "And you're *really* not in a position to consider it seriously?"

He looked at her reproachfully. "That's what I've been telling you."

"No—you've been telling me that your commitment to Mather College is such that you haven't been able to write for seven years, and you've suggested that even now, to return to the campus is to invite immediate submergence."

"That's true," he admitted. "But *mxmx* Professorship *mxmx* false auspices—"

"— You wouldn't *have* to take it under false auspices. You could tell Trinity College you hesitated to make a permanent commitment right now because of your wife's recent death, but that you would love to come for a year or two. If they really want you, they'll make it possible—and that would give you a chance to work on the book."

His eyes followed the light that reflected off a faraway car on the road to Westover. "That assumes the reason *mxmx* unfinished book *mxmx* lies without, not within."

"I doubt anybody who's read your work thinks the problem lies within."

He looked at her coldly. "You can have no idea."

No idea! So he thought that days, weeks, months of cleaning houses had no effect on intellectual momentum? He didn't realize that loss of momentum was a terrifying prospect to *anybody* who'd witnessed the ossification of middle-aged scholars? It hadn't occurred to him that being universally perceived as half-witted might make the matter worse? Christ almighty!

He moved uneasily. "Eleanor—"

She dropped her gaze from the mountains to the overgrown pasture below them, trying to summon up a look that wouldn't turn him to stone. He didn't deserve it; he'd only snapped because she'd touched a raw spot. And who was she to blame him for that?

A hand dropped gently on her knee—and stayed there as she looked at him in astonishment. He was obviously searching for words that she could understand, but he had no need to. Sorrow for his coldness mingled in his face with regret for what he'd become, then, with an electric snap as their eyes met, a craving for intimacy so deep, so long denied— It was gone almost before she saw it, and with it, his hand. Whatever he might have wanted, what remained in his face asked only for forgiveness.

She reached over and quickly pressed the hand he'd retrieved, then jumped off the wall. "Let's go back."

He nodded and joined her, throwing a stick for Derri with his usual athletic grace. She sighed as she fell into stride next to him, wishing he were not going. He would probably come back once in a while—after all, he still had to decide what to do with the Ward Place. But whatever it was they'd tenuously created over the past few days was so fragile, so dependent upon proximity, that it had little chance of being renewable.

She glanced at him as they reached the house, half hoping to see some regret in his face; but he had withdrawn into his inner self. He moved about the kitchen automatically, producing them an omelette with admirable efficiency, and he said a polite word or two as they ate it, but his mind was evidently elsewhere.

"Would you like to read?" she asked when they had finished.

"I'm sorry?" he said, looking up abstractedly.

Now *there* was a switch. She smiled and repeated the question.

"Oh yes—yes, of course." But as he and Fou settled themselves in his usual chair he looked up. "I was just thinking…"

She tried to look receptive as he paused.

"I was thinking *mxmx* submerging. And about how nice *mxmx* the rest of the summer writing at the Ward Place. And I was wondering" —he stroked the cat— "*mxmx* intruding if I came back here *mxmx* more weeks, while I finished the work over the hill?"

She lifted *Bleak House* off the coffee table. "This can hardly be called an intrusion."

"Then I'll come back *mxmx* week or two," he said. "If that would be all right."

"It would be more than all right. I really enjoy our evenings."

"So do I," he said.

12. Infidelities

No lesser personage than Peggy, the executive administrative secretary, ushered Joel into the President's office, and Andrew actually stood up as he entered. "Well, well! Vermont has made a new man of you!" he said, shaking hands warmly. "Tanned, fit—you put the rest of us to shame. You'll come for dinner at our house tonight, won't you? There'll be nobody but you, Margaret, me, and three steaks on the grill. Promise."

Joel smothered a smile. Nobody's fool, was Andrew, when it came to subtly applied pressure, but that pressure was certainly preferable to dinner with the absent presences in his own house. "Thanks, I'd love to."

"Great." Andrew sat down again and chatted about Vermont, carpentry, and the weather for an appropriate interval, then leaned back in his chair. "So, tell me the details of this offer."

Joel enumerated them briefly—so briefly that only prior knowledge could account for a failure to request elaboration. Amazing, how quickly one's political instincts redeveloped.

Andrew did not request elaboration. "Not bad, by English standards," he said grudgingly. "And there's no denying the label's got class. How long did they give you to decide?"

"They were generous; but I'd like to return the favor."

"Of course. Well, since your call on Tuesday, I've talked to Dean Rice and a couple of trustees, and we agreed that though we can't offer you antiquity and a river—at least, not the right river—we can offer other things. All negotiable, you understand. Let's start with teaching. How about a junior seminar in the fall and a senior seminar in the spring?"

"In addition to—?"

"Nothing. We think you could use the leisure profitably." Andrew glanced at him. "Oh, I know: *the purpose of a college is to teach young men, not to subsidize professors.* The damn phrase was ringing in my ears all the time I was talking to Rice, and in his ears too, I bet; Brantford has a way of ruling from the grave. But we can't possibly compete for good senior scholars when everybody knows a full professor's teaching load here is triple anyplace else's."

"Even though everybody also knows that Mather's curriculum— alone in an academic world that routinely exploits young scholars— doesn't depend on a floating bottom of adjuncts?"

"Well, if it's conscience that's bothering you," said Andrew, smiling seraphically, "ask Cambridge who teaches the majority of its undergraduates."

Perhaps one's political instincts didn't redevelop quite fast enough. Five weeks ago, he would never have given Andrew an opening like that.

"On to our other terms," said Andrew. "We were thinking about your house on Elm Street. It must look pretty empty right now, and of course, handsome old places like that are expensive to maintain." He tapped his fingers together. "Supposing we were to buy Elm Street from you at market price, and set you up somewhere else? For example, the College just bought the Victorian across from the gates, and we're going to divide it into four faculty apartments. The largest of them, if you're interested, could be yours. Rent free, of course. That would be in addition to the raise I'm currently discussing with the trustees. I don't have a figure yet, but it should be considerably more than they've offered you at Cambridge."

"That's...generous."

"Well, you know," said Andrew, "there are a lot of people who want to keep you here, and not just because you're a big name."

Something in his voice made the sentence more than a carefully worded presidential line. He was a good man, Andrew Crawford. They were all good men, in fact. Joel stood up a little too quickly. "Let me think about it, all right?"

"Sure. Take a few days to con it all out; then we'll talk again." Andrew stood up, too. "Not tonight, of course—that's pleasure. Make it around six, okay?"

They shook hands, and Joel walked out into the summer silence of the corridor. Sorted through the hodge-podge that had built up in his mail box. Sauntered to the English Wing. Unlocked his office door. And stood on the threshold, stunned by its familiarity.

There had been no comparable leap into the past at Elm Street: the echoing rooms were so changed that he'd felt like a stranger. But here—his eyes traveled across the crowded bookshelves that lined the walls to the window-framed campus, then across the worn Oriental rug to his desk. He walked in slowly, feeling the events of the last month fade with every step. Sitting in his desk chair, he could almost believe that he had slipped off into a fantasy of days filled with carpentry and evenings listening to *Bleak House,* and just returned to reality. He spent an hour dealing with the backlog of memos and queries, then started home.

Queen Elizabeth Professorship of Renaissance Studies. The 'chunk' of the English wing door, the worn steps, the Mather Arms on the gates—every detail of the landscape accused him of infidelity. How could he possibly have let a passing fancy for Gothic architecture and a label tempt him to desert the campus that had for so long been his second self? The ideals of Nathaniel Brantford's Mather College— devotion to learning, to teaching, to the subsidy not of professors but of young men from factories, villages, farms—commanded respect even in today's fast-track educational world. Separated from the reactionary context with which they had become associated, those ideals could be adapted to an age of technological change. It would take a man of Nathaniel's dedication to do it, of course. He who tried it would have to give up all thought of further scholarship, and perhaps also... No, if Nathaniel's devotion to his ideals had limited the love he bore the people who had cared for him, that was a condition he'd shared with Milton and Newton. Faced with the achievement, one felt ungrateful for having occasionally wished more of the man.

He strolled down Elm Street, gazing at its handsome federal houses. An apartment made sense. To maintain two houses in the absence of Letty's income would be to pile debt upon debt as he furnished them and bought a car in which to drive from one to the other. How fashionable. How absurd. On the other hand—he looked at the house as he turned up his walk, wondering how he could bring himself to sell it. Its empty rooms and unmowed lawn should have made it unattractive; but instead they reminded him of the days in which he'd bought it.

Nathaniel stood in the middle of the walk, looking at the front yard. "The lawn needs mowing. Sure the place is good enough for Letty?"

He smiled. "She seems to think so."

"It's a good house. 1780's, I'd say. You're going to make an offer?"

"This evening, since you approve. And, Nathaniel, you really must let me thank you for your generosity. You know perfectly well I could never buy Letty a house like this without—"

"—That's quite enough."

It was; the words were said. But as they surveyed the neglected garden, he still felt the strain that developed between them on the rare occasions when it was necessary to speak of personal things. Finally, when they returned to the front yard, Nathaniel looked at him in the fading light. "You know, Joel, you're pretty quiet for a young man who has just gotten back from his honeymoon and found the perfect house for his bride. Everything's all right, isn't it?"

Could he...should he...? His eyes roved irresolutely over the house then, as the streetlights blinked on, back to Nathaniel's waiting face. And saw what he'd heard was not a question, but a plea.

He straightened up and smiled. "Of course it is."

Joel shook his head as he unlocked the door. This house was as bad as the Ward Place; ghosts lurked in every corner. As Eleanor said, though, ghosts were easily dispersed by activity. He hurried upstairs, found an old shirt, and went out to mow the lawn.

E leanor eased her car up the Ward Place driveway, wondering what she would find in the papers Joel had left for her on the dining room table. The night before he left, he said he'd searched them for clues about Henry Ward and his children, and had found nothing—but that she might be able to use the names in the accounts to find some trail to follow. She had taken the request as a gracious way of offering her the Wardiana she hadn't yet gotten to, but this morning's chance encounter with Lucy Davis had made her think that maybe—

A flash of brown and white caught her eye, and she braked, expecting a deer. But it was a horse that blazed by on the far side of the mowing wall—Cocoa, galloping at a perfect cross-country pace under Charlie's guidance. As she watched, the two swung away from the wall for a few strides, then turned straight towards the house and soared over the gate into the dooryard. They had slowed to a walk by the time she reached the dooryard herself, and Charlie waved, but she had the sense not to say anything. No need to, anyway; Cocoa was going to have to walk to the bottom of the driveway and back before he was cool enough to tie. Eleanor watched them fondly as they started downhill, then glanced respectfully at the gate, reflecting that she'd lost her youthful confidence in her immortality. Gone were the days when she would put a horse—even this horse—at a solid obstacle four feet high.

She started toward the house, but paused in something like disorientation. She'd seen it a few weeks ago, of course, and Joel, Ray and Charlie had updated her on its progress, but in her imagination it had retained the aura of the forlorn house she had kept up surreptitiously for six years. And that aura was gone. In the spot where the ruined barn had stood, there remained nothing but hand-laid foundations, carefully preserved and cleared of brush. Near them, the usable beams and siding that had not already gone to Ray's were neatly stacked, awaiting transportation. The repainted house glowed softly white under its maples; Mary Ward's porch swing, refinished and re-hung, swung gently over a floor that no longer listed towards the steps; the sheds stood straight, their rebuilt doors securely closed; the missing slates on the roof were replaced, the chimney re-pointed.

Five weeks. Joel Hendrickson had done all this in five weeks. Not alone—Charlie had scraped and painted part of every day; Ray and his equipment had obviously been invaluable. But the bulk of the work and time had been Joel's. She felt a surge of regret mingle with her admiration. She'd thought she had gotten to know him fairly well, but in letting her busyness serve as an excuse for not coming here more often, she hadn't seen the part of him that emerged when he picked up a hammer. The transformation before her revealed as much about his inner self as his misery in the face of political wrangling had revealed at Helena's tea. It was a product of skill and craftsmanship—and above all, of care—worthy of Rob Ward.

A voice interrupted her thoughts, and she turned, startling as she realized Charlie and Cocoa were standing right next to her. "Pretty nice, huh?" repeated Charlie. But her face was sad. "What do you suppose *mxmx* do with it?"

"I don't know. I don't think *he* knows."

Charlie checked Cocoa's chest for sweat. "Yeah, *mxmx* appraised *mxmx* few days ago. On the other hand—*look* at it! It's impossible *mxmx* work and love, and then *sell* it!"

"Well, practically speaking, if he sells it, he'll be able to retire and

166

do nothing but write for the rest of his life. No teaching, and most of all, no politics."

Charlie pursed her lips. "He hates politics, all right. But *mxmx* loves teaching. I mean David's okay, I suppose, but Joel *mxmx* books and ideas and, well..."

"And what?"

"Students. He *cares* about them. *Mxmx* hope I find professors *mxmx* Yale. *Mxmx* awesome four years."

Eleanor looked at her closely, but all she saw was genuine affection and respect. She'd been right, then, to laugh at David's worried query, and silly to let even one drop of its poison pollute her mind. If there was any man to be trusted with a teenager still unconscious of the power beauty gave her, it was Joel Hendrickson— "I'm sorry?"

"**I don't think he will sell it for the money,**" repeated Charlie. "*Mxmx* can't see it. But there's something funny *mxmx* legacy thing. I mean, if he had known his wife owned it—"

"—Right. That's why he's looking for a family quarrel to justify her silence. If that's what it is, it's still not great, but it's at least understandable."

"*Mxmx* have to wonder *mxmx* married her in the first place. Of course, David's stories *mxmx*." She turned her face away to feel Cocoa's chest. "*Mxmx mxmx* boss *mxmx mxmx* those."

"Wait, wait! You're losing me."

"Sorry." Charlie turned towards her and spoke slowly. "I said, David's stories are unjust to Joel. Only a wimp or a politico would marry the Great Nathaniel's niece or cousin or whatever to please the boss, and he's not either of those." She waited patiently. "I said—"

"—I heard you. It's just difficult to imagine a situation as unusual and complex as Joel's was. To begin with, there is (or at least was, before the ham-fisted psychology of this enlightened age knocked all nuance out of human sensibility) such a thing as a friendship of a lifetime. It's very rare, and it rarely *lasts* a lifetime, but it exists. I'm fairly sure that Joel and Nathaniel Brantford had such a friendship."

"But *mxmx* nothing to do with Joel and Letty."

"I think it does. Everything I've ever heard about the Great

Nathaniel makes him out to have been intellectually imposing, and I think his friendship with Joel was based on literary discussions—"

"—boy, I bet they were something!"

"I'll say. But that means that if Letty wasn't intellectual, she was left out."

"You're saying Joel married *mxmx* include her?"

"To—? Oh, just to include her. Well, not 'just.' Don't forget, she was stunning—so beautiful that neither David nor Helena ever talks about her without saying so, even when they're angry at her policies. That's rare. All the same, I'm fairly sure including her was part of it. And then, I think that having married her, he loved her."

Charlie blinked. "*Because* he'd married her?"

"There are people who work like that."

"You're not saying *mxmx* happy marriage, are you?"

"Oh, no. Just that he loved her."

"But that's *terrible!*"

Eleanor smiled. "Is it?"

Charlie frowned pensively. "Okay, not necessarily. *Mxmx* abstract, anyway. *Mxmx* if she loved him *mxmx*, even backasswards."

"Even backasswards. I like that. Let's hope that what we find in the archives proves that she did." Eleanor stroked Cocoa's neck. "Hey, this horse is in great shape. Not even hot."

"He has to be. Rhinebeck event *mxmx* next week. *Mxmx* potential buyers *mxmx*." She chattered away cheerfully as they led Cocoa to the old maple and unsaddled him, and while the activity made it impossible to understand most of her words, the confidence and enthusiasm that manifested itself in her riding was clear in her voice. Making real money this summer, painting and training. Looking forward to the fall and a whole new life. Thinking about a history major, thanks to Clara Ward. What wonders the future held. Eleanor smiled a little sadly as they walked across the dooryard together.

Inside, the house was still largely its old self, though it was about to change. In preparation for Joel's return, Charlie had been commissioned to steam the wallpaper off the downstairs bedroom and paint it if the condition of the walls allowed. The furniture had been moved upstairs, and Charlie, changed out of her riding clothes into cutoffs and a T-shirt, went to work, as innocent as Joel of the knowledge that the room had been the one in which Mary Ward died, alone and unattended. Just as well. Eleanor picked up the pile of papers Joel had left and took them to the porch swing, along with the old edition of Longfellow's poems as a paperweight. At first, the act of sitting on the swing begot memories so strong that they competed with the documents before her, but after a few minutes she forced herself to concentrate, and she slowly paged through folders of Robert's careful accounts, then Mary's, marveling at their unthinking portrayal of a lost way of life, but finding nothing of specific interest to Joel except—

—"*mxmx* quiet," said Charlie, suddenly appearing next to her. "Anything interesting?"

"Only a lacuna."

"A what?"

"A gap in the evidence. Actually, it's more a premature end than a gap. There's nothing after 1930. Are you sure this is everything?"

"Pretty sure. Joel said everything *mxmx* the stenciled chest, including the journal and the Longfellow, *mxmx* hidden under the false bottom. I looked *mxmx* big wardrobe, tapped floorboards...nothing."

"The Longfellow was hidden with the journal?"

"Right. I checked *mxmx* secret letters *mxmx* nothing. Not even a pressed flower."

"Well, it's a lovely old edition. Did it belong to Grandfather Ward?"

Charlie moved the documents to the middle of the swing, sat down and flipped open the front leaf. "It sure did," she said, smiling at the bold hand in which "Henry Ward, 1875" was written. "But hey, look!" She put the book down between them and pointed. "There's something slipped under the whaddycallits."

"Endpapers," said Eleanor automatically, but she quickly placed her hand on Charlie's excited fingers. "Take it easy—sometimes there are pages of lost books stuffed in endpapers. "

"Okay." Charlie wiggled the paper gently back and forth and gradually slid out an old snapshot of a young man and woman standing on the Ward house steps. Eleanor bent over it eagerly. The girl had Grandpa Ward's soft, intelligent eyes and Robert and Alice's determined chin. But unlike the other Wards, she was lovely—poised, graceful, and heartbreakingly young.

"Wow!" said Charlie. "Look at those Twenties clothes—oh, hey! Twenties!" She bounced up and down on the swing. "Remember? *Gid back. Brought a Kodak.* It's got to be Clara! And look! If it was *mxmx* the journal, the guy must be—!"

Eleanor shifted her attention to the young man beside Clara. There was no doubt about his lineage, even though he was in his shirt sleeves. His stance made it obvious that he was used to giving orders, that in fact it wouldn't have occurred to him not to. But his face was a study in contradictions—chaotic eyebrows that seemed to have nothing to do with the immaculately oiled hair, eyes much too dreamy to go with the strong chin and stubborn nose. Eleanor followed his affectionate gaze back to the girl. "That's the most interesting pair of faces I've seen for a long time. What a pity—not that it would have been an easy marriage."

"Yeah," said Charlie. "But tell me something: does he *mxmx* the kind of guy *mxmx* leave a girl *mxmx* parents didn't like her?"

"Does he—? No, I got it—and no, he doesn't. But that's a very aristocratic face; he may simply have come to his patrician senses at the end of the summer."

"But he asked her to marry him!"

Eleanor shook her head. "That's a classic story, I'm afraid. And I admit, when I came to that awful break in the journal, I assumed it was theirs. But looking at that face—I don't know. Maybe we should check the outside information."

"Outside information! You mean there is some? Where?"

"Remember Clara's references to Susan Wheeler, who married into the Howe family?

Well, this morning I talked to her grand-daughter—Lucy Davis, who works at the bank—and I asked if she was still alive. She is. Lives in Florida with her grandson's family, and Lucy says she loves to answer questions about old times. She'd lonely these days—just about blind, I gather. But she can still talk." Eleanor pulled a piece of paper out of her pocket. "Here's her number."

"Susan Howe! That's fantastic! *Mxmx* as soon as I get home!" She hesitated. "Unless you'd rather do it."

"Don't be ridiculous," said Eleanor. "The phone is not my medium." That was certainly true, but when she looked at Charlie's excited face, she felt a twinge of self-sacrifice.

Helena looked up from her roses, her eyes widening in surprise as a silver sports car purred into her driveway and stopped. David? So soon after the tea?

"I'm over here!" she called as he turned towards the house.

He strolled through the gate with a jauntiness that suggested something was troubling him deeply. " 'Persephone gathering flowers, herself a fairer flower'— How are you, Helena?"

She got up so slowly that if he had been Nathaniel or Joel, he would have seen that she was not as well as she would wish. "I'm fine, thank you. Are you here about Joel?"

"Well, in a way." David looked over the far gate to the fish pond.

"Good news, I hope—at least good news for the college."

"For the college? Oh, I see... No, this isn't college business. Or good news either, for that matter. In fact, it's sort of a mess."

"Perhaps you should tell me what it is."

"It's Charlie." He jingled the keys in the pocket of his whites. "You know, she's gotten awfully good looking in the last year. Oh, she hides it most of the time, with those cut-offs and old shirts—you'd never know her from the old Charlie that used to hang around Eleanor's place with Hattie. But when she cleans up..."

"She's beautiful," said Helena. "Quite extraordinarily so. I noticed at the tea."

"If you noticed, maybe you also noticed how Joel was looking at her when they took those kids to see the fish." He glanced at her. "You did, didn't you?"

"Yes, I did. Though I think there's very little to worry about."

"Little to worry about! He's old enough to be her grandfather!" He began to pace up and down, endangering the lobelia that lopped into the path. "I blame myself, of course; I've let her go to the Ward place every day to paint. But who would have thought it? I swear, I never saw Joel's eyes move towards a well turned ankle, let alone anything more provocative."

"Letty Hendrickson was a very beautiful woman," said Helena mildly. "And there is such a thing as fidelity."

"That's irrelevant; Joel's free now. When he comes back—"

"—He's coming back? I didn't know that."

"Neither did I, but I saw Eleanor yesterday, and that's what she said. I suppose Charlie knows; she's been really cheerful, all wound up in some historical project she's doing for him." He looked at her tragically. "Please, Helena, don't just smile. Tell me what to do."

She eliminated the smile. "You could always call him out."

"Call him out? You mean—? Oh, come on, that sort of thing went out a century ago."

"Then so should the cast of mind that went with it."

"If you think I'm going to watch my daughter be seduced by an old widower—"

"—You'll be spared that, I should think. Seductions rarely take place under parental scrutiny."

David looked sheepish. "Okay, laugh if you must. But dammit, I've known perfectly decent guys in Joel's position who've succumbed to girls a lot less attractive than Charlie."

"So have I. But Charlotte has an understanding heart, as well as youth and beauty. There would be no disaster if he did succumb."

"No disaster! As far as the eye can see, the landscape is piled high with the psychological ruins of girls who have been seduced and abandoned!" He stopped pacing and looked at her defensively. "Oh, I know what you're thinking; but don't. Salome is old enough to take care of herself, and I'm really serious about her, God help me."

"I'm delighted to hear that."

He would not be deflected. "Please, Helena! Charlie's the only daughter I've got, and a false move in this sort of situation makes kids throw over their parents forever. I know I'm hardly the perfect father, but believe me, I—"

She observed his distress with relative sympathy. Beneath David's bravado lay the humility that made him likeable; and his love, however flawed, went deep. "Supposing what you fear were to happen," she said. "Charlotte, being who she is, could give Joel a tenderness he deeply needs. And Joel, being who he is, could give Charlotte a rare and precious love that would make the rest of her life sweeter. Is that a possibility you want to take from them, just because it doesn't coincide with your ideas of paternal responsibility?"

He looked at her oddly. "That's a romanticism I wouldn't have expected from you, Helena."

"Well, that's good to hear. It's always nice to surprise old friends, especially at my age."

"I suppose you have a point," he said after a moment's silence. "Though it certainly goes against the grain."

"Certainly. But there's a reward for parental tact. If you leave them alone—if in particular you leave Charlotte alone, trusting to Joel's thoughtfulness, if not to his restraint—"

"—Well?"

"Then someday, she may be grateful."

"She'd be more likely to throw my lack of care in my face. She's been doing that lately."

"I doubt it. Not in this case." She looked at her watch. "I think I'll go back inside. Can I offer you a cup of tea?"

"It's only four o'clock. You're quitting two hours early?"

"I'll come out in the early evening, when it's cooler."

He looked at her with a shadow of concern as he gave her his arm and, to her relieved surprise, tactfully declined tea. "I'll think about your advice," he said as they reached the steps. "It might not be a bad thing to have a grateful daughter."

"No, indeed." She began to slip her arm out of his, but he stopped her.

"Helena," he said, not looking at her, "have I ever told you how wonderful you are?"

"I should hope not. I'd have to take it as a sign of your advancing age."

He laughed, kissed her hand, and left; she watched him go, pleased at his unexpected receptiveness. If there were a situation to be handled, it would be good if he handled it with delicacy. Having once been a grateful daughter herself, she knew how much parental restraint could mean.

There seemed to be no end to it. Joel suspended a memo between the 'to file' heap and the waste basket. Cleaning up one's desk was always an interesting pilgrimage into the past, but he'd had no idea it would take this long. Well, the misery was over now; it was time to meet Jed Smith. He tossed the memo into the waste basket and moved a heap of papers from one side of his desk to the cleared space in the middle, uncovering a bulging portfolio...portfolio?

Good God. It was a measure of how deeply he'd been submerged last year, that he hadn't even known where it was—and a measure of how deeply he was still submerged that he hadn't even thought to look for it in the week he'd been here. He sighed and looked at the handwritten labels on the sub-folders: *Pastoral: Theocritus, Virgil, etc. Romance 1: Ovid and the Art of Love. Romance 2: Medieval Concepts of Romantic Love. Romance 3: Italian Romance: Ariosto, Tasso. New Genre: Sidney, Lodge, Greene etc. Culminations: Shakespeare. Spenser. Milton.* It was all there: notes, xeroxes, initial thoughts, faithfully awaiting his return.

He stuffed the portfolio into his briefcase and walked—since he'd had no time to go running lately—from Mather to the Whitby high-rise in which Smith and Sons Attorneys had recently established new offices. He'd expected to enjoy it, but once he'd crossed the river, he was conscious mainly of the heat, the blowing garbage, and the scrutiny of the shirtless men who sat smoking in boarded-up doorways. One forgot many things, living in Vermont.

Inside the high-rise, he took the elevator to the fifteenth floor and was in the midst of telling Jed Smith's secretary that he had arrived when Jed himself emerged from his office.

"Joel! Great to see you! Come on in. I have everything all laid out."

Joel sat down at the mahogany table, and the two of them spent the next half-hour embroiled in legal language. "It looks as if everything is going well," he said finally. "I'm glad you could get the advance on Letty's—"

"—It's called the Brantford Fund, now," said Jed, taking the papers to his desk. "Terms of the bequest. And as for the advance, it's done all the time. We just leave out twice what it looks the taxes are going to be for safe keeping." He frowned. "But rumor has it you're going to open the gates to women. I *told* Letty that would happen if she didn't put in a restrictive clause."

Joel looked up sharply. "And what did she say?"

"Well, she was a bit down, I thought—not that I had any idea she was so close to the end. But what she said was along the lines of wanting to be remembered without restrictions." The phone rang, and he reached for it apologetically. "This will just take a minute."

Remembered without restrictions. So she'd somehow recognized not just her coming death, but her past restrictiveness. Let go. And he, frantic with term papers, senior theses, exams, committees, hadn't—no, he had noticed. In fact, he'd wondered a little at her unusual silences, and at a series of unprecedented small gestures. But he'd been so busy and so weary he'd put off thinking about possible meanings. Even when...

Letty sat in Nathaniel's favorite chair—gaunt, tense, her suitcase waiting in the hall. He had already put on his trench coat; they were due at the hospital at four.

"You know that Chopin piece you used to play all the time? The one with the repeated note in the base?"

Of course he knew it, though why she should bring it up now...

"It's been going through my head all day. I wish you'd exorcise it for me."

There was some change in her face. Illness, maybe, or an increase of pain. No, this was different. He looked at her, unbelieving. "You want me to play it? Now?"

She leaned back in the chair. "If you would."

He played it, not terribly well—he was out of practice, and his trench coat caught at his shoulders. But she seemed not to mind his occasional fumbling, if indeed she noticed it. At last he reached the ethereal coda and faded the pulsing A-flats into the final chord. As it died away, he sat looking at his hands. Silence hovered in the room.

She stood up. "Well, I guess we'd better go."

He followed her out into the rain and opened the Dodge's door for her. She had never asked him to play for her before.

Jed hung up the phone. "Sorry about that—Joel? Are you all right?"

He took out his handkerchief and hastily wiped his eyes. "Allergic to—" What was there in this office to be allergic to?

"Must be the new rug; I was a wreck the first week it was in. Someday somebody will sue Bigelow, and I'll find out what they treat carpets with these days." He smiled. "Anything else? —Oh, I know! I dug up the background of the Ward Trust. And I mean dug. My dad handled it years and years ago. It turns out that Nathaniel Brantford *did* have something to do with it. He established it in 1959, when Letty inherited the property."

"*Nathaniel* established it?"

"You bet. He took care of all the details of the estate. When he died, Letty gave our firm the power to handle taxes and upkeep out of the trust, but since I've taken it over—that's 1987—I've dealt only with the taxes. I assumed she took care of the upkeep with Dr. Brantford's local agent." He frowned. "I hope everything's going smoothly."

"Everything's fine. I just wanted to be sure no orders got crossed or duplicated."

"Of course. I wish I could be more helpful, but Letty's only instructions about the place were to bother her as little as possible, and to maintain the confidentiality Dr. Brantford had insisted upon." He opened a small folder and glanced at it. "The cash in the trust is currently worth fifty thousand dollars, give or take a little; it's a certificate account, and since it was used only for taxes since Dr. Brantford's death, it has appreciated considerably. Will you be wanting to handle it yourself?"

"Eventually. But not for a few more months, if it's no trouble."

"No trouble at all."

"Thank you. This is my number in Vermont in case you need to get in touch with me in August. If you get a woman on the phone, be very patient. My landlady is deaf."

Jed smiled. "A real Vermont old-timer, huh? That sounds colorful. Going back soon?"

"In a week or so. I'm going to sell 54 Elm Street to the college, and it will take a while."

Jed looked up quickly—and no wonder. He, too, was surprised by the decision.

But it was the right decision. Trudging home through the rush hour exhaust that hung in the humid air, he felt not a single quiver of regret. It would simplify his life. The cash would enable him to buy a car. He'd be able to fix up the Ward place properly, which would please Eleanor. But most of all—he looked bitterly at the gracious, familiar houses as he turned down Elm Street. Most of all, it would enable him to forget.

Nathaniel stood in his office door. "I'm leaving tomorrow. Take good care of Letty."

"Of course. England again?"

"There and some other places; I'll be back in August. What are you working on?"

Nathaniel knew perfectly well what he was working on; they'd talked about it yesterday. But he told him. It filled the space that seemed to grow between them every year at this time.

Letty was dressing for a party when he got home. He knocked at her door and leaned against the jamb, watching her put up her hair. "Nathaniel won't be there tonight," she said. "He's leaving tomorrow."

"He never says where he's going, does he?"

"That's the point; he needs to be inaccessible. Can you blame him?"

"No, not at all. But I wish he felt he could tell us where he goes. If he were in an accident—if something happened to you..."

She turned to him, radiant, beautiful, desirable. "He knows you'd take care of everything that needed to be done, if something happened to me." She kissed him so affectionately that he decided to let the matter drop.

Yes, but she had been similarly affectionate the day Nathaniel had left the previous July, as she had been on that day in all the Julys before and after that. And he, poor fool, had never allowed himself to ask why she was most affectionate on the day Nathaniel disappeared.

Inside the house, he laid his briefcase on the old dining room table he'd brought back down from the attic, sat down, and opened the portfolio. He should start by looking over material again, testing the validity of the new ways of reading that had arisen in the past few years. He'd not thought much of them last summer, but if he used the approach Abe Lefkowicz had mentioned at Helena's tea, he could at least get a feel for the methodology in action, as it were. He leafed through his notes. Virgil, Mantuan...

"Everything's all right, isn't it?" The expression in Nathaniel's face had been very like the one that accompanied *"I'll be back in August."* And very like the expression Letty had covered in her own face by kissing him. That should have told him there was a great deal Letty had known about Nathaniel and never revealed. And a great deal Nathaniel had known about Letty and never revealed. More than the Ward Place. Much more than the Ward Place.

Spenser's pastoral. The landscape of Ireland, like the landscape of Vermont, loved by the very people who, from the Irish point of view, had betrayed it...

One would not have thought betrayal was in his nature. Nathaniel, who had remained faithful to his ideals throughout his life. Nathaniel, whose unexpressed affection for Helena had moved everybody who saw it. Nathaniel, who had wept for Orpheus's loss of Eurydice.

Milton's use of the pastoral in *Paradise Lost*. Adam and Eve, the Garden...

But one should not be hurt by the Milton or the Newton in Nathaniel. There really was greatness that passed petty human concerns.

Spenser. Milton. Newton.

Cambridge.

For a long time he sat staring at his notes in the gathering twilight. When it got too dark to see them, he stood up, turned on the lights, and picked up the phone.

13. Seductions

"Sorry, old dog," said Eleanor, as Derri followed her to the barn with tragic eyes. "I'm not thrilled about going myself." She heaved the vacuum cleaner into the car, looking sadly at the magical late-afternoon light. "But I have to keep you in biscuits—Derri! Down!"

Derri dropped obediently as a Toyota Alltrac with temporary plates turned into the driveway. Probably somebody about to ask directions to the lake, which she— The driver's door opened, and Joel stepped out. She released the trembling dog quickly to keep him from breaking, and followed his joyful bounces across the lawn, her own delight qualified only by embarrassment.

"Joel! I thought—!"

"You thought I *mxmx* tomorrow," he said, tossing Derri's excitedly proffered stick. "If it's inconvenient—"

"Not at all! Unfortunately, I've got to take off soon. Special post-wedding cleanup job."

"Don't *mxmx* make you late."

"Ten minutes won't matter. It's good to see you."

He looked down the road to the valley, then up to the neighbor's distant mowing and the mountains. "I can't even begin *mxmx* good it is to be back."

There was no need for him to try. His face was drawn, positively ashen, and every muscle in his shoulders was knotted with tension. "Things were difficult at Mather?"

"Yes." The monosyllable spoke volumes.

"I'm sorry. But everything's all right, isn't it?"

He looked up with such a peculiar expression that she added, "I mean, Cambridge—"

"—Oh, Cambridge." The expression passed, all but its shadow. "Yes, that's settled. As of noon today, Trinity *mxmx* two years *mxmx* no commitment to stay. Mather *mxmx* two years' leave *mxmx* no commitment to go back." He smiled wryly. "That's why I'm early. I fled an hour after *mxmx*, lest somebody *mxmx* amendment."

She returned the smile. "Very sensible. That kind of politics is so draining."

"Actually, *mxmx* tedious, not draining. The difficulties lay—elsewhere. But not within. *Mxmx* pastoral romance notes *mxmx* reading, thinking *mxmx* wonderful escape *mxmx* crowd the East Wing." He pointed to the computer boxes in the car.

"There's no need to crowd the East Wing," she said. "You can set up in Hattie's room."

"I wouldn't be intruding?"

"How could you? Hattie's in London, and the state-of-the-art computer station Ray built for her is just sitting there. Let me show you where it is."

He extricated an enormous monitor from the car and followed her inside. Upstairs, he looked out of scale in Hattie's slant-ceilinged room, but he also looked pleased, which was great. Heaven knew what had drained him so terribly, but if he could write, time would work its usual miracles.

As they started downstairs, he suddenly turned around. "Want *mxmx* phone?"

The phone. She hadn't heard it. She was going to *have* to get some kind of flasher. She stopped, but after he'd listened a second, he pointed to himself. An amendment? Already? She hurried downstairs to assemble the rest of the cleaning things she'd need tonight. Surely anybody who'd seen him lately would—

Joel appeared in the doorway, his face shaded with puzzled irritation. "*Mxmx* Colleen Rickerts," he said. "*Mxmx* appraisal of the Ward Place, *mxmx* wants a 'business evening' *mxmx* tomorrow at eight. What do you suppose that means?"

She kept her face carefully neutral. "Probably dinner someplace, with talk about real estate."

He sighed. "*Mxmx* not delighted. *Mxmx* looking forward to *Bleak House mxmx* couldn't think of an excuse. And I *did* write, reminding *mxmx* appraisal. *Mxmx* could hardly refuse."

"Of course not. We can always read a little extra day after tomorrow."

"No, that's when she wants me. But we can read tomorrow— and maybe tonight?"

"I'm afraid I won't be home until almost midnight," she said regretfully. "And I really have to go now." She tossed some cleansers and a few sponges in her bucket, hating them all.

He picked up the bucket and held the door for her with a graciousness that somehow made her feel better. "How *mxmx* been here?" he asked.

"Well, Charlie has found some information about your wife's relatives, but I'm afraid you won't get it right away. She's off to a three day event at 5 AM tomorrow."

He smiled. "*Mxmx* enlighten me?"

"I wish I could, but we haven't been able to get together long enough to talk about it. She's been going every minute between the painting and the training; Colleen's recommendations have given me a flood of the kind of work I'm doing tonight—and then there's Helena."

"Oh, yes," he said, frowning. "Andrew *mxmx* concerned. What's the matter?"

"I'm not sure. I first noticed it last week, when I dropped by to pick up those magnificent black irises she'd promised me. She'd forgotten all about them."

"*Mxmx* hardly cause for alarm."

"Maybe. But I went up there in the afternoon, and she wasn't gardening, which *is* cause for alarm. And then—well, she was charming as always, but she seemed a bit vague."

"Vague." She could see her own concern reflected in his face as he put her cleaning things into the trunk. "*Mxmx* Andrew said. I suppose *mxmx* some forgetfulness at her age, but there was no sign of it when I left." He pursed his lips. "A minor stroke?"

"That's what David and I think, and each of us has gone there several times to be sure everything is okay. It isn't; she spends more time on the porch than in the garden, and she dreams off, even when somebody's there. Still, she's articulate—even a little testy—and there's nothing so *obviously* wrong that we feel we can do anything." She sighed. "It's hard. She's been so magnificent for so long that I don't even want to *seem* to intrude on her. But I'm running out of excuses for visiting."

"I'll go up there tomorrow," he said. "*Mxmx* natural; she's been *mxmx* Cambridge negotiations— Hey! Look who's here!"

She turned and saw Ray's tractor bouncing down the driveway across the road. "Oh, no!" she said, looking at her watch. "I just *can't* stay. Give him my regards—and a beer, if you feel like chatting." She slid into the Honda and started it. "Oh yeah, and ask him about the Wards. I saw him down street yesterday, and he said something about 'a piece of Ward news,' but I didn't get it put together until after I'd taken off, so I didn't ask him for details."

Looking at him, she wasn't sure he'd caught what she'd said; in a world of diminished sound, it was easy to forget that engine noise made it necessary to shout. But the way he greeted Ray made her feel better about leaving. It would be good for him to have a man to talk to; lord knew, he had more than his share of burdens. Legacy. Mather. Cambridge. Colleen. Helena.

He'd been glad to see her, though. Very much so, in his understated way. How nice.

— — —

$\mathcal{S}$addles (3). Saddle pads (4). Bridles (2, plus spare). Lead ropes (3). Blanket. Cooling sheet. Galloping boots. Shipping boots. Bandages. Buckets (4). Hunt cap. Helmet (plus spare). Flak jacket. Dress jacket. Boots (2 pairs). Muck boots. Paddock boots. Chaps. Breeches (3). Shirts (3). Stock pin. Gloves (3 pairs)— Charlie looked up from the checklist as Ray's tractor stopped next to the trailer and shut off. "Hiya! You all set?"

"Are *you* all set, is more like it," said Ray, peering in the trailer's side door. "Who would have thought you needed all this stuff to take a horse to a show?"

"A three-day event is for high maintenance horses only," she said. "Wait until we get there—you'll see equipment that makes this look like peanuts."

Ray frowned. "You guys outclassed?"

"Depends upon what you mean by 'class.' Cocoa is definitely *not* outclassed. There's nothing he won't jump: walls, gates, picnic tables, ditches, drops, the bed of your pickup truck—"

"—You're kidding!"

"Nope. You left it in a tempting place last week, and over we went, coming and going, no problem. But see, a lot of high maintenance horses who jump like that are lousy at dressage, and he's terrific. So if by 'class' you mean athletic ability, he's got it—unless I screw him up, of course. That brings us to me."

"You look like a pretty top class rider to me—but what do I know?"

"You know that David could bankroll my four years of apprenticeship with Herr Greisemuir, plus schooled horses for the summer. Because he could afford those things, I got to be a better rider than equally talented, hard-working kids whose parents couldn't. That's unjust; that's class."

Ray shrugged. "There's no point in turning money down if you got it."

184

"I didn't. When I got old enough to notice it, I thought, well, David gave me a leg up; I can do the rest myself. But I can't. 'The rest' involves owning a horse like Cocoa, who will be worth as much as your house if he does well in this event—"

"—holy crow!"

"Right. And it involves owning a trailer like this, and equipment like this—almost none of which, outside the clothes and my cross-country saddle, was financed by me. Subsidy's okay when you're a kid, but if I went professional, I'd depend on it for the rest of my life. That's why I decided not to go on. If you don't have money behind you, you're *nothing* in this sport."

"That's nothing new," said Ray. "When I was your age I did some car racing—"

"—You *did?* Wow! I always knew you were cool, Ray."

"Not cool enough. Got beat time after time by folks who could pay for these amaaaazing cars. I did okay, at least okay enough that some of them started to ask me to drive for them, but the War came along, and by the time I was discharged, rich folks could choose drivers from a whole new crop of youngsters with no wives and kids. So I came up here—"

"—And became your own man in a way you never could have been if you'd sold your soul to the system, and you've got no regrets, right?"

Ray looked out over the pasture. "Not as many as I used to."

That wasn't quite the answer she'd expected, and she was still trying to think of what to say when he turned around smiled. "I got a piece of news for you. Joel's back."

"He is? I thought Eleanor said it was tomorrow."

"Seems he skipped out early, and from the look of him I'd say not a moment too soon." Ray shook his head. "But he was real happy to hear you got that room all painted for him. *And*" —he shot her a look— "he said something that made me think you've been holding out on us."

"Holding out? No way!"

"Okay, okay. But what he *said* was that Eleanor told him you'd found out something important about the Wards. He was kind of hoping I would know what it was, but I figured since you hadn't let on to anyone here, you were saving it for him, so that's what I told him. Well, of course he was interested. In fact, if he was anyone else, he'd be down here now, but being Joel..." He looked around the trailer. "Looks like you've got everything set."

Charlie studied his patient face. "You think I should go see him, right?"

"I don't say that. But I do say he looks kind of down. If you have anything new, it would sure give him a lift if you had time to tell him tonight instead of waiting til you get back."

Damn. If only she'd had time to talk to Eleanor! It was her fault: at first she'd been so excited about her find that she hadn't wanted to share it—which was lousy in itself. Then just as the pre-event hectic-ity started up, she'd realized she'd gotten caught up in the thrill of the chase again, instead of thinking about the dreadful implications of her find.

"There's another piece of news," said Ray. "He's going to spend the next two years teaching at Cambridge, in England."

"You're having me on!" But she knew he wasn't. The phone had been ringing every half-hour, and David had disappeared for a whole day without saying where he was going. So, given that Salome knew the whole thing was about Joel, it was a no-brainer that there had been major politics afoot.

"Nope," said Ray. "And except that he makes such a great neighbor, I'd say that was a good thing. I don't know what those fancy folks deal out, but I'd take a fist-fight any day."

She thought of the way Joel had looked at Helena's tea, then mul-tiplied by two weeks. "Okay," she said. "Let me just get through this list and do some final checking, and I'll go talk to him and Eleanor."

"Eleanor's not there—some big money cleaning job. But I prom-ise you, Joel's not going anywhere tonight." Ray looked at his watch. "You want dinner?"

She didn't, really, but she did want time, and it was sweet of him to offer, so after they had gone over every possible thing and left Cocoa munching happily on a pound of cut-up carrots, she joined Ray and Connie for Sloppy Joes and potato salad, absently chatting with them about tomorrow's drive and the scene at Rhinebeck while she tried frantically to think of what she should say to Joel. Inspiration didn't dawn, so she drove off with no better plan than telling him the historical part of her news and saving the rest until she'd had a chance to talk to Eleanor.

Joel was sitting on the front steps, presumably watching the sunset but so lost in thought he didn't even look around until Derri barked. He waved and stood up as she returned the dog's enthusiastic welcome, so everything seemed fine—until she got close enough to see his face. Totally shut down. No feeling at all. Brother.

"Welcome back!" she said, forcing herself to smile. "Ray said I would find you here."

"No secrets in this neighborhood," he said, smiling back. "But we still have surprises. When I heard you and Cocoa were off at some ungodly hour tomorrow morning, I figured I wouldn't see you until next week."

"Well, I found out something about the Wards, and I thought you might like to hear it before I left." She glanced at his abstracted face as they walked to the steps. "But it can wait."

"Oh, no," he said, sitting down. "A little Wardiana is just what I need."

Maybe it was, if she could just keep to the past. "Okay. I hit a gold mine—Susan Wheeler Howe, Clara's friend in the journal. Eleanor gave me her phone number in Florida, and the two of us ran up a humongous bill—because she knew what happened to Brent and Clara."

He settled himself back against the doorstep and gave her the first real smile of the evening. "Oh, wonderful."

"It really was," she said, smiling back. "But the story is—well, you can judge for yourself. Brent took Clara down to Newfane to meet his parents. And they were just *awful*. Remember the dress she and Mary made especially for the visit? When she put it on for the first party, Brent's mother said something like 'you can't go in *that*, dear—let's see if we can find you something more suitable.' And at the party, they introduced her as "Brent's little farm girl," with a sort of apologetic snigger, and 'translated' her Vermont accent for their friends. As Mrs. Howe puts it, that didn't sit very well with Clara."

He shook his head. "I can imagine."

"So after the party, she told Brent that if he didn't take her back home in the morning, she would walk every step of the way, starting right then. He said he would—what else could he do?—and I suppose he talked to his parents, hoping to smooth things over. But she'd have none of that; she wouldn't even speak to him. Not the next day, not any of the days after it. Mrs. Howe says he went back to the Ward Place time after time, but she'd never see him, and finally— Well, nobody knows what Asa said to him, but he left."

Joel looked out at the mountains. "That's very sad," he said. "I suppose she was just too young to realize how careful Brent had been with Mary and Asa, and see— Well, who knows? I confess, though, I feel as sorry for him as I do for her."

"Oh yeah," she agreed. "Mrs. Howe said he came to see her as a last resort, and he was really torn up. In the long run, though, Clara's the one that really suffered from it. Brent went back to his patrician thing, whatever it was, but she— Well, it was sort of the end of her life."

He raised his eyebrows. "She didn't go to Smith, just to show him?"

"Nope. She didn't even go back to school in the fall, just stayed up on the hill with Asa and Ma, because—" Oops.

"—because?"

Shit. "Well, there was a lot to do and—"

"There was a lot to do before," he said, "and that didn't stop her." He looked at her closely. "Are you sure you're telling me all you know?"

"I...well..."

"Charlie," he said gently, "you're not going to begin your career as a historian by withholding evidence, are you?"

She looked desperately at the red rim of the sun as it sank beneath the mountains. If only Eleanor were there! If only—

"You know," he said, less gently, "sparing people's feelings is a form of condescension."

She looked at the irritation that mixed with the other things in his face. "Maybe. But I also know that a lot of messengers who *didn't* spare people's feelings have been killed."

"That bad, eh?" he said lightly, raising his eyebrows. "Well, if it's any comfort to you, the messenger I dealt with in Whitby is still alive and well."

It wasn't a comfort, if the Whitby message had anything to do with the way he looked, but there didn't seem to be any way she could stop now. "Okay. Remember that picture of Henry Ward, looking like he's off to school? He was. Later he became a high school teacher in Middlebury, married, and had a daughter named Emily. Sometime in 1929, Henry and his wife were killed in a buggy accident. Mrs. Howe says Mary Ward wrote right off to Emily, who was Clara's age, and offered her a home with them, but Emily wanted to stay with her friends, so she hired out up there. It seems, though, that she was a little too friendly with her friends, especially a Middlebury student called Joseph Brantford."

He tapped his fingers on the stone step. "I thought it must be something like that," he said. "I suppose it sounds very strange to somebody your age, but illegitimacy used to be—"

"Oh, it wasn't a matter of illegitimacy," she said hurriedly. "He married her. As Mrs. Howe puts it, the Wards always looked after their own."

His eyes opened. "You mean, Mary and Asa made him—?"

"Absolutely. But this time it really was a matter of 'looking after,' because Emily died having the baby, and Mary went up north and brought it back here. That's why Clara never finished high school or went to Smith. She and Mary were raising a baby."

"That's a terrible shame. All that intelligence and spirit."

He hadn't asked the crucial question, thank God. Maybe she could keep him deflected. "Yes, but she kept those books, and there was the library, and she was only 31 when she died—she may have been hoping ...well, you know Smith has that program for women that age. At least they do now."

He nodded, watching the clouds go pink and orange. "Pride has a hell of a price," he said reflectively.

"You mean, about Brent? But she was *right!* Why should somebody like her, who worked hard for everything she had, have to put up with the snobbism of people who lived off their husbands' money?"

"There may have been a middle ground," he said. "Brent was obviously trying to find one. But so far as I can see, part of the problem was that Clara had never encountered snobbism before, and didn't recognize it for what it was."

As usual, he had a point. And since it was a point that allowed her to avoid the message she most wanted not to convey, it seemed a good place to close. She got up and smiled back at him. "I should take off—tomorrow's a long, long day."

"Sure," he said, standing up too. But as she turned to go, he said, "Just out of curiosity, what happened to the baby?"

Oh, no. "Just what you'd expect," she said evasively. "She grew up on the farm and went to the Draper school—"

Something changed in his face. "She?"

"Um, yeah."

"What was she like?"

"Very pretty, Mrs. Howe said, and really social, which I guess got to be kind of a problem as she grew up, especially between her and Asa. And when Gid saw that, he stood up for her when the others scolded her, bought her ready-made dresses, offered to drive her to town—imagine what *that* did to family harmony! Mrs. Howe said if Asa had been a whole man, he'd have chased him off the farm with a—"

"—What's this about Asa's being a whole man?"

What a mess she'd made of everything! "I'm sorry. I should have started with that. Asa lost his right arm in the War."

"For God's sake!"

"Yeah. That's why it was such a crisis when Gid disappeared during haying season, and why Clara had to write that letter to Brent. In fact, judging from the way Mrs. Howe talked about Gid, that's the only reason Asa and Mary put up with him at all. I guess he was pretty disreputable; Mrs. Howe wouldn't even talk about him. All she said was that he took after his father, which seemed odd. Would you have thought Gid was alcoholic, from what Clara wrote?"

"No," he said. "But when Ray stopped by this evening, he said he'd helped Mike Wolfington, the owner of 'my' heifers, fix his tractor. They got talking about the Wards, and Mike said his old man used to say Gid Bartlett was a bootlegger."

"Wow! No *wonder* Asa was so mad when Gid got home!"

"Exactly. Before '33, there was a real danger of arrest, not to mention that liquor must have been an anathema to the respectable Bartlett children. Especially since it seems to have been connected with—other vices." He pursed his lips, and for a minute she thought he'd let the rest go. Then he said, in that voice that gave a command without seeming to, "But you were telling me what happened to the girl."

"Well, it's confusing; Mrs. Howe wasn't very clear about the chronology. Because of the family arguments, I think Clara and Mary wanted to send her to her father, but then Pearl Harbor happened, and he got stationed overseas, so they said they'd wait until the war was over. But then Asa had a stroke, Gid got into some sort of trouble (Mrs. Howe didn't say what it was, but I guess there was plenty of talk) and left—and in the midst of all that, Clara died. And that was the end for Mary. She sent the girl away, and she became the recluse Eleanor met when her family bought this place."

"I see," he said, his face a mask in the fading light. "And since she couldn't send the girl to war-time Pacific, she sent her to Nathaniel Brantford, her father's cousin. Is that correct?"

She nodded. A bat flew by, the pulse of its wings loud in the silence. Fou got off the warm rock steps, stretched, and trotted off for an evening's hunting. Derri pricked up his ears as a dog in the valley barked twice, then twice again.

"You've been very discreet," he said at last—quietly, but in a tone that made her shiver. "Still, I'd appreciate it if you validated Mrs. Howe's evidence by telling me the girl's name."

191

"Letitia," she whispered.

A breeze rustled in the trees, and the first stars began to come out.

"I'm sorry," she said finally. "I really am. I should have handled it…differently."

He shook his head.

"And look, nobody knows but you and me. For starters, I didn't say a *thing* about the connection to Mrs. Howe—it would be all over Draper in fifteen minutes. You know even Ray and Eleanor don't have a clue, and I'd never tell David and Salome anything like that."

"Thank you."

They stood there for so long she began to wonder if she'd ever be able to move again.

"I really have to get going," she said finally.

He startled like a man coming out of a dream. "Of course you do."

His voice sounded normal, but when he opened the Toyota's door for her, its little light shone on a face barely recognizable as his.

"Joel," she said, her voice trembling, "would you accept a messenger's hug?"

For a second she thought he would refuse, but then his terrible expression melted and he opened his arms. It didn't last very long, but it was a real hug, and as she drove off she was pretty sure everything was still okay between them.

Something was very wrong. It had been for several days, but gardening seemed to have made it worse. It shouldn't be this difficult to get up. Helena reached for her shovel, hoping to balance herself with it, but her right arm was stiff and uncooperative, and her attempts to move it only rolled her over on her back. She shut her eyes against the sunlight that poured into the garden. It felt rather good, actually.

Perhaps she'd been unduly prejudiced against sunbathing all these years. And surely, after she'd rested a few minutes, she'd be able to get up and call Nathaniel, which she really should do. He had always worried about her being up here by herself. As usual, he'd try to insist that she get someone to live with her, and perhaps he was right. It was inconvenient not to be able to get up when one fell.

She must have dozed, because when she woke, the sun was in a different place, and someone was shaking her gently. That was ridiculous; she was fine. She'd just fainted. He was the one who— No, she would never think of that again. What was done, was done. Her father would resign; he'd finally see that Mussolini and his *Fascisti* promoted themselves through brutality, not politics. He'd go back to New York, and she'd go with him, forget, start over—

The sun was certainly hot. She was very grateful to the stranger who sat between it and herself, bathing her face with water.

Of course they were all very upset, the people who were running about the piazza. He'd told them, he'd tried to warn them, and they had laughed. Even her father—but no, he hadn't felt he could speak to her father. What a foolish thing honor was.

"Helena—Helena, can you understand me?"

"*Si, ma non bisogna parlare Inglese...*"

The cool cloth brushed her forehead again. "Don't try to talk. They'll be here soon."

In the distance, she could hear a siren, but they were stupid to waste gas on her. It was he who needed— She turned her head away from the cloth as a terrible certainty blazed into her mind with the sunlight. The ambulance was for her because the *Fascisti* had done their work too well. He hadn't just fallen; she'd seen the blood. She pushed herself up. "Lorenzo!"

Somebody caught her as she began to fall again, and she opened her eyes. And it was—! No, it couldn't be. This was the dream she'd promised herself not to have, this was sentiment. But she knew the face that looked down into hers. Dark curly hair, graying at the sides, blue eyes—what other face could be this familiar, this welcome? "*O, Lorenzo...carissimo...pensavo che tu fossi morto...*"

But they wouldn't leave her alone with him; they clustered around like pigeons, talking to each other, pushing him away. "Lorenzo!"

"Is that your name, sir?"

He said something she couldn't hear as he came back into her crowded line of vision. It was hard to focus on his face with them bending over her, moving her, and the only hand she could reach out to him was on the wrong side.

"Just a minute, Mr. Hendrickson. When we get her inside, you can go with her."

Suddenly the light changed, and they were swaying back and forth. This was wrong. This was not the right kind of siren. And above all, he was there—he was there, wasn't he?

"Lorenzo?"

A face bent over hers. *"Ecco."*

And it was he. She smiled and reached up with the only hand that would do her bidding. *"Non piangere,"* she whispered, laying it on his cheek.

But he must not have heard her, because she felt his tears fall on her hand long after he'd taken it.

⸺ ⸺ ⸺

Joel leaned back in the plush bucket seat and looked out the window. "I'm sorry you had to pick me up, after putting off work on the appraisal for so long," he said. "But there was no way around it. Eleanor wanted to go to the hospital to visit our friend, and her car's in such poor shape that I simply couldn't let her take it to Bennington."

"Don't think of apologizing," said Colleen. "It's no trouble at all." She turned off Route 100 onto a side road. "And how is Miss Woodhouse doing?"

"As well as can be expected. She'll be home soon; David Reynolds and I have arranged for a private nurse. We think she'll be happier there than at the hospital."

"I'm sure she will; it's a beautiful place."

"You know the place?" he said with some surprise.

"Everybody does. It's the last estate left, up there by the Mountain—a piece of the past, like Miss Woodhouse."

"I suppose it is." He stared out the window, seeing not the opulent vacation houses that flashed by, but Helena's garden, blooming softly inside the protective enclosure of the barn foundations, unaware, untended… He felt Colleen look at him.

"It must be hard for you, seeing her so helpless after you've known her so long."

"Yes, it is," he said. "I'm afraid it makes me poor company."

"Not at all," she assured him. "And we'll see what we can do to cheer you up." She turned right between two stone pillars and pulled up in front of a large clapboard building with Palladian windows.

He looked for a sign, but apparently he'd missed it as they drove in. "This is a handsome place," he said. "What inn is it?"

"It's called Casa Rickerts," she said, smiling. "I thought since you'd had a tough week, you'd prefer a quiet evening on the deck to waiters and music."

Somewhere in the back of his mind, he heard a little beep, like the warning his computer gave when it had dealt incorrectly with a program—a sound which experience had taught him one ignored at one's peril. Fool that he was, he should have made a reservation at the Alphof Inn. But she had drawn up at the house, and protest at this point was impossible. He would have to hope for the best, which was not unreasonable. She had been nothing but professionally sympathetic, and as for the perfume that scented the car, she wore that even at work.

He got out of the car in silence and walked to the house, taking in the mountains and the immaculate lawn that stretched down to the pond. "It must take you a great deal of time to keep this up so beautifully."

She laughed as she unlocked the front deadbolt. "It would be more accurate to say it takes my gardener a great deal of time to keep it up—outside, anyway. Inside, it's your landlady who does the keeping."

"Eleanor?"

"Best cleaning lady I ever had," she said warmly. "Never have to tell her anything, and the place is just spotless when I get home. She's a real treasure. What would you like to drink?"

He stared at her, a horrified reproof checked only by years of experience with wealthy College donors whose disheartening political attitudes had perforce to be ignored—and saw that she had not intended to be demeaning.

"I'm going to have a daiquiri, but there's scotch, bourbon, gin—"

"A tall glass of seltzer would be great," he said, smiling.

Her eyebrows rose, but she said "Fine," and pointed to the French windows on the far side of the living room. "Make yourself at home; the deck's out there."

He strolled across the Aztec-design area rugs and shot the three bolts on the French doors, cursing himself internally. Forget the Alphof Inn—he should have used the necessary postponement as an excuse to pick up the appraisal at her office, thus shutting down the "business evening" idea completely. The sense that he was participating in Eleanor's reduction quite aside, "at home" was the last way he felt in this aura of…what? Emptiness? He looked back at the tastefully chic furniture, the framed silk-screened flowers on the white walls, the accent pillows on the sofa, the carefully chosen books on the coffee table. Not emptiness. Absence. A lack of the pervading sense of private self that graced Helena's house—and for that matter, Eleanor's, despite its shabbiness.

He turned away uneasily, but the view from the deck restored him. In spite of the rain clouds that obscured its top, the Mountain looked enormous; this house was four or five miles closer to it than Eleanor's, and he could see how it rose from the valley floor. There were drawbacks to the proximity, though: he could also see—he counted thoughtfully—twenty houses, interspersed on ten-acre lots whose contours hid them from each other.

The tap of high heels behind him made him turn. Colleen hurried through the doors, bearing their drinks and a plate of micro-waveable hors d'oeuvres.

"Like it?" she asked, jerking her head towards the view.

"Very much." He took a welcome pull at his seltzer; he'd gotten himself back to three miles now, and this evening he'd really pushed himself. "Did you build the house?"

As he had hoped, the question relieved him of any necessity of talking. Seating herself on the rattan chaise longue, Colleen began with her architect, then went on to the Valley, the recession's effect on real estate prices, and the love of country living that had brought her to Vermont. He listened with more interest than he had expected to; her businesslike attitude to the area was entirely different from the perspectives he'd previously encountered, and it suggested considerable savvy. He smiled, thinking of Ray's recommendation. *For an official appraisal, you gotta go to Colleen; she'll be fair. Just watch your step. She's straight, but when it comes to getting what she wants, she's not dumb.*

No, she was not dumb. And dinner, when they got to it, demonstrated a talent the hors d'oeuvres had not led him to expect, for it revealed great care in preparation. The water-cress soup had been chilled for a full day, the cannelloni had a delicacy that could have been achieved only with homemade pasta, the Chateau Margaux was the best wine he had drunk since his days with Nathaniel—and by the time he had finished the perfectly textured chocolate mousse with which the meal concluded, his admiration was qualified only by a few random beeps. "You've missed your vocation," he said, leaning back in his chair. "You should have become a chef."

"Oh no, I'd be a terrible chef," she said. "I only enjoy cooking for an appreciative audience." She smiled at him between the candles. "There will be a brief intermission while I make Irish coffee," she said, pointing towards the living room. "Make yourself comfortable."

She tapped into the kitchen in a way that somehow made refusal churlish, so he rose and walked back to the deck. Clouds had covered the Mountain, and the breeze brought the smell of coming rain, but a few stars still shone overhead. He leaned on the railing, looking at the scattered lights of the twenty houses and sensing the tree-filled spaces between them. Vermont was beautiful still, in spite of the changes it had undergone since Ambassador Woodhouse had resigned his post in Italy after Mussolini's march on Rome and chosen Westover as a refuge for his grieving daughter.

Carissimo...pensavo che tu fossi morto. A Black-Shirt assassination of an early anti-fascist activist, Eleanor had dimly recalled from overhearing her parents' circle reminisce about Woodhouse's resignation; but nobody had thought to relate the incident to Helena herself. After all, she had been—as closely as he and Eleanor could figure it—no more than Charlie's age at the time. Hardly more than a child, though not in all ways: years later, the woman who had survived the loss had been capable only of a deep friendship that had never developed into a marriage. No, seventeen, for Helena as for Clara Ward, was plenty old enough to suffer irremediable loss. Perhaps it was just as well he didn't have a daughter. To watch a dearly-loved young life fade away before it had properly begun—

Colleen's heels tapped to the doors, then stopped. "Let's take these into the living room, shall we? It's going to rain any minute."

He was loath to leave the deck, but a glance at the disappearing stars above him convinced him of her practicality. He followed her, stopping to close the French doors behind him. When he reached the living room, she smiled from her seat on the sofa and held out one of the two glass mugs to him, handle first.

"Here you go. And be careful. The whipped cream's about to slop."

It was, indeed. It rose like a meringue above the lip of the coffee-dark glass; there was no chance its surface tension would survive a journey to a chair. He sat down a cushion away from her and took the handle. "Cheers," he said—and sipped hastily. "Ah, excellent."

She smiled as she picked up her mug. "It's my grandfather's democratic recipe: equal rights for the Irish and the coffee."

He laughed and sipped it slowly while she, crossing one attractive leg over the other, talked a little of her family, then ushered in questions about himself. He answered with the circumspection evolved over countless evenings on questionably neutral territory, but as the equal Irish rights began to exert their influence and she steered the conversation towards cross-country running, he found himself talking about his halcyon days at Exeter and Yale, finishing with modest reference to his Ivy League record run of '57.

"How wonderful!" she said, running her eyes appreciatively over his torso. "What a star you were! Well, it comes as no surprise."

"Those days are long over," he said deprecatingly—and was brought up short by the cliché. Looking at his watch, he was further humiliated by realizing how long he had spent in self-glorification. Good God, by his usual Vermont schedule, he was well in bed by now, dreaming in Eleanor's inflection of Dickensian London. "It's getting late," he said, putting his empty mug on the coffee table. "We should go on to the business of the evening."

"Is there any rush?" she asked, tucking one unshod foot underneath her.

In all the accessible folders of his mind, the beeps urgently resumed. "Yes, there is," he said firmly, "I have some important decisions to make, and I was counting on your help."

"Of course," she said, sitting up straight. "Well, for tax purposes, I wrote up an assessment of $250,000. That's ridiculously low, but it's what farm property is worth, and I figured you wouldn't want to be beggared by American taxes if you're living in England."

"How on earth did you know—?"

She laughed. "What you'll have to learn about Draper, Joel, is that its residents have no secrets from each other. It's true, isn't it—England, I mean?"

"In a manner of speaking. I'll be teaching at Cambridge for two years, but I'll come back in the summers."

"To the Ward Place?" The sharpness of her look made him suspect she had given herself coffee less democratic than his own.

"That depends on…circumstances." One of which, though he was not about to tell her, was that the Ward Place, once peopled only with the unobtrusive ghosts of an unknown past, was now so filled with Letty's evasive presence and Nathaniel's unconscionable betrayal that he wasn't sure he could bring himself to do further work on it.

"I assume you're referring to maintaining your home in Massachusetts?"

"No. I sold it."

She seemed unfazed by the bitterness in his voice. "I wish I had been able to help you," she said sympathetically. "It's so much easier to part with years of memories when somebody else takes care of the details." She paused, looking at him. "Perhaps you aren't interested in a market assessment of your farm, then."

"I can't tell you until I've heard it."

"That's businesslike," she said, laughing. "And there's no need to sell the whole place; many people sell all but the house and twenty acres; it makes their lives so much more comfortable. If you did that, you could get $150,000 for the four lots with lake frontage, and $120,000 for the nine view lots in the sugar grove and the pasture near that little graveyard."

"One hundred twenty thousand *apiece?*" He stared at her. "You can't be serious."

"I was never more serious in my life. I have a sketch of the property and its possible divisions sitting in the hall." She slipped off the sofa to fetch it; he got up and walked to the dining room table, reversed the dimmer and put on his glasses. The surprise in her face when she saw he had done so told him the beeps had served him well, but the matter was not settled even when they sat in separate chairs, for she managed to lean forward a little more than necessary over the papers she placed before him, her perfume wafting around him. *Watch your step.* "This is just provisional, of course," she said, "but it'll give you an idea. Here's the house. Just for now, let's block off the two lots nearest it." Her finger traced their outlines on the paper. "That leaves you with thirteen lots, and frankly, you could probably sell them all by the end of the year. One road here, and you've got four lots as near the lake as zoning will permit; another one here, and you've got a way to those gorgeous views."

His mind, he was pleased to find, was capable of doing the required multiplication despite the Irish. The total, though a little larger than the one he had come to on Helena's porch two months ago, was in the same ballpark. But then he'd believed, or at least wanted to believe— "It would require an investment of around half a million, of course," she said. "But since you've just sold your other house, you're in a fine position for that. And the return would be considerable."

There was no denying it. With resources like that, he could retire early. Give up academia entirely after his two years at Cambridge. Write. Move to England—move anywhere in the world—and live unburdened by the past. The golden thought hung temptingly before him; he stared at it, dimly aware that the rain outside was now accompanied by occasional flashes of lightning.

For some time, she sat as still as he did; then she turned down the dimmer and stood beside him, slipping her bare arm over his shoulders. "Forget the business for now," she said softly. "You poor, dear man—you've had a hell of a time."

The beeps crescendoed into a chorus of alarms, but courtesy— or something less laudable—made him refrain from getting up. "It's been a difficult summer," he admitted. "But my friends have been supportive, and that's helped a great deal."

"I was hoping," she said, very softly indeed, "that I counted as one of those friends."

"You've been very kind," he said. "I certainly didn't mean to imply..." But as he turned to look at her, he saw that he had implied far too much; not even the poor light could obscure the message that had suddenly appeared in her eyes.

System Failure.

"You're very attractive," he said, trying to smile. "But I'm in no condition to—"

"—Oh, I wouldn't say that," she said, sliding her hand down his back.

He swallowed hard over the desert in his throat. "I'm afraid I'm not expressing myself clearly," he croaked. "What I meant was, I don't want to—"

"—You don't *look* as if you don't want to. Why don't you just let go, Joel?"

He was all too well aware of how he looked, but he stood up with what little dignity he could assemble. "I think it would be better if I went home now," he said coldly. "Thank you for the excellent meal and the...er, appraisal." It wasn't much of an exit line, but at least it got him to the exit. He had almost escaped when her voice stopped him.

"Joel, please wait! There's no reason for you to walk home in this."

Oh, Christ; Eleanor had his car. He leaned his forehead against the half-open door, listening to the thunder and wishing death would come quickly.

Her shoes tapped across the floor, detoured to a nearby closet, then stopped just behind him. He turned reluctantly, but there was no further danger. Before him stood an immaculately groomed woman, her face a mask of professional poise, and her trench-coat buttoned to her chin. Smiling, she offered him one of the two umbrellas in her hand. "Shall we go?"

He took the umbrella and opened the outside door, then the car door for her with a gratitude he would not have possibly imagined five minutes earlier, and, following her cue, discussed meteorological conditions all the way through Draper. When they finally pulled up in Eleanor's driveway, Colleen switched off the lights, but left the motor running. "You know, Joel," she said, "I was thinking about what you said earlier— about your having no more to give—no, no, not that." She shook her head as he raised a hand in apology. "What I meant was, after what you've been through, the last thing you need is more trouble, and subdividing an old farm is a real hassle. Suppose I were to write up a detailed offer for your property. Not for a couple of weeks—this is a very busy time of year—but well before you go to England. Would you be willing to discuss it?"

Something behind her businesslike tone told him that to say no was to admit it would be worth a million bucks not to have to face her again. "Possibly," he said. "Let me think about it."

"Fair enough."

More than fair enough, given the circumstances. He reached for the door handle. "Thank you, Colleen. I really appreciate your—" He paused as the door opened, shocked by the pain the light revealed in her face. "—your understanding. And I'm extremely sorry I've needed it."

"That's perfectly all right," she said, with a professional smile. "These things happen."

"So it seems," he said unhappily—and fled into the deluge.

Why don't you just let go, Joel? The question followed him into his room, tugging at his mind as he tugged at his damp tie. Why the hell hadn't he? He certainly hadn't been insensible to her charms. Closing his eyes, he saw, or rather felt, her breasts brush against him as she slipped her arm around his shoulder... He threw his tie across the room and sat down on the bed with his face in his hands. Let go. Right. If he'd just be willing to let go, he could have listened to the continuing invitation in her voice as they sat in her car and apologized, explained, invited...and she could have been here now. He groaned and lay back against the pillows. It would have been better here, amidst the affectionate, tolerant companionship of the Randalls' books. So much more private, so much more companionable. He turned the bedside lamp to its lowest setting and moved over, making room for her beside him. And then...

And then, lying together in the undemanding half-light, they talked. Running, poetry, memories, observations—it wasn't the subject that mattered, but the closeness the words engendered, the gradual dissolution of the contours that separated person from person. Slowly, as the talk drifted into comfortable silence, and from there into equally comfortable embrace, he felt all the remnants of fear, both his and hers, slip away.

He raised himself on one elbow and looked into her face; she smiled, and he brushed her hair off her forehead and kissed the spot where it had been. Slowly he moved from there to her eyelids, to her mouth—and there he met a tenderness nearly smothered by the desire to please. He stroked her cheek and rolled over onto his back.

"Kiss me," he whispered.

And she did—shyly, at first, but gradually with increasing confidence. He reveled in it, gently holding her face between his hands until her mouth left his and started exploring his neck and chest. He tilted his head at an impossible angle, and what he saw through the chaste veil of hair that covered them both was so beautiful that he parted it with his hands so he could touch her...there, and...there. She hesitated, then sank down by his side. Too much, then. He went on more carefully, softly transferring his kisses from her mouth to her neck, her breasts, thankful that the inexpertise of the hands that slid down his back and flanks allowed him to be patient. But finally, he braced his elbows and looked at her serious face, wishing he weren't breathing so hard.

She studied him. "Don't stop."

"Are you sure? I don't want to hurt you."

"Yes, I'm sure," she said. And kissed him—really kissed him.

And so, gently, carefully, he moved her legs slightly apart and... God, she was so perfect, so fragile...

He came to himself lying prone on his bed, and looked down at the phantom in his arms. It was not Colleen Rickerts. It was a beautiful child with long chestnut hair and hazel eyes that gazed levelly into his own. The girl who, in his darkest hour, had hugged him with all the sympathy and remorse in her affectionate soul and demanded nothing in return.

Oh Christ, what had he done?

He put his head down on the empty pillow and burst into tears.

14. A Confession

Eleanor woke up with a start and looked at the rain that beat against the windows with the moths. It was awfully late. Joel should have gotten back hours ago, but apparently he hadn't. She sighed, thinking with some bitterness of spirit of the hours she had spent at Colleen's house earlier in the day, washing sticky dishes and putting finishing touches on the bower of bliss upstairs. She got up so suddenly that Fou catapulted off her lap onto the floor, and shut the north window. There were no lights coming down the road; and even if there had been, waiting up for a grown man was unnecessarily reproachful. She'd better mop up sills and go to bed.

She moved from window to window, talking consolingly to Derri, who pressed against her legs at every absent-minded flash of lightning. When she reached the kitchen, she saw a dim light in the East Wing and, feeling martyred, nipped out to close Joel's windows, too.

She was halfway across the room before she saw that he was lying face down on the bed. She stopped, embarrassed, and was about to tiptoe away when she realized his shoulders were shaking in great, long sobs. She stepped closer and leaned over him. "Joel?"

He turned his head, but he didn't get up.

"I didn't realize you were home—Derri's afraid of storms, so he didn't bark—and I came out to shut your windows. I'll go away if you want, but is there anything I can do?"

He muttered something incomprehensible, but not entirely negative.

"Look," she said, "why don't you come into the living room? We wouldn't have to talk; we could just sit."

"I'm afraid *mxmx* to drink," he said apologetically.

"Not enough to do any good, it seems."

He looked down at his sodden pillow. "All right. Give me ten minutes."

"Of course. I'll make us some tea." She left him to himself and banished Derri and Fou to her room, stopping along the way to put on a kettle. He joined her within his ten minutes, his damp hair and changed clothes suggesting he'd tried to drown the signs of misery in a cold shower. But the misery itself clearly remained.

"Can you tell me what it is?" she said gently, after they had sat in silence awhile.

He poured himself a mug of tea and sipped it—more, she suspected, to give himself time than anything else—then slowly, hesitantly, began to speak.

And she couldn't hear him.

It wasn't the light; that was just the way it always was when they talked. Nor was it his voice, though it was certainly subdued. It must be that whatever he was saying distressed him so much that he couldn't bring himself to look directly at her. But the reason hardly mattered. She *had* to hear him; she couldn't let him pour out his soul to a blank wall. Turning up her aids until his voice pounded at her ears, she moved closer to him. That helped a little; she caught a few words about Colleen and—*Joseph Andrews?* Well, clearly his evening had not gone swimmingly, but beyond that, she could ascertain nothing. And yet, to stop him, to beg him to look up, was impossible.

He finished, and she could feel him waiting for a response. Desperately, she studied his face, hoping for some clue that would enable her to say the appropriate thing, but all she could see was self-loathing—and some indefinable aura that suggested he had kept a great deal back. She hesitated, then, praying that she was doing the right thing, laid her hand on his knee. "Things like that are always upsetting," she said. "But it's not really what's bothering you, is it?"

He looked at her hand for what seemed a long time; then, as she withdrew it, he transferred his gaze to the raindrops that trickled down the window. "No," he said. "But I don't know how I can *mxmx* what is. It's terribly complicated—*mxmx* elements involved."

"You could always start with the simplest element and proceed from there," she suggested. If he did, she might at least catch some of it.

He shook his head with a wan smile. "There is no simple element. *Mxmx* long history *mxmx* convoluted relationships *mxmx* weakness."

She sat still, sensing that the slightest motion would discourage him from continuing.

"I suppose," he said finally, "that the efficient cause *mxmx* state you found me in *mxmx* surprise *mxmx* nobody but myself. In my own defense, I can only *mxmx* my age *mxmx* safe to return *mxmx* seventeen-year-old girl."

Seventeen-year-old girl. She struggled to keep the alarm out of her face. "Charlie?"

He nodded.

"You mean, the night she was over here, and you were so upset, you—you and she—?"

He sat bolt upright. "Good heavens, no! *Mxmx* 'weakness,' not mortal sin! I promise you, *mxmx* only in my thoughts, *mxmx* grieving for those when you came in." He looked at her pleadingly.

"I'm sorry," she said, blushing. "The thought was unjust."

"No, it wasn't. I deluded myself *mxmx* enjoyed her vitality. *Mxmx* convinced myself my feelings were paternal." He set down his mug. "Fool that I am."

"Nothing foolish about it! She's at a very dangerous age, both girl and woman. So far as the girl is concerned, you've been positively saintly: given her employment, an historical project, companionship, and consistent—not to mention, tactful—support. If you haven't been able to do that without being taken unawares by the temptations of the woman—well, you're only mortal, and thoughts are only thoughts."

"Thoughts are _not_ only thoughts," he said. "Fantasy _mxmx_ drug _mxmx_ man of my history _mxmx_." He shook his head and his voice dropped. "_Mxmx mxmx_ infidelity to my wife."

This time she couldn't let it go by; she'd missed too much, and it was too important. "Joel, forgive me, but what I put together was that you had a history of infidelity to your wife. And I can't believe that's what you really said." She jumped up and pulled a legal pad and a pencil out of the slant-topped desk. "Would you mind—?"

"Of course not. _Mxmx_ should have suggested it. Given my state, _mxmx_ miracle you can put anything together." He took the pad from her and moved from his accustomed chair to the sofa. After a second's hesitation, she sat next to him, watching him write: 'What I said was, it's difficult for me to say what's really bothering me without posthumous infidelity to my wife.'

She searched for the right apologetic words, but he wrote on without looking up.

'The common brand of infidelity simply wasn't an option. We lived in a world of 1200 people, and because she was who she was, our marriage was a source of 'community interest.' In such circumstances, fidelity has more to do with self-defense than with virtue.'

"Wait a minute," she said. "If you spare your spouse the humiliation of community gossip and pity—not to mention personal pain— isn't that virtue?"

'Only if you call it virtue to be sensitive to politics—or to a difficult emotional situation.'

He glanced at her, then began a new line. 'I suppose David has told you all about Letty's attachment to Nathaniel Brantford.'

"He's mentioned it," she said, trying to keep her voice neutral.

He smiled. 'Letty and David didn't get along well, either personally or politically. But of course, David wasn't the only person who saw that Letty's love for Nathaniel bordered on worship. Or the only person who talked about it. Not that he (or they) meant any harm.'

She glanced at his profile. "You never told them to go to hell?"

'Only in my thoughts. Telling them in fact would have added to the inherent interest of the situation and thus increased the talk.' He flipped over the page, a hint of bitterness showing in his carefully controlled face. 'And it might have led to some goading.'

"Undoubtedly," she said, with bitterness of her own. "So you rose above it?"

'' 'Denied it' would perhaps be more accurate. But it was important to ignore it, because to Letty, 'learning' meant being bored in the classroom, and 'literature' meant women's magazines. And that meant that while she loved Nathaniel, she had no access to him.'

"Oh, how terribly, terribly sad."

He nodded. 'Sometimes I'd come home from an evening with the two of them ready to weep. There she'd sit, with the banquet of his intellect before her, unable to partake; and there he'd sit, appreciative of her charm and even (in his way) fond of her, but—' He rubbed his forehead reflectively. 'It's hard to describe. There seemed to be a' —the pencil hesitated— 'a void where his feelings for her should have been. It was nothing I could put a finger on; he listened to her attentively, and he went out of his way to make her happy. But there it was.'

Poor Letty. "Did she know that?"

'That depends on what you mean by 'know.' Letty tended to resist unpleasant knowledge. But at some elemental level, she knew.' He looked up from the pad into some unfathomable distance, then flipped to a new page. 'That's the real reason infidelity wasn't an option. It was painful enough for her to doubt Nathaniel's love. If she'd ever had cause to doubt mine, it would have been the end of her. And it wouldn't have taken much to make her doubt that, because—' He stopped and flipped back through the densely-covered pages. "Look at all that!" he said apologetically. "You've mxmx patient."

"Not at all!" she began—then paused, realizing that he'd stopped for reasons quite other than the one he'd given. Quickly, she searched for a way of asking him to continue without seeming to become— without becoming in fact—one of the "interested" spectators who'd made his life so difficult. Literary truth came to her rescue. "Conversation always looks longer on paper than it is in fact," she said, smiling. "Spoken words take only time, not space; and memory foreshortens them."

"Mxmx suppose that's true," he muttered. "But mxmx very late. Mxmx keep you up."

"I'd been asleep for a couple of hours before I shut the windows."

He looked down at the pad for perhaps a half minute, then picked up the pencil and turned to a new page. 'To understand the situation,' he wrote slowly, 'you must realize that I was raised by a widowed father and educated in the 50s at Exeter and Yale. I suppose it's hard these days to understand the effect that had on—'

"Oh, not at all," she said. "My parents were very much products of that tradition, and I married a man who had spent his entire adolescence in a practice room."

He nodded, but he didn't look up. 'Then I hardly need to tell you it's not a background that prepares one for' —the pencil hesitated— 'marital difficulties.'

"No," she said gently. "Though I don't suppose any background really does."

'Probably not. But in this case, knowledge might have helped. And I had none. On our wedding night, I was inexper' —he crossed it out— 'totally ignorant, in a hurry, and embarrassed. In the midst of everything, I didn't even think of what she might be feeling until she—" The pencil paused again, then stopped altogether.

"Froze up?" she suggested.

'No. She didn't freeze up. She—' He looked across the room. 'It was quite a shock. I'd never seen violence like that, even at Exeter. For a while, I thought she'd gone mad.'

Gone mad. For a moment, she was sitting again in the cheap folding chairs of the Cambridge Woman's Crisis Center, looking into the stunned eyes of girls Charlie's age, the bruised, denying faces of women whose silent children hung on them with guarded looks. Evening after evening of listening to fear, denial, weariness, anger. "Did she hurt you?"

He shook his head as he wrote. 'It turned into hysterics before she could do any real harm. And when that was over, she cried for hours. If I'd known anything at all—about women, about sex, about psychology, about anything that wasn't inside the covers of a book— I'd have realized something was seriously wrong. But as it was, I just blamed myself for frightening her and told myself that things would be all right in the future.'

"And I take it they weren't?"

'No. Not all her fault, of course.'

"Oh, I seriously doubt that. From what you've said —"

He held up a hand. 'I haven't said everything. The situation obviously required tact and patience, and I realized that.' He looked up defensively. "I'm not a brute."

"Of course not! But my own days of ignorance taught me that frustration brings out the savage in even the most civilized of men."

He stared at her in unalloyed surprise, and in the instant before he looked back at the pad, she saw years of self-recrimination and despair. 'That's what it did,' he wrote slowly. 'I was simply appalled. I'd had no idea I could feel like that, especially towards someone I loved.' He sighed. 'And fear of what you call the savage made it impossible for me to do the one thing that would have helped, which was just to hold her, night after night, until she stopped being afraid.'

"You do realize, don't you," she said softly, looking at his averted face, "that it was impossible to do that because the demand was one no mortal man in his twenties could meet?"

He smiled wryly. 'I do now—though exactly when age brought me wisdom, I can't say. The point is, on our honeymoon, I confused mortality with lack of discipline—don't forget, I was a runner—and I blamed myself for continual failure. Of course that made it worse. By the time we'd been married a month, we could hardly talk to each other during the day, for fear of what was sure to happen at night. Finally, after we bought the house on Elm Street, I suggested that we not share a bedroom. That made it possible for us to live together.'

"So you never —?"

The pencil hovered indecisively over the page. Finally it wrote: 'She said she wanted children—only because she knew how much I wanted them, I think—so she did the thermometer thing, and when the time looked right, we tried to make a baby. The business of it seemed to make things a little easier for her, and she tried—know she tried—to cooperate. But all I can remember about those nights is that I was terrified.'

"Of her? Or of yourself?"

'Of both of us.' His eyes drifted across the room, then back to the page, carefully not meeting hers. 'Eventually, I just couldn't face it any more. Not even for a child.'

And this was the man who'd sat so happily in the sunlight of Helena's garden, talking to the girl-child who rocked a baby, while a little boy slept in his lap. "I'm sorry," she said inadequately. "When I asked what was bothering you, I hadn't realized it was so—so much. Or that I could say so little."

He shook his head quickly. 'It wasn't as bad as it sounds. Once we stopped doing the one thing that came between us, things became much easier. There was the college, there was work, there was running—'

There was the admission that fantasy became a drug to a man of his history. There was the scrupulous care to avoid physical proximity with women. There was the momentary hunger for intimacy on the top of the hill. There was the crash that had come after an encounter with Colleen's assumption that Sex Had Something For Everybody. —But he'd gone on writing. She looked hastily at the page.

'What's really been bothering me is that Nathaniel knew.'

She stared at him. "Knew about the—marriage?"

He shook his head and wrote hastily: 'Knew about EVERY-THING. Knew about the Ward Place. Oversaw its upkeep until he died. Went there every summer, unknown even to Helena. Knew Letty had grown up there. Knew what was wrong with Letty. AND NEVER TOLD ME.'

She looked in bewilderment at the sprawling words on the page. "Are you—sure?"

He nodded and turned to a new sheet, though the previous one was only half filled. On the new page, he wrote: 'New research.

'1. Source for Nathaniel's overseeing the Ward Place: Smith and Sons Attorneys, who formed the Ward Trust for Nathaniel and took care of all Ward Place taxes for Letty (without my knowledge) after Nathaniel's death.

'2. Source for Nathaniel's going to the Ward Place in the summer: personal knowledge that he took summer vacations at an undisclosed place, clearly (in retrospect) known to Letty, but not to me.

'3. Confirmation of 2: your testimony that the agent for the Ward Place lost contact with Clarence Wolfington before his death in 1981. Nathaniel died in 1977.'

"My God," she whispered. But the pencil wrote relentlessly on.

'4. Source for Letty's growing up at the Ward Place: Clara's friend Susan Wheeler Howe, who says Letty was the daughter of Henry Ward Jr.'s daughter and Joseph Brantford, raised by Mary and Clara after her mother died in childbirth. Same source says Letty's beauty and social nature, encouraged by Gid, exacerbated the problems of the Ward family so much that after Clara's death she was sent to Nathaniel—not after her father's death in the Pacific, as Letty and Nathaniel had told me, but before, so sometime in late 1943 or early 1944—aged 13.'

Oh, no. If she'd only—! But who would have thought Charlie would uncover something so devastating? Or that Eleanor Klimowski, who had in her day seen so many students lose perspective in the thrill of historical chase, had trusted the discretion of a kid not yet in college?

'5. Source for Nathaniel's knowing what was wrong with Letty: personal experience. Nathaniel had obvious reservations about the courtship—didn't talk to either of us about it for its whole nine months. Continued to be reserved despite his expressed pleasure when the engagement was announced. Concerned about my silence and tension after the honeymoon, to the point of mentioning it (extraordinary for Nathaniel)'—his chest rose and fell unevenly— 'and asking if everything was all right. Do you begin to see the reason for 1–4?'

"Joel—" She put her hand on his to stop him, but he shook it off.

'Think about it. What other reason could they possibly have to lie about her past? What other reason could HE possibly have, knowing what was wrong with her, for not telling me?'

He dropped the pencil and watched, unseeing, as it rolled off the pad onto the floor. She bent to pick it up, and as she sat up again, gently took the pad from him and forced her tear-filled eyes to look over what he'd written. Think about it. Think about the unthinkable—? No. If she wanted to offer him more than paltry sympathy, she was going to have to think beyond the unthinkable. Think about it. The evidence. The text. She wiped her eyes fiercely and read over his numbered statements.

His hand appeared between her and the page; she looked up into a face devoid of emotion. "Well?" he said.

She drew a long, shaky breath. "I—I see your point. But it—but I—" This was absurd. She'd have to ask him. "Do you believe it?"

He glanced dully at the pad on her lap, then took it from her. 'I have to. He lied. Repeatedly. For years. The evidence is overwhelming.' He drew an arrow to the top of the page.

"About the Ward Place, yes. And I'm not defending it. It's— well, it blows me out of the water, so I can imagine what it has done to you. But there really is no evidence that he lied to you about the Ward Place because he knew at first hand what was wrong with Letty. That's conjecture, backed up by memory, and perhaps by the assumption—completely understandable in the wake of recently-discovered betrayal, but extremely dubious philosophically—that a man who is capable of lying to his friend is also capable of raping his ward."

"Raping!?" He stared at her in horror.

"Well, yes," she said, confused. "Isn't that what you—?"

"No, no! I never mxmx deepest condemnation mxmx!" He shook his head in frustration and went back to the pad. 'I never thought RAPE. Letty was beautiful in a way very hard not to desire—

surely as a young girl, she was as close to him as Charlie is to me—if he was 'taken unaware' as you so kindly put it, by the temptations of the woman, who am I to accuse him?'

Then he'd thought—? Unbelievable! No. A widowed father, Exeter, Yale, Mather, with none of the rending, revealing experience of the Crisis Center— "Joel. Are you really trying to tell me that a woman who, as a teenager (possibly even later), had sex with a man she worshiped, would react violently and hysterically every time her husband approached her?"

He hesitated. 'I thought guilt. The '40's, remember.'

"Possibly. But the words you used were —" she flipped back through the pad and ran her finger under the phrases: I'd never seen violence like that. I thought she'd gone mad. It turned to hysterics before she could do any real harm. And further down the page, I was terrified.

He looked at them, then at the windows. After a long time, he shook his head. "Oh, Letty," he murmured, so quietly that she could only see the words, not hear them. "Dear love."

He picked up the pad. 'Why didn't she tell me?'

"It's not unusual. Traumas like that get buried very deeply, and take years to come out." She looked at him. "Do you still think Nathaniel—?"

"No," he said. And wrote quickly. 'Impossible. It was simply not in his makeup. Though why he would lie—'

"If she didn't tell you, she may very well not have told him. And if he only sensed something was wrong, how could he have told you, without violating a confidence she'd never placed in him?"

He doodled thoughtfully on the page: little zigzags and circles. After a moment, he wrote: 'That's a tremendously sustaining thought.'

She prayed that it was also true. Not just for his sake, but for the sake of the man whose brilliance, commitment and integrity had once been a byword in academic circles.

'But if he didn't know—why would he lie about the Ward Place? And why would she?'

"That's a poser," she said. "And at this hour, I have nothing to suggest. What about we work on it tomorrow?"

He looked at his watch and raised his eyebrows. "It is tomorrow," he said, smiling. "Mxmx the day after. And look—mxmx aspirins, would you? Mxmx red wine, loaded Irish coffee. Mxmx terrible headache coming on."

"I should think so," she said, shuddering. "Let's see what we can find."

He followed her to the kitchen and sat down at the table, his forehead in his hands. She fetched him four aspirins and a glass of ice water, then watched with sympathy and a vague sense of superiority as he downed them.

To her surprise, when she reached out for the glass, he took her hand. "Thank you," he said. "I—" He stopped and lifted her fingers to his lips.

She looked into his eyes as he raised them—and saw nothing but exhaustion, a headache, and deep gratitude. Well, gratitude was something. And what more could she ask for? Gently, she brushed the graying curls off his hot forehead, then left him and went up to her room.

And what more could she ask for? She slipped off her clothes, watched only by the reproachful eyes of her banished animals, and pulled her nightgown over her head, looking out the window. Outside, the rain had stopped, and the moon lit up the side of a fast-blowing cloud, then, suddenly, the whole range of mountains. She watched the harrowed pasture across the road turn silver through the faint reflection of herself, still beautiful in the inconstant light. And what more could she ask for? What she could offer him now was as unlike the self she'd once been as the bulldozed field was unlike the wall, the orchard, the trees that once had been. The world of music silenced, the world of learning limited to a computer screen, the love of a kind and difficult man long in the past, the child of that love grown and gone— The clouds covered the moon, and in the darkened window, she saw the pig-tailed phantoms of Charlie and Hattie, then one of Joel, sitting in Helena's garden, a little boy asleep in his lap.

No. She couldn't even offer him that.

216

Sorrowfully, she pulled the shade, glancing across the hall at the nearly completed stack of pages on her desk. Boccaccio. Love melancholy. How much the man had known, had understood. How little the tragedies and absurdities of the heart had changed in the six hundred years since his death. How comforting, finally, that was to know.

15. Enlightenments

Charlie slung a 35 gallon bag of wallpaper shavings into the back of Ray's pickup, belatedly looking over her shoulder to see if the action had made Cocoa startle. It hadn't; he'd come a long way since the scene with the heifers. Smiling, she walked across the dooryard towards his tree— and he nickered. Oh, brother. She stroked his neck as he politely pulled the carrot out of her back pocket. Two more weeks, and they'd never see each other again. It seemed impossible, standing here in the shade of the old maple, but in fact it was just business. The talent scouts at Rhinebeck had seen instantly what she'd told Ray before they left: that Cocoa was one of those rare horses that was equally at home in all three phases of an event. The result of which had been a ten-day bidding war, and the price agreed upon last night had been so much higher than the syndicate had anticipated that they'd called to offer her thanks—and a cut. No problem, except that every friendly nicker made it feel like thirty pieces of silver.

She scratched his ears sadly as he draped his head over her

shoulder. What was going to happen to him? Nothing terrible, given the money involved. But as she'd told Tom last night when he'd called, all it would take to wreck a horse like Cocoa was somebody who demanded obedience instead of cooperation in the dressage ring and strong-armed him over jumps rather than staying out of his way. She'd half expected Tom to laugh at her for worrying about the horse instead of celebrating about the money, but he hadn't. In fact, he'd said he would ask around about who might be doing the riding—sometimes you could pass on information like that not as advice but as part of a horse' s reputation. That was Tom all over: not just vaguely supportive, but quick to see what would make the situation better. It made for a heck of a rider.

But it made for other things too. When the couple he rode for pointed him out as a fellow Yalie, she'd kind of thought *oh no,* but when they'd walked the cross-country course together, she'd realized that this long, lanky guy was in a different intellectual league from the other people there. That evening, they'd sat on hay bales and slipped from shoptalk into the kind of discussion she hadn't had with anybody except maybe Joel—completely out of place at an event, but fun, because he was really up on history, and the way he thought was more professional (government and politics and that sort of thing) than the academic way she was familiar with. Meanwhile, he was putting himself through college by riding for fancy people, and during the school year he was on the Yale polo team, which he'd assured her she was more than qualified to join. So there were all sorts of things to look forward to...

But there was no time to dream off. She was picking Eleanor up in an hour and a half—just long enough to get back to Ray's, put up the horse, and slip into something decent. She hurried across the dooryard, but as she started through the house to get her riding clothes, she paused to take in its changes. The living room and dining room walls looked much better painted than they had with the grape arbors and pink cherubs she'd steamed off (dreadful job). The old pine floors looked a bit skinned after being sanded (another dreadful job), but Joel and Ray had promised her they would darken to a beautiful color. Around the corner, the floor-to-ceiling bookcases Joel had built in Mary Ward's downstairs bedroom looked spectacular. It was all great; they had done good work, and maybe the most wonderful thing was that they had done it at all, because that meant Joel had made his peace with the place and was going to keep it. But even when people did this sort of thing carefully, a farmhouse that had been "restored" somehow lost its farmhouseness. She leaned against the door frame to the dining room, so lost in mixed feelings—about the Wards, the house, Cocoa's sale, Tom—she barely registered the sound of a car in the driveway.

Behind her, the front door opened and shut. "Admiring your work?" said Joel's voice.

Turning, she saw the carefulness that had shown in his face ever since she'd come back. At first she'd thought maybe it was her status as a messenger, but it seemed not to be; he was perfectly friendly, and they had even had some good talks. Still, something always seem to come between them in a way she couldn't remember its doing before she'd left for Rhinebeck, and that was sad. "Actually," she said, "I was wondering what happened to the Wards."

"They haven't been much in evidence, have they?"

"Nope. They weren't even around when I got here early the other day. Maybe they resented your giving their furniture away."

"Maybe they did," he said sorrowfully. "But don't you see—?"

"—sure I do." Under the circumstances, it was surprising he'd kept even the Niagara Falls picture and the stuff in Clara's room. "Are you coming to Helena's with Eleanor and me?"

"I'd like to, but I promised David and Salome I'd drop by for a drink on my way home. Salome wants to talk to me about her dissertation."

"Oh yeah. She was *ecstatic* when you offered to read it." She looked at her watch. "I've got to be off—I just came in to change."

"Okay," he said. "How much did you get done upstairs?"

"The whole of the big bedroom and most of the first little one."

"Really?" He headed for the stairs; she headed for the little bathroom, listening to his footsteps overhead as she slipped into her jeans and chaps.

"This is wonderful!" he said, coming down just as she emerged. "It'll be all done next week!"

Yes, he was as terrific as ever, and they chatted cheerfully as he helped her saddle up. But as she waved and rode off, she couldn't help wondering if it were a coincidence that he was going to David's the one afternoon she'd promised to go to Helena's.

She and Eleanor took the Toyota, and since Eleanor (unlike David) allowed people to drive their own cars, conversation was technically possible; but both of them were silent until they'd come out on the far side of Draper. Then Eleanor sat forward and pointed to the left. "That's Mrs. Howe's house."

Charlie glanced at the approaching condominiums. "Where?"

"Up on the hill, behind the last condo on the right."

"Oh, poor little house! I guess I sort of remember it from when I was a kid. Where the condos are now, was their mowing, right?" She pointed, to facilitate understanding, and Eleanor nodded. "That's a shame."

"Well, yes. But it bought college educations for her grandchildren. They were luckier than Clara Ward."

"I suppose that's true." On the other hand, would Clara have wanted the Wards to build an upscale development on their mowing in order to set her free? Charlie watched real estate offices, ski lodges, and souvenir shops slip by the car, thinking about the days when the only buildings along the road to Westover had been farmhouses and barns. A different world, and not just visually. If you worked your own farm, you could look WASP aristocracy like Brent in the face and say you would have nothing to do with a man whose family looked down on you. But if you worked for the tourist industry (and what else could you do here, now?), you either put up with people who looked down on you or starved. That wouldn't sit very well with Clara.

Slowing down as they reached Westover, she looked up at Helena's mowing, in what she suddenly realized was an habitual action. "What will happen to Helena's place when she—?"

"Sorry?"

"Helena's place. What will happen to it?"

"It will be sold, and the proceeds will go partly to Mather College, but mostly to a school she founded after the War on a big estate near Fiesole. I know, because she told me quite frankly the last time we had a real visit. But there's no danger of something like the Howes' mowing; she tied it so the lots can be no smaller than fifteen acres—more or less like Colleen's property across the road from me. That's about the best you can hope for, these days." Eleanor sighed as they started up the familiar driveway. "You haven't seen Helena since her stroke, have you?"

"No, I've been meaning to, but—" The excuse faded away as the car stopped on the gravel circle by the woodshed.

"You'll find it difficult."

She was *already* finding it difficult; everything looked just the way it always had.

"Over here," said Eleanor. "She usually sits on the porch."

She led the way through the open kitchen door, tapping the knocker as she went by. As they walked between the beautiful, familiar antiques that furnished the living room, a nurse hurried in from the porch. "Oh, hello, Dr. Klimowski. She'll be so glad to see you." She glanced at Charlie. "And this is your daughter?"

Charlie saw Eleanor struggle with the question and answered for her as they stepped out on the porch. And there was Helena, small, bent, and almost transparent in her wheelchair. The nurse leaned the over her. "Miss Woodhouse, company's here."

Helena's gaze remained fixed on the open photograph album on her lap. Eleanor walked around to the front of the wheelchair and knelt down, taking her hands. "Hello, Helena."

"Letty," said Helena, smiling. "What a lovely surprise." She looked over Eleanor's shoulder. "And who is this?"

Charlie gulped as she met the vague eyes. "I'm Charlie, Helena. Charlotte. Don't you—?" But of course she didn't, not if she didn't even know Eleanor.

The nurse broke the awkward silence. "She's had a good time with that album today. I think she's been wanting it for quite a while;

she kept asking me to look in her desk drawer for somebody named Nathaniel, and I thought—well, you know how she is. But finally I opened the drawer, and I found this. It's made her real happy."

Helena looked up from the album. "We'll have tea now, Mrs. Roberts."

The nurse looked slightly resentful—probably not because of the request, but because of the tone of voice, which was clearly the one in which Helena had once addressed her servants. She left obediently, however, and Eleanor, who had been looking confused, realized what was up and went to help her.

It didn't seem right for everybody to go, so Charlie sat down shyly next to the wheelchair, watching Helena's fragile hands turn over a leaf of the album. "Are those pictures of Nathaniel Brantford?" she asked.

"Nathaniel." Helena considered. "Yes, some of them are of him." Using only her left hand, she turned the album a little so they could both see it. "Not this one, of course."

Charlie looked at the offered picture; it was a portrait of a girl about her age, maybe a bit younger, looking absolutely gorgeous in a strapless evening gown with a wasp waist and a full three-quarter length skirt. Charlie glanced at the caption, but all it said was '1946.' "Who's that?"

"Letty Brantford," said Helena, looking surprised at her ignorance. "That was her first formal; she was more excited about the dress than about meeting President Truman at the reception." She turned to what was obviously a series of pictures of the reception, which, judging from the evening dress and nearly all-male company, had been held at Mather College.

Charlie's eyes ran over them quickly, then landed on a shot of a stunning woman with dark hair coiled around her head talking to Harry Truman—and making him look totally undistinguished. She reached across the page and pointed. "Is that you?"

"Yes," said Helena, smiling. "A long time ago, of course." She turned another page, to two enlarged shots, one on each leaf. On the left was her beautiful younger self, standing arm in arm with a powerfully-built man whose face was turned towards her as he said something that made her laugh.

"Is that Nathaniel?"

Helena nodded. "It's not a good likeness, but he got an enlargement because it was a good one of me." She pointed to the opposing page. "The one with Letty is much better."

Charlie looked eagerly at the picture; and it was well worth looking at. Because the Great Nathaniel wasn't just handsome, he was... well, *great*. Everything about him—the way he stood, the way smiled, the way he wore his tuxedo—made it obvious that if he'd been born in another country and another century, he would have been a king on the scale of Charlemagne. Everything, that is, except his face, in which you could see the intelligence and sensitivity that had drawn Joel to him. She looked at it contemplatively, then blinked a couple of times and was about to look again, when Mrs. Roberts and Eleanor came in with the tea things.

"Thank you," said Helena, in her gracious dealing-with-servants voice. "Letty, perhaps you'll pour?" She closed the album with her left hand, but the right hand that should have supported it didn't move, and it slid off her lap, sending odd pictures flying across the porch.

It was nothing, really; but Helena looked so upset that Charlie was glad to jump up and collect the things that had escaped. A picture of a beautiful old car—maybe the Dodge David always talked about. A picture of Mather College, with acres of gardens where there was only grass now. But no more pictures of Nathaniel, unfortunately.

She slipped the pictures back into the album, but she didn't dare open it again; it was several minutes before Helena could be persuaded to drink her tea, and even after that, the atmosphere was so uncomfortable that it would clearly be unkind to do anything that reminded her of the accident. So she sipped her tea instead, making herself join in the disjointed and incoherent conversation. It hardly seemed fair to leave all the talk to Eleanor, who couldn't possibly have been able to follow the numerous changes of subject and mental slips, but who responded to everything just as if she understood.

After what had to be one of the most painful half hours ever known, Mrs. Roberts came back out on the porch and caught Eleanor's eye. Eleanor stood up. "We must go, Helena."

Under Helena's veil of perfect decorum there shone a glimmer of relief. "You should take a turn in the garden first," she said, smiling. "I'd take you through it, but I'm afraid I'm indisposed at present."

Indisposed. Charlie swallowed hard. Then, breaking a long-standing rule, she leaned over and gave Helena a kiss. "I'm leaving for college soon," she said, "and I probably won't be seeing you again—this summer, I mean. So—goodbye."

Helena smiled graciously, but without complete comprehension. Fortunately, Eleanor rescued her by coming up to say her own good-bye, and soon they were out of the house. But when they reached the garden, and Charlie looked over the familiar white gate, she found she couldn't leave quite yet. Not until she'd stood here a moment and thought about the secret garden, the fishpond, Helena's white tea dress. Helena, charming Harry Truman. Helena, leaning on the Great Nathaniel's arm, laughing.

Eleanor slipped an arm around her shoulder. "Want me to drive?"

She shook her head. "No, I'm okay. I was just—" She shouldn't have said anything, because it made her cry. But Eleanor was really nice about it, so it didn't matter.

◦≡≡◦ ◦≡≡◦ ◦≡≡◦

Joel turned over the last page of Eleanor's Boccaccio section and leaned back in his chair, locking his hands behind his head. He hadn't expected anything like this; in fact, coward that he was, he'd put off reading her manuscript out of fear that it might not be good. But it was—no, 'good' was a word that applied to well-informed, intelligent studies like the dissertation he'd read last week, and encouraged Salome to expand and publish. This was on a whole different order of magnitude, a work whose depth of insight could have come only from years of intense intellectual and spiritual engagement.

Pursing his lips, he thought of the conditions of that engagement. Eleanor, coming home after cleaning houses to write about the issue all other Renaissance scholars had uneasily chosen to ignore in *The Decameron, The Prince, Utopia*—the fact that each of them had conflicting, double meanings. Eleanor, suspended between the worlds of the hearing and the deaf, writing about Janus-faced books that looked forward to a world unthinkable, backward to a world irredeemably lost. Eleanor, returning from visiting Helena to write about Boccaccio, whose *brigata* gathered in a garden to tell each other stories culled from a civilization that was dying all around them. Eleanor, writing through a Vermont winter on Machiavelli, who had himself spent long, lonely evenings 'conversing' with the Ancients. If she understood the deprivation of exile, the pain that accompanied witty analysis of a civilization adrift, and the inner, atemporal companionship that made intellectual isolation bearable, that was no accident.

He gazed down at the manuscript, feeling a twinge of envy— not at the quality of the work, but at the state of mind that had engendered it. It was this engagement, this complete submersion in intellectual inquiry, that he had lost during the years of Letty's illness; and he seemed to be incapable of writing without it. Of course, given time and the absence of college politics, he might be able to submerge himself in literature again. But at the back of his mind, there lurked the memory of the day long ago when he had read Nathaniel's dissertation and come upon a place where the brilliant criticism of the early chapters stumbled, faltered, and turned in a matter of paragraphs to pedestrian analysis. Reading on, he'd realized, with a long, slow chill, that whatever had stepped between Nathaniel and the page had remained there permanently; its presence was visible not just in the dissertation, but in the undeveloped, unsustained flashes of insight that illuminated Nathaniel's literary conversation. If such a thing could happen to Nathaniel, who loved literature more than he loved any human being, it could happen to—

He shook himself. There was no point in dwelling on thoughts like that. Right now, he should find Eleanor and tell her how much he liked the manuscript. She was home; he'd heard her come in over an hour ago, and, judging from the smells that were drifting into his room, she was cooking dinner. Putting the pages back on the scarred roll-top desk, he started towards the kitchen. But as he shut the East Wing door and started across the grass, he paused, then stopped altogether. Through the busy noises of chopping and stirring, somebody was singing.

> *How should I your true-love know*
> *From another one?*

It couldn't be Charlie; Ray had said David and Salome were taking her out to dinner. He stepped to the kitchen window and peered through the screen. Inside, Eleanor put the domed lid on the wok and turned to the sink, rolling up her sleeves.

> *By his cockle hat and staff,*
> *And by his sandal shoon.*

The wistful, flute-like voice was as sad as the song, and fresh from the power of her work, he stepped to the door, longing to comfort her. But as his hand touched the knob, wisdom alerted him to the inevitable result of such an intrusion. She would stop singing immediately, as she had stopped playing the piano upon those rare occasions when he, hearing her, had come to listen. She would look at him in a way that declared his sympathy unnecessary, then turn away. Her pride was as frustrating as Clara Ward's; but it required the same respect. He sat down on the stone doorstep, listening sorrowfully to the rest of Ophelia's song, and more sorrowfully still to the silence that followed. Just as he thought he could bear it no longer, footsteps crossed the kitchen—and he jumped up hastily, looking as if he were just emerging from the East Wing as the door opened.

"Perfect timing," said Eleanor, smiling. "Dinner's ready."

"Great," he said, and followed her in.

He wished to discuss the manuscript immediately, but he'd

learned by now that she could attend either to what he said or to her food, but not both. So with impatience exacerbated by her song, he waited until he put the last plate into the dish rack before he began. "I finished your book this afternoon. It's wonderful. Superb, and not just in a scholarly way. I—"

"I'm sorry," she said, looking up from the silverware drawer. "What's wonderful?"

He was about to try again, when a car pulled up in the driveway. "Someone's here," he said.

Eleanor glanced at Derri, who had trotted towards the door, wagging his tail. "Must be Charlie," she said. "Nobody else gets a welcome like that."

It was Charlie, resplendent in wide black pants, a silk shirt, and the earrings she'd worn the day he'd first met her. "Hello, everybody— easy there, old dog!—you got time to listen to two interesting pieces of information?"

Eleanor took in her quivering expectancy with a smile—and Joel suddenly saw the kitchen as it had been for many summers before this one: full of half-grown children, animals, and noise. "Two pieces of information?" she said. "Sure, but only one piece at a time."

"Okay," said Charlie, grinning. "Here's number one—you ready? Salome is coming back next summer."

Eleanor stared at her. "Did you say Salome? Coming back?"

"You got it. That's what they took me out to dinner to tell me. David's so happy, it's absolutely touching."

"That's worthy of a small celebration," said Eleanor. "We're short on champagne, alas—but how about coffee and ice cream?"

"Super!" said Charlie, opening the freezer. "David and Salome never eat desserts, so of course I couldn't order one. Oh, yum! Rain Forest Crunch." And for the next half hour, she chattered on about David and Salome with a delight no less whole-hearted for its irony.

When they'd finished their coffee, however, her face became more serious. "The second piece of information is historical," she said, pulling an envelope out of her shoulder bag. "At least, I think it is." She slipped a picture out of the envelope and handed it to Eleanor, who looked, nodded in recognition, and passed it to Joel. "Do you know who these people are?"

He glanced down at the yellowed print, his hand traveling to his shirt pocket for his reading glasses. "Of course. Letty and Nathaniel." There was a significant silence as he perched his glasses on his nose. "No, I'm sorry, it's not Letty—couldn't be, if Nathaniel was that age."

A small sound from Eleanor made him look up, but it was Charlie who spoke. "You're absolutely *sure* it's Nathaniel?"

"Oh, yes. There couldn't possibly be two faces that extraordinary. The girl with him, though—" He looked at their silent faces. *"Should* I know who she is?"

"Yes and no," said Charlie. "You should recognize the porch she's standing on, anyway. And if it helps, the picture was in the chest with Clara's journal, slipped under the endpapers of Grandpa Ward's *Complete Longfellow.*"

He stared into the quiet, intelligent eyes of the girl standing arm in arm with Nathaniel on the porch. His porch. "Clara Ward," he said wonderingly. And then, his mind somehow unable to absorb the inescapable corollary: "But Nathaniel wasn't a sergeant; he was a lieutenant."

"He might have been promoted," said Charlie eagerly. "Lieutenants *are* higher than sergeants, aren't they?"

"Yes." And Nathaniel would have been the last man in the world to mention a promotion that might remind Asa of his injury. Joel looked at the picture once more, then at Charlie. "How long have you known this?"

He hadn't meant to sound reproachful, but Charlie blushed. "Just since this afternoon, when I remembered to check it out. I mean, Eleanor and I found the picture while you were gone, and I was going to show it to you, but I—I thought maybe you'd had enough of the Wards. Besides, I had no idea it had anything but historical interest until last week, when Helena showed me a picture of Nathaniel at a reception. And then, well, I was upset about Helena, and I put off checking because I didn't want to think about her." She glanced at Eleanor. "I should've told you on the way home, but if you remember—"

Eleanor nodded, though it was impossible to tell whether she completely understood.

"And anyway, I wasn't completely *certain* until right now." She pointed to the picture. "I mean, the face is one you just don't forget, but in Helena's pictures, he was a lot older and—well, different, somehow."

Different. Joel gazed down at the snapshot. She was right; in spite of his unmistakable face and bearing, the open, affectionate young man who looked proudly at Clara Ward bore little resemblance to the Nathaniel he had known.

Eleanor's hand touched his shoulder. "Joel—are you all right?"

"Of course," he said automatically, but his eyes remained on the picture. Orpheus at his wedding. Orestes before the onslaught of the Furies. Hamlet before his father's murder. If one had known them then, would one have recognized them later, when they walked on stage? He pondered the question absently, letting the rest of Charlie's explanation drift around him like leaves in a night wind.

After some time, Charlie stood up. "I've got to go; I promised I wouldn't be gone long, and I think I'd better deliver. It has just hit David that this is the last week of my last summer up here, so I'm trying to be good daughter."

He stood up too; there was a little pause.

"You know I won't tell David," she said finally.

"I didn't imagine you would."

"I feel sort of bad about finding it out, even. I mean, it was *theirs*; nobody else really needed to know."

"No," he said, "but I'm glad you found out."

It had been the right thing to say; all the apology went out of her face. "Really? I was afraid maybe I'd done it again."

"Not at all," he said. "It explains all sorts of things."

"Yeah, I was thinking on the way over, if he *was* Brent, that story about Emily—" She caught Eleanor's eye. "I mean, it does explain a lot. But nobody needs to know but us. And they won't. Ever, ever. Okay, I'm outta here. Thanks for dessert and listening."

"Take care," said Eleanor. "And give Salome and David our congratulations."

"I sure will." She hesitated, then stepped between them and put one arm around each of them. "You know, you guys are fantastic, wonderful, fabulous people— Oh, yes, and you too, Derri." She hugged the jealous dog, waved, and left.

Joel watched her lights disappear down the road, then sat back down at the table, drawing the picture to him. Behind him, he vaguely heard the clink of dishes as Eleanor washed the bowls and cups, then the sound of footsteps quietly approaching his chair.

"Joel," she said. "You *sure* you're all right?"

"Yes," he said absently. "Yes. It's amazing."

"It is, though when you think about it—"

"No, I mean the resemblance."

She sat down, peering in frustration at his face. "I'm sorry?"

"Come with me," he said. "I'll show you something." Picking up the picture, he started out to the East Wing, turning once to be sure she was following. It was under the desk, somewhere; he'd seen it just the other day, when he'd been hunting for the box with tax records in it. There it was! Or rather, there *she* was: Letty at eighteen, slightly remote, in 1940's high school graduation picture style. He put the portrait on the desk, and placed Nathaniel and Clara next to it. "*That's* amazing."

She bent over them, then looked up. "Good God."

He nodded. "The observation you wouldn't let Charlie make is hard to—" But he was confusing her again. He slid a pad of paper out of the side desk drawer and wrote, 'I'm surprised that the good citizens of Draper accepted the story about Henry Ward's daughter.'

"Well," said Eleanor, "of course we don't know what the good citizens of Draper really accepted, only what Clara's closest friend chose to tell Charlie." She looked back at the two pictures. "But part of the resemblance is seeing pictures of them at the same stage."

He smiled and wrote, 'As Ray says, they're all beautiful at that age.'

"Ray should know," she said, laughing. Leaning to the side, she opened the bottom left drawer of the roll-top and rummaged through a stack of envelopes. "And without a doubt he's right—he, and Sidney, Spenser, Milton, Shakespeare—all your pastoral romance friends who know a woman is of no poetical interest after she turns 25." She sat up again, pulling two 5x7 picture folios out of an envelope. "But when it comes to mother-daughter resemblances—"

She flipped open one of the folios, revealing a shiny black and white print of a girl sitting at a grand piano, her forearm resting lightly on its case. Not a pretty girl, feature by feature: the cheekbones were a little too high, the nose a little too roman, the chin a little too sharp, the large, dark eyes a little too competitive. But as a whole, the face had a peculiar blend of poetry and dynamism that was more than attractive. And yes, familiar in a vague sort of way. He looked down at Eleanor's sharp features and smiled. "Hattie?"

She nodded, looking at the picture affectionately. "Last year." She moved it up the desk and opened the second folio underneath it. "And then there's this one."

"Hm," he said, and wrote 'Less professional—but I think I like it better.'

"Thank you."

The irony in her voice, and in her smile as she glanced up at him, made him look at the picture again. The piano, the girl, the—no, it was not the same face. The nose was straighter, the hair lighter, the eyes far softer. An interesting, intelligent face, but unworldly. Undefensive. Unscathed. He looked back at Eleanor in disbelief. "That's—you?"

She nodded. "At the same age." She closed the two folios and slid them back into the drawer. "That's my point. You see the resemblance most strikingly when you isolate it from time—but if you saw Hattie and me together now, you'd hardly notice it." She slid the other two pictures under the light. "And it was probably the same with Letty and Clara. Those are lovely faces, but beyond the beauty, they're not all that much alike."

He pulled the leather chair closer to the desk and sat on its arm, looking at the two portraits. Beyond the beauty. Perhaps he'd never seen beyond it. Perhaps in Letty's presence, it had simply not been possible to notice that her face had none of the elements that made her mother's countenance so arresting. At least, not possible to him. But to others... Slowly, the young man who stood with his arm around Clara dissolved into Nathaniel, watching Letty at the bridge table, at dinner, at parties. Not proudly. Not affectionately. A void, he'd told Eleanor. But it was more than a void. To a man led by physical resemblance to hope he would re-encounter in his daughter the intelligence and pride he'd loved in Clara Ward, Letty must have been a continual disappointment.

He shook his head and picked up the pencil. 'Charlie said Clara was the real loser after the breakup, but she was wrong. Or at least half wrong. It was the end of him.'

"The end of Nathaniel?" Eleanor's voice was incredulous.

'Maybe just the end of Brent—but Brent was the scholar and the lover; Nathaniel was just the public man. Where Brent should have been, there was a black hole. I was always aware of it. Even' —He could not make the pencil write 'hurt by it.' If she could only—! No, it was hardly her fault that the permanence of words distorted fleeting, inconsequential moments of pain. Spoken or written, it made no difference— 'Even intellectually. Someday, when I get all my books sorted out, I'll show you his dissertation. It's finished, but it died in the middle. Terrifying. Just today, I was thinking' —The wayward pencil stopped again, and Eleanor looked up, puzzled—as well she might. Surely he was the only man in history who'd managed to stammer on paper.

"Are you saying Nathaniel's dissertation died because he lost Clara?" she asked.

He nodded. 'Definitely. He left Harvard in December of 1929, with it undone. Finally finished it in 1935; was made president of Mather the following year. Clearly he finished it for administrative reasons.'

"That's very sad," she said. "But you shouldn't find it terrifying. Total emotional trauma—depression, nervous breakdown, whatever—is one thing. Getting stuck at the beginning of a huge project is quite another."

'Not if it's gone.'

"It?"

'Intellectual engagement,' he wrote impatiently. 'Creative fire, if you want. Ability to—' to hell with the whole discipline of writing! He rose off the arm of the chair and walked up and down the little room "Ability to write, dammit! To sit down with a great work of art and have something to say. It's there—everywhere, everywhere—in your book! Every line, every word! It's so damn good, Eleanor, and God knows, I'm not jealous, and I don't think I'm just being small—it's just hard to read something like that and say to yourself 'once upon a time, I, too, could write something of real—!" Christ, what kind of a way was this to tell her he liked her book? He stopped by the desk and picked up the pencil. 'Nothing I said bears writing down. I'm sorry. There really is no —'

"As a matter of fact," she said mildly, "I got most of it. At a certain decibel level, speech becomes intelligible. And I'm delighted that you think my book is good. As for the rest—"

"—Please!" he said, flushing. "The less said, the better."

She shook her head, deadpan. "Oh, I don't know. You do romantic agony rather well."

He stared at her, almost unable to believe his ears or eyes—and then joined her as she laughed. 'All right, all right. But it's so frustrating not to be able to—'

Her face changed. "You think I don't know that? The manuscript you read today is the one that might have saved me from being 'let go' at John Adams because of my hearing—if the loss of my hearing hadn't made me incapable of writing it."

God. And he, in the picturesque, all-male cloister of Mather College, had been oblivious. 'How long was it before you could work on it?'

"Quite a while. For years, I didn't even want to look at it, and of course, between keeping the place up, keeping the ship afloat and keeping Hattie in lessons—which included driving her to the Conservatory two or three times a week—I was pretty busy. But after she could drive herself, I realized that soon the only company I'd have would be the dog and cat, and I began to worry about sinking to their

intellectual level." She smiled. "So I gave myself a paper assignment:
a five-pager on Patient Griselda's place in The Decameron. And of
course I was in over my head in five minutes, reading all the tales,
nipping down to the U Mass Library, catching up on feminist criticism—"

"—And writing?"

"In every spare moment. At first, it helped that the spare moments were short—you know, the threat of imminent death that
concentrates the mind so wonderfully. But pretty soon, I got into the
rhythm of it." She glanced at the slightly skewed pile of pages he'd left
on the desk. "And in the long run, I'm glad it happened the way it did.
It's a much more interesting book than it would have been if I'd written it under normal circumstances."

Normal circumstances. Grants. Sabbaticals. Leaves of Absence.
Summers at Bellagio. Winters at Research Triangle Park. *The leisure
of the theoried classes*, Nathaniel had called it. And who was Joel Hendrickson to scoff? NEH grant, Guggenheim, Queen Elizabeth Professor of Renaissance Studies at Trinity College, Cambridge. With a
deep sense of shame—as much for his privilege as for his outburst—
he pulled the notes he had written about her chapters from underneath her manuscript, and, alternately writing, speaking, and pointing, he talked with her about her work. Quite apart from his interest
in her chapters, he found the dialogue fascinating, for as soon as she
was liberated from the struggle of trying to hear, her responses came
so quickly and with such nuance that he was glad that the necessity
of writing gave him extra time to think. As he enjoyed the power of
her intellect, he slowly gained insight into her experiences at John
Adams College. No matter how tactful she might be, a woman with
insights this intelligent and original could only have been a threat to
her orthodox, tenured colleagues. And yet she was not in the least
competitive; he felt nothing behind her arguments and clarifications
except the love of her subject and the immense pleasure of discussing
it with another scholar.

After a couple of hours, she reluctantly stood up. "This is just
great, but I'm afraid we must stop. I have to have a condo ready by

ten tomorrow morning, and it's going to take me at least three hours to get it respectable. And then I have Colleen's house and one other of about the same size. But before I go..." She looked at him hesitantly. "It seems a shame to waste all these wonderful insights" —she pointed to his scribblings— "on a pad of paper. Have you thought of assigning yourself a five-pager?"

He smiled politely, but she saw through the subterfuge.

"I'm serious. It doesn't make any difference if you see through the exercise—at least, I saw through it, and it worked anyway. Of course, it can't be just *any* old five-pager. It has to deal with a real problem, or you'll just polish it off overnight and turn it in."

"I suppose that's true." He rummaged in his mind for such a problem, but as usual, his mind refused to consider anything that had remotely to do with the pastoral, and also as usual, the refusal set off a wave of panic. He looked up to stave it off. "Any suggestions?"

She considered a moment, then her eyes fell on the two portraits, and she smiled. "Try this," she said. "'They're all beautiful at that age,' right? Viola, Rosalind, Pastorella, Miranda, Perdita—all those lovely creatures. But the most deeply moving female character in pastoral romance is Hermione, who by the end of the play has to be well over thirty, possibly—horrors!—even in her forties. And yet there she is, reducing the audience to tears. What does she have that makes her so much more affecting than the lovely maidens?"

Ah. That *was* an interesting question. He eased himself off the arm of the chair and pulled Robert Randall's *Complete Shakespeare* off the shelf. As he paged through it, she got up, smiling. "I'll leave you to your assignment," she said, and slipped out the door before he could protest.

He sat down at the desk and found *The Winter's Tale*. Hermione. For all his work on the pastoral, he'd never really thought about her. The wonder of the final act was one of those things he'd always accepted in his heart, and her dignity, her triumph over time—

That was it. He pulled out the pad he'd written on for Eleanor and jotted down 'Triumph over time.' Well, that was obvious. It was *how*—he jotted a little more. But in terms of the whole play—he

236

flipped back to Act I and began to read.

Long past midnight, he closed the book gently and looked at the two portraits underneath it through the tears that filled his eyes. Where had it been, this forgiveness and reconciliation, for Nathaniel? How unnecessary, somehow, that his pastoral romance had turned to tragedy. How sad (and not just for Nathaniel) that Letty had not been a Perdita. He folded the picture of Nathaniel and Clara into Letty's folio and leaned on his elbows, his palms over his eyes.

And how unjust, how blind, he'd been during the past weeks to attribute Nathaniel's reticence about his courting Letty to some dark motive. He leaned down to put the folio back in its box, and, on his way back up, opened the desk's left bottom drawer. There, on top of a pile of miscellany, lay the envelope Eleanor had put away. He drew out her picture and looked at it, first with sadness for the passage of time and the injustices of the world, then with a surge of bitterness. Whatever Nathaniel might or might not have known about Letty's history, nobody could have known better than he did how different Joel Hendrickson's life would have been if he'd married a woman with a wonderful face like this.

16. Departures

Eleanor pushed Derri out of the way as she dropped two bags of groceries on the table. Milk, butter, cheese— "Must you stand in front of the refrigerator, you dumb dog?" He scuttled under the table, and she put things away, ignoring his reproachful look. There were days when brown-eyed devotion was really irritating—or maybe it was just that the atmosphere of late August made the limitations of canine companionship all too obvious. Back to School. Paper, pencils, binders, star-crossed plastic lunch sacks in The Grand Union. Yellow busses in the Texaco station. Cheap imitations of name-brand clothes at Tru-Value. And in the outlying areas of town, summer academics shifting into campus mode. Charlie off to orientation tomorrow, high as a kite. Salome the day after, no doubt equally high (and equally terrified), but too cool to show either. Then one by one, David and the other veterans, straggling to their offices a day or two before registration. And finally, the day after Labor Day, Joel. After that, there would

238

be just the cleaning lady, the dog, and the cat on the hill.

But that was hardly Derri's fault. She reached under the table and gave him a penitent pat. "It's all right, old dog. You can come out now."

He did come out, so happy at her restored affection that she was ashamed of herself. She fussed over him for a minute, then started to fold up the grocery bags. As she picked up the second bag, she saw a note she should have seen the minute she came in. *10:00—Came over, hoping to find you—loading Cocoa at 11, then off as close to noon as possible—will try to stop by on way out—Love, Charlie.*

Noon *today?* Damn. And she'd been so sure it was tomorrow. She stuffed the bags into the recycling basket, repressing a tremor of fear. She could *too* manage by herself; it was just that with Joel around to answer the phone or write important information down, she'd gotten dependent. And now that he was ensconced in the Ward Place— But she'd taken care of that. The TDD and flashers she'd ordered were sitting in the Honda; all she had to do was set them up, and she'd be able to use the phone again. And as for verbal information, she'd just have to get it in writing if it was important. Pride or no pride.

Meanwhile, it was only eleven; thanks to the cancellation at Timber Creek, she had time to catch Charlie, if the short cut to the Walkers' through the woods was still passable. She whistled to Derri and let him out the door in front of her, smiling at his enthusiasm. However limited it might be, a relationship with a dog was blessedly straightforward.

She walked up the rise across the way, then, skirting the enormous half-framed house, hurried down the path that Joel had worn to the Ward place, looking anxiously around the shorn hillside for the sugaring track that had once branched off in the direction of Ray and Connie's. Here, right? No, maybe a little further. She stopped, looking back at the house and trying to remember what the land had looked like without it. The orchard had been here—or had it been a little to the left? The high bush blueberry patch had been where the corner of the house was now, or somewhere near it—it was hard to tell with the maples gone. She closed her eyes, and the whole scene rose before her, every hummock indelibly imprinted in her memory; but when she opened them again, she could see the landscape only as it had become. Like Hattie and Charlie, it still resembled its former self, but its familiarity couldn't even help her get her bearings; it served only to remind her that it was no longer intimately, belovedly a part of herself.

Ahead of her, Derri paused and looked back questioningly. Ah. To those who were untrammeled by the past, the way was apparently still clear. She pointed to the left and followed the dog as he climbed over a pile of roots and trotted down the old trail. In two minutes the land before her eyes matched the land of her memories. Too bad that's the way she liked it; the phenomenon suggested, once again, that she had come to oppose change in any form. She preferred not to think that, having always considered herself to be reasonably progressive, but all her deepest feelings were of a piece. Her retreat from deafness, her rebellion against Vermont's development, her dislike of postmodernism, her mixed feelings as she read Hattie's excited letters, her resistance to the idea that Joel was leaving—yes, they were, without exception, symptomatic of a cast of mind and heart that sought to keep things she loved as they once had been. To see the dangers that lurked behind that cast of mind, one had only to think of Brent and Clara, forever imprisoned by the results of a six-week romance, or of their daughter, who in the name of love had nearly turned a great college into a fossil.

No, she was going to have to stop looking back. She'd done it before: dried her tears, picked up the pieces and marched on. If there were more pieces now, less youth and energy to march with, no child to march for—there was still herself, and she would *not*, dammit, *not* let herself become what she was becoming. There was the book, already in the hands of an editor with a letter she had been too practical to forbid Joel to write. It wouldn't work wonders, of course—even if the book were accepted, it would be only one among thousands more fashionable—but it was a start. And though it was too much to hope that a deaf woman pushing fifty could land a full-time position, the law was on her side now, applications cost very little to send out, and there were always grants. In the meantime, there was the Community College of Vermont, which offered education to the Clara Wards of the current world, and paid at least as much per course as a steady condominium job. She ducked through the fence behind the Walkers' barn, shuddering at the prospect of professional phone calls on a TDD, interviews with a typist to transcribe—no, such thoughts were *not* allowed. The past was crumbling everywhere around her; there was no place to go but forward.

She squared her shoulders and walked down the driveway, marveling at the absence of golden dogs and the size of the six-horse van that nearly blocked the road.

"Okay, boy—easy." Charlie stroked Cocoa's neck and led him up the ramp into the van.

"Wow," said Ray. "That's impressive."

Charlie nodded. "Sure, he's a pro. —There you go, Cocoa. Be a good boy." She hugged him and walked down the ramp without looking back. There were larger events to be sad about today than saying goodbye to a horse.

"Okay," said Ray, after they'd helped the driver fasten the door. "Let's get over to—hey, great! Somebody found Eleanor."

Charlie ran towards her, then made herself slow down. Tomorrow morning, she was going to be a Yale freshman; she would *not* bawl like a little kid with a scraped knee who'd been okay until Mommy appeared. "Hi, Eleanor. Glad they found you."

"Hi," said Eleanor, including Ray in her smile as he caught up. "Glad what?"

"Glad they found you," she said, raising her voice. "Joel and Connie. They've been looking *everywhere!* Colleen didn't have your schedule, just the places you—" She broke off as the confusion in Eleanor's face merged with concern. "You mean, they didn't find you?"

"Nobody found me but your note. What's up?"

God. She didn't know. Which meant— Charlie turned to Ray.

"Um," he said. "Your friend in Westover—"

"—Helena," said Eleanor. Then, looking at the two of them, she got it without words.

Behind Charlie, the truck started up. "Okay, all set!"

She swallowed hard. "Thanks a lot! Have a good trip!" She waved, and the three of them watched the van as it started carefully down the road.

"Any details?" said Eleanor finally.

"No. The nurse went in around 7 to get her up, and—" She watched the van disappear around the corner. "David says the nurse should have been on the ball."

"Uh-uh," said Ray emphatically. "Much better just to go if you're on your way out."

"That's what Salome and I said, but—well, you know how David is." She rubbed the toe of her boot in the dust, then looked up guiltily at Eleanor, wondering if she'd caught any of it.

"David's just *devastated*. I knew he liked Helena and all, but I didn't realize—"

"Oh, yes." Eleanor smiled sadly. "Of all the women in his life, she's the one he cared for most deeply."

Most deeply. She thought of the way she'd found David this morning, sitting in his study, staring out the window, his face blank with grief. It was a good thing Salome was there. "He and Joel are executors of her will," she said. "It will cheer him up to have something to do. Jed Smith—he's the lawyer for Mather College—called, and one of them's got to go down there while the other one sorts through the stuff in Helena's house." Oops. She shouldn't have said that. Just the thought of that house, without Helena in it—

Ray put a heavy hand on her shoulder. "So Connie and I are going to run this kid down to Bridgeport today, where we're already booked to arrive at 4. New grandson. Big deal. Then tomorrow we'll get her to New Haven first thing."

"Think that will be okay?" said Charlie, looking up at Eleanor. "I could call Yale and explain I had to stay for the funeral, but orientation's supposed to be important." Not to mention, it was unbearable to think of a funeral for Helena.

"Orientation *is* very important," said Eleanor in the voice that made you love Eleanor so much. "And it will be several days, maybe even longer, before the funeral is arranged. So you should absolutely go." She smiled at Ray. "And since it's your stable boy you'll be driving south, I'll do the horses tonight and tomorrow morning ."

"Thanks," said Ray. "Figured you'd do it. Left a note on the feed bin about that stuff you wanted me to ask Mike Wolfington, in fact—afraid I'd forget again." He paused, about to repeat it, but then he turned. "Will you look at that!! Here's Joel and Connie back to check up, right on schedule. Looks like we'll make it to Bridgeport before the traffic gets bad."

And that was that—or almost that. Amidst all the dust and talk and confusion, Eleanor gave her a big goodbye hug, and Joel promised once more to visit Hattie first thing in London, and to write her at Yale. His face showed how deeply *he'd* cared for Helena, but the hug he gave her didn't have a shadow of carefulness, and when they looked at each other through all the things they couldn't say, she knew everything was more than all right between them. Then she was in Ray and Connie's car, unbelievably off to pick up her stuff and say goodbye to David and Salome. And tomorrow, even more unbelievably, to Yale and orientation, and pretty soon Tom, who'd promised to drive her out to the polo stables the very first moment she had free.

17. A Commencement

Joel parked in Helena's driveway and walked for the last time across the lawn. The house looked just as it had when he'd first seen it in June, placed with inconspicuous decorum in its cluster of maples and overlooking the mowing, the Westover steeple, the Mountain. Only the absence of the white wicker porch furniture testified to the changes of the past two weeks—that, and the Hume and Rickerts 'For Sale' sign that swung at the bottom of the driveway. When he and David had assumed their executors' duties, they'd found (not entirely to their surprise) that Helena had made those duties light indeed: her property had been surveyed, divided and appraised in April, and the two of them had been able to put it on the market as soon as it became clear that combined resources of the people who cherished Helena's memory were insufficient to preserve it intact. The listing had appeared in the latest *Vacation Homes*: 'WESTOVER ESTATE SALE: beautifully restored 19th century farmhouse with 15 acres, fabulous views, established perennial garden. Fifteen additional 15-17 acre lots with spectacular views of Westover and the Mountain, minutes from the lifts. Exceptional value.'

It would be done, Colleen had assured David, in the very best of taste. Nobody doubted that; people who could afford fifteen acres 'minutes from the lifts' would be sure to build houses worthy of the site.

Fifteen worthy houses.

He looked down the mowing once more, then strolled back the way he'd come, feeling the shadows of bygone tea guests part to accommodate his alien corporeal substance. After a quick stop at the car, he went on through the gardens and sat on the bench by the drained fishpond, not next to Charlie and a baby this time, but next to the urn he'd taken from the front seat. *I would prefer*, she had specified, *that there be no memorial stone, and that my ashes be scattered in Fiesole, if my death occurs in Italy, in Westover, Vermont if it occurs in the United States.* David had confessed himself unequal to the task, and so he, Joel, was fulfilling her wishes alone—appropriately, as it materialized, and now he was glad he'd thought better of weakly asking for Eleanor's company. He'd tell her in due time, of course. Perhaps even show her the letter, if it revealed what he was almost certain it would. But though Helena's silence could not possibly be construed as betrayal (for to break it, she would have had to violate a sacred promise to Nathaniel), he wished to read it alone. And read it before he performed his task here, so nothing would remain between them and himself as he did it.

He felt in the inner pocket of his suit and drew out the unopened envelope that the Mather College librarian had sent to Vermont with Andrew, who'd arrived in mid-morning for this afternoon's memorial service. It was addressed to him at his Draper Post Office box number, but—in sad testimony to Helena's fading capacities—it had been sent to the library with what was now officially labeled the Brantford-Woodhouse correspondence, sealed to all eyes for fifty years. How typical of the librarian's archival care that she had checked every one of the twenty boxes. And how thoughtful of her to forward his letter to him, rather than letting it wait in bureaucratic correctness for the passage of fifty years—by which time his own ashes would have long been dispersed. Smiling thoughtfully, he drew out his penknife and slit the envelope.

It did not contain the fifth-act explanatory epistle he'd imagined; instead, it contained two smaller envelopes, both unopened. One of them was marked 'Joel' in Helena's elegant calligraphy; the other was addressed to Helena, in Nathaniel's unmistakable bold hand, and canceled May 7, 1977. How peculiar. He drew out his penknife again and opened the envelope with his name on it.

July 8, 1991

Dear Joel,

I have been sorting through the correspondence between Nathaniel and myself, in preparation for following Letty's example and donating it to Mather College. In the process, I found a letter which Nathaniel sent me a few weeks before he died, with instructions to open it after that event. After some consideration at the time of his death, I decided not to open it; our farewell had been satisfying, and I felt that rhetorical expression of something long understood was unnecessary. My sentiments in that regard remain unchanged; yet I do not wish to send a letter that I have not read to the archives. I have, therefore, decided to pass it on to you. If, in keeping it this long, I have inadvertently kept you from knowledge that would have spared you pain, I apologize. The possibility occurred to me only this evening.

Yours truly,
Helena Woodhouse

Only this evening. So she had not known—had not deceived him, as he'd thought with passing bitterness the other day when he remembered that during his first visit here, she had said that she hadn't known Nathaniel owned land in Draper. Had not known either, then, of Letty's parentage or history. No, she had not deceived him. And here he'd 'forgiven' her last week, and sanctimoniously planned to forgive her again before he scattered her ashes! He looked around the garden, feeling the late-summer blossoms reproach him for his unworthiness. It was *he*, not Helena, who stood in need of forgiveness. It was *he*, not Nathaniel, who stood in need of forgiveness for thoughts still more unworthy. But who could bestow it on him now?

Sorrowfully, he picked up the second letter and turned it over in his hands, thinking of Nathaniel and Helena walking through the Mather College gardens arm in arm, growing older, but never diminishing. If the letter contained a rhetorical expression of something they had long understood, what right had he to read it? Whatever the two of them had shared was, as Charlie put it, theirs. The past was past, and the present had no right to it. He would simply keep the letter, unopened, and everything would be—

Everything's all right, isn't it?

He started, restraining himself only with an effort from looking behind him for a phantom that could not possibly be there. Yet the letter, if not the phantom, was before him, still open: *If, in keeping it this long, I have inadvertently kept you from knowledge that would have spared you pain...* Was it possible—could Nathaniel have once told Helena something about his suspicion that everything might not be all right? What, in fact, had made Helena think there might be something in Nathaniel's last letter that might *not* relate to her?

For perhaps a minute, he gazed at the letter, then he slit it open and unfolded—with a shock at its forgotten familiarity—Nathaniel's handsome letterhead.

> *May 7, 1977*
>
> *Dear Helena:*
>
> *The enclosed letter should be self-explanatory.*

Enclosed letter? Opening the envelope again, he discovered it: a page of carefully rounded script on lined notebook paper, dated May 2, 1944. *Dear Brent*—ah. He skipped to the signature: *Mary B. Ward.* Quickly, he ran his eyes over it:

I am sure you are surprised to get a letter from me, since it has been so long. In the Depression, we saw in the paper that you had been made president of your college, that is how I knew where to write to you.

Asa passed away a year ago. He was poorly a long time, and glad to go. Gid is gone, too. Not dead, just left for good. Clara passed on last November. She never did marry, just worked the farm. She had a little girl May 7, 1930, and she named her Letitia Brantford. We call her Letty. I thought Clara should write to you when she found out she was expecting, but she said, no, it didn't make any difference, and Asa said the same. Nobody knows Clara is Letty's ma, including Letty. We let on she was the daughter of a cousin up north that had to get married, and we took Clara up there the last month, so the birth certificate would fit what we said. It was easy in those times, and people have such wicked tongues, Asa told Clara how the baby would suffer if it got around. Clara wouldn't have cared for herself.

Yes, of course Mary Ward would have written; she could hardly have ventured to Whitby to find Nathaniel. But while the letter contained little he didn't know, he looked up with blurred eyes. The subterfuge of the proud. The determination not to let a daughter suffer. The spirit of the eighteen year old girl, bereft of the education and life she'd dreamed of, who had named her child Letitia: gladness. If only, if only—! He shook his head as he scanned the remaining short paragraph, then turned back to Nathaniel's letter.

You may, if you wish, share it with Letty and Joel, who are as ignorant of its contents as you have been until this moment. I should warn you, however, that while I originally intended to tell Letty what her mother had not, I quickly found that she wished to expunge all remnants of the past from her memory, and I hesitated to take a step that would force her to link her new life with the old until such time as she expressed a desire to reconcile the two. That time never came. And in fact, it is because that time never came that I have decided to set aside a long tradition and write this letter to you. I would not have dared to do so if you had not set aside the tradition yourself on our last meeting in Vermont, by suggesting that I accompany you to Italy. With that invitation, you opened the possibility that we might share, perhaps not past sorrow, but at least the landscapes which saw that sorrow—and which, revisited, evoke both grief and felicity long past. Perhaps we should have opened our landscapes to each other years ago. Such places are the Edens of the soul; I would have liked to have seen yours.

That, however, is by the by. My concern at present is that my landscape does not belong to me, and that I consequently have no way of ensuring that it will be cared for after I die. It is a farm just south of Draper, locally known as the Ward Place, and it belongs to Letty, as by right it should; it was the place her mother lived all her life. To me, it is all that your refuge in Fiesole is to you; I have spent every morning of my Vermont visits there, first with Letty's grandmother—a woman of courage and dignity worthy of Hecuba—then, for the past eighteen years, with the land and its memories. To Letty, however, it is nothing; if it has remained what it was, it is because I have overseen the details of its care.

What I want to ask you, then, is that you attend to the farm after my death. It would take you very little time. All you would have to do is stop by the farm of Clarence Wolfington (off the Westover road, just behind the Howe Place) each July and renew the oral contract by which, since 1959, he has used the pasture and the mowing in return for keeping up the lawn and the cemetery and doing light carpentry on the house. I realize there is a certain irony in this request; if I have not been to you all that I should have been, that is because the essence of myself has lived apart in the fields of the Ward Place for nearly fifty years. Yet I can make the request of nobody else—not even Joel, for Letty has never told him about the place or her past, and for me to do so would be unforgivable. I trust that you will understand—and understand also that leaving in your care the thing I have loved most dearly is itself an act of love.

That is all, except that I would not have you think I came to Vermont each July only to relive the past; I came also to see you, to share your wisdom and your patience, your blessed reticence. I have long awaited the passage which is soon to be granted to me; and yet I find it difficult, as always, to take leave of you. For you have been all in all to all of me that lived.

Nathaniel

Somewhere in the woods, a thrush sang a long, descending melody. As it died away, there was nothing but the hum of bees, and, far away, the faint noise of cars passing through Westover on Route 100. Slowly, Joel folded the three letters, returned them to his inner pocket, and stood up. There was very little time left; the memorial service was due to start in less than a half an hour, and although the real memorial to all that might have been—and to all that had been, in spite of all that might have been—lay next to his heart, he had to be present for the ceremony. Ashes unto ashes, dust unto dust. And where should he scatter them but here, where the old walls protected the Garden from the sorrows of the world?

Eleanor stood at the side door of the Westover Congregational Church, watching people get out of their cars and walk in hushed twos and threes towards the church door. Most of Helena's mourners, it seemed, were associated with Mather College and the aristocratic circles to which it, like Helena, had remained attached; but some of them were not. Near the steps, there was a group of young Italians—students, no doubt being educated at Helena's expense. And climbing the steps were Susan Howe's granddaughter, Mike Wolfington and his wife, and several other people whose bone-set, eyes, and bearing proclaimed their affinity to Mary Ward.

The door beside her opened, and David looked out anxiously. "*Mxmx* Joel?"

"Not yet." She looked at her watch. "He still has ten minutes."

"Yeah, but—" He came outside, then turned back, looking at the gray-haired man who waited in the doorway. "*Mxmx* not here yet."

"*Mxmx* will be," said the man. "Joel's never late." He turned to her and smiled. "*Mxmx* Eleanor Klimowski?"

She nodded, trying to place him. Clearly Mather College, and if he was waiting in the vestry for the front pews, clearly close to Helena. But how had he known her name?

"Andrew *Mxmx*," he said. "Joel's *mxmx* your place, *mxmx* book. *Mxmx* impressed."

Ah, Andrew Crawford. The President. She murmured an appropriate response, smiling into the appraising eyes that graced his otherwise undistinguished face. While she'd never heard David mention his name with anything other than respect, she'd always felt a little sorry for him; it could not be easy to walk in the shadow of Nathaniel Brantford. But if he had none of the Great Nathaniel's imagination and originality, he was nobody's fool; whatever his reason for assessing her merits, he was certainly doing it carefully, behind his conversation.

"Here he is!" David hurried off to the parking lot as the Alltrac turned into the last remaining place. Andrew watched Joel get out, and sighed.

"*Mxmx* very sorry Joel is leaving."

She nodded with some feeling. "Yes, but he really needs to leave for a while."

He gave her an odd look. "That's *mxmx* Helena said. *Mxmx* right, maybe. *Mxmx* looks much better than *mxmx* last May. *Mxmx* a way to go before *mxmx* old Joel Hendrickson."

She looked at Joel as he strode across the lawn, wondering a little sadly what the old Joel Hendrickson had been like—a Joel without a Titian face and a tendency to withdraw. She'd probably never know, Cambridge or no Cambridge. Like herself, he'd picked up the pieces

too many times to be the whole he'd once been. But what remained—
She returned his smile as he came up to them, then stood by silently,
observing with interest the respect with which the other two men
talked to him, though they were obviously just making desultory conversation while they waited for the usher.

The service was every bit as beautiful as she, David, and Joel
had taken care that it should be, and thanks to Joel's thoughtful tran-
scriptions, she could follow it—or at least, follow the readings. Music,
hopelessly distorted for the past couple of years, was now not even
that; when she closed her eyes, she was hardly aware it its presence.
Profound. Yes. Very different, this, from the loss that had initially driv-
en her to Vermont, but in its way, easier to cope with. With hearing as
with people, loss was less painful than losing. She watched the bows
of the quartet stop at the end of the Lydian Canon that Beethoven
had been no more able to hear than she, seeing in her mind's eye the
image of Helena, bent and helpless on her porch, only partly compre-
hending her condition. A great kindness, was loss, if one could only
bring oneself to accept it.

— —— ——

$\mathbb{T}$*hough I speak with the tongues of men and of angels, but have not
charity, I am become a sounding brass or a tinkling cymbal...*

Charity. Joel shifted a little in the pew, mulling over the word.
He, David and Eleanor had decided to use the King James version,
not only because of the seventeenth century prose, but because (or
at least, so he assumed; none of them had dared say it), while 'charity' definitely applied to Helena, 'love' seemed too personal. If he had
read the letters, perhaps he would have objected...no. With Helena,
as with Nathaniel—and even, in a very different way, with Letty—
personal tragedy had damaged precisely the indefinable quality that
allowed charity to develop into love. No doubt that explained the peculiar absence at the heart of what had, for so many years, been the

three central relationships of his life. It was strange he hadn't noticed the absence until this summer. No, that wasn't true. He had noticed. He'd loved in spite of it, accepting charity's passionless affection as return in kind.

Eleanor touched his hand. Looking about him, he saw with embarrassment that the service had come to an end, and people were getting up. He moved up the crowded aisle, returning hugs and handshakes, and thinking of the visit Helena had quietly paid him after Letty's funeral. Had that only been charity? And had it only been charity on one of their last evenings together, when Nathaniel, violating a twenty-year precedent, put one arm around his shoulders, and told him to take care, not of Letty, but of himself?

He walked down the narrow steps and found Andrew, who was talking to David; they both turned to him as he approached.

"Lovely service," said Andrew. "And lovely place, that farm of yours. Thanks so much for showing it to me. And look—have a good trip and keep in touch."

"Of course. I may spend Christmas in Vermont. If I do, I'll call."

"I don't recommend it," said David, "With no central heat, you'll spend twenty-four hours a day keeping warm. But then, if the cold drives you down to Providence, Sal and I would sure be glad to see you. Meanwhile, I've got to get down to Providence myself, this very evening; classes start day after tomorrow. Take care."

Joel shook hands warmly with both of them, then, as they started to the parking lot, looked across the dispersing crowd for Eleanor. She was standing a little apart from it, as she had stood at Helena's tea, and again before the service, patient, observant, alone. It was high time he took her back to a world that had content as well as form. Catching her eye, he smiled and started towards her across the lawn.

Eleanor, duly changed into jeans and a work-shirt, sat at the kitchen table looking at the three letters and scrap of paper spread out before her. *Nothing we didn't know already,* Joel had said when he'd given her the letters. But she hadn't known. Not known that the man whose car she'd occasionally seen leaving the Ward Place when she'd ridden her pony over to visit Mary had been the Great Nathaniel. Not known about Nathaniel's unexpressed devotion to Helena Woodhouse, or of Helena's affection for him. Not known—she looked down at Mary Ward's careful, familiar writing. No. She'd vaguely suspected (enough to ask Ray to find out what he could from Mike Wolfington) but she couldn't say she had *known*. But now— She perused the letter again. *Gid is gone, too. Not dead, just left for good.* May 2, 1944. She slid the scrap of paper next to it, and read Ray's working man's hand, slightly smeared from being carried around in his pocket, then left on top of the grain bin.

Mike says GB left town just after sugaring season in '44. Mike just a kid, so no details, only knew M Ward had finally kicked him out, but remembers how upset his mom was, and now thinks Clarence may have helped, but nobody ever let on.

Well, there was room for doubt, and God knew, she'd prefer to doubt. On the other hand— She read Mary's last paragraph again.

Now Letty and I are alone on the farm, which is what she wanted, but she has been very poorly and wants to leave. I told her she wouldn't want to be on her own at only age 13, I would write to a cousin of her pa's and maybe he could help her. She said all right, she would wait until her birthday, but if there was no word by then, she would go. If you could write to me before then, that would relieve my mind. It has gotten so I can hardly hold my head up, otherwise I would have left you alone, the way Clara wanted.

She pushed her chair back, folded the letters and shoved them in her back pocket, then let Derri out the front door and followed him across the road. The path between her house and the Ward Place had become a carefully seeded lawn; clearly, it wouldn't be long before the familiar walk was closed to her. But today she could still skirt the new grass, and that was a comfort; for this particular walk was not a commute between two houses, but a pilgrimage into the past.

She hurried through the remaining woods and ducked under Mike Wolfington's gate; then, calling Derri to heel, walked slowly on, alternately looking out at the view and down at the cow-pies on the close-cropped grass, until she reached the graveyard and went in. *Let the dead lie easy.* Henry. Alice. Robert and his infant sons. Clara and her roses—past their blooming now, and dying down for the winter. She passed them all, and stopped before the newest of the tomb stones. Mary Bartlett Ward. 1894-1959. *A woman of courage and dignity worthy of Hecuba.*

Had Nathaniel known the extent of her courage or her grief? Clarence Wolfington's wife had known; Susan Howe also, no doubt, as she'd been deliberately vague about the chronology of Letty's leaving. But Nathaniel? Could any man of patrician background—no matter how much that background was mitigated by intelligence, imagination and love—have known that there was only one thing that would make Mary Ward bow her head? Probably not. To know, he would have had to know the history, not just of Mary Bartlett, but of a Vermont closed to outsiders. Would have had to know the rhythms of farm life that necessitated work apart. Would have had to know how long necessity had conditioned a family to trusting the untrustworthy. He might have known the second two. But the first—the determination to put the shame of incest behind forever, the desperate propriety which led her to hide a daughter's pregnancy, to risk a trip north, to lie— He could not have known. She would never have told him. Not about her father and herself, not about her brother and her grand-daughter. And the friends who protected her secret would never have betrayed her.

Noli me tangere. Oh, Mary. Oh, Hecuba. She reached out and placed her hand gently on the warm stone.

255

$\mathcal{C}$harity. Joel paced up and down the living room floor, and finally went outside. With Nathaniel and Helena, there had been moments when charity had become, if not love, at least the acknowledgment of love's existence. With Letty, though— He vaulted over the gate and walked moodily up the hill. With Letty, it was more difficult, because 'charity' was not the first word one would apply to her, in spite of her bouts of generosity. Her deepest wound had been more profound, and deliberately inflicted, with the result that she had never—

Ahead of him, a dog barked; looking up quickly, he saw Eleanor at the graveyard gate.

He waved and increased his pace. "Hello! I tried to call, bu —" But what was he doing talking to her at this distance? What was he doing talking to her at all, when her face looked like that?

"It's nothing," she said, looking past him at the view. "I read the letters, and I came here to—to commune."

He nodded. It was a good place to commune, as Nathaniel had well known. "Would you rather I went back?" he asked—and instantly regretted it. If she said yes, there would be no way he could reasonably stay.

She looked back from the mountains. "I'm sorry?"

Ah. "Why don't you come down to the house?" he amended, speaking more slowly.

She hesitated, then slowly nodded. "Thank you," she said. "I appreciate—"

She stopped, clearly aware of how stiff she sounded. But that was all right. The miracle was not that she accepted implicit support stiffly, but that she accepted it at all. And the stiffness dissolved almost immediately; as they walked down the hill together, she talked about the letters with all the sympathy and understanding he always marveled at in her. It was only as they reached the porch that she paused.

"Joel. About Letty. When you said there was nothing in the letters you didn't know, did you include—Gid?"

There was no mistaking what she meant. "Yes and no," he said hesitantly, and added, "Let me get some paper."

Inside, he pulled a pad out of the computer station he'd built for himself and wrote hurriedly: 'Not right away. It took me most of the afternoon to admit the likelihood. But I've done that, now.'

He walked back out to the porch and found her seated on the porch swing, rocking slowly back and forth. "I've just taken a Proustian journey back to my childhood," she said, looking up at him with a peculiar smile. "I used to sit out here for hours, shelling peas."

How strange that she should have been part of the prologue to his present without his knowing it. He sat down next to her, feeling for the first time in several days the quiet presences that occasionally flickered on the edges of his consciousness. He turned the pad so she could see it, and added, 'If you have any concrete evidence about Gid and Letty, please spare me. It's difficult enough to think of her regarding him as Prospero and discovering Caliban.' He shuddered and looked away. Thirteen. Not just violence and horror, but betrayal. He picked up the pencil again and wrote 'God, I wish she'd told me,' then began to scribble it out. What difference did it make now?

She stopped his hand. "I was just thinking, sitting out here, that she did tell you."

"Oh, no," he said. "I assure you—"

She shook her head. "I don't mean in words. I don't even mean in a way that would have changed your lives together. But in the end, she left this place to you. That might have been a way—not of admitting everything, but of saying she cared."

He glanced at her, then wrote, 'She could certainly have chosen a more direct and less painful way of saying it.'

"Possibly. But having been through what she had, she probably couldn't separate love from pain. And since she'd denied the pain for so long, and repressed the past for so many years, there really was no way she could tell you. But she could leave you the Ward Place."

He looked over the porch railings at the old maples that hid the view of the lake. Was that possible? Could she have? He frowned.

'When I was in Whitby and found she'd taken all the restrictions off her legacy to the college, I went through all her papers at Elm Street, and I found absolutely no explanation—even a hint' —he stopped, looking at what he'd written. Taken all the restrictions off her legacy to the college, so greatly to Jed Smith's surprise. Been so quiet, so gentle, so greatly to his surprise. Asked him to play the Raindrop Prelude, perhaps to her own surprise. Certainly it was not, in the phrase at the top of the page, concrete evidence. But— He started a new line, and wrote, 'Maybe you have a point.'

"Well," she said, "I certainly wouldn't have thought so when I first heard of the legacy, but now—it's a possibility, anyway."

It was. But he never could have come to think of that on his own. Left to himself, he would probably have sold the place for whatever he could get and borne the pain as best he could. As it was—how could he tell Eleanor? *What* could he tell her? If he were wise, he'd tell her nothing. There was no need to; the understanding between them was —

I felt that rhetorical expression of something long understood was unnecessary.

Well, that might be, but an acquaintance of three months was hardly a friendship of forty-five years. Not to mention that in less than a week, he'd be three thousand miles from Vermont. Or to mention that at the moment he had very, very little to offer, intellectually or emotionally.

If I have not been to you all that I should have been...

He glanced sideways at her. She was looking off at the darkening maples, her face relaxed into the expression that he'd wondered at so often when he'd caught her at times she thought she was alone. The one he'd seen in Nathaniel's face, and occasionally in Helena's.

He was wiser now than he'd been two months ago; he knew what it was. Loss.

But *her* essential core had remained whole. It was simply a matter of getting to it, through the peculiar mixed layers of fear and toughness. And when she released it—

Such places are the Edens of the soul; I would have liked to have seen yours.

If only he were only not so much adrift himself—but surely he would not always be so. Thanks to his five-pager, he could write again, even now. And after two years—after one year—in a few months—

"Eleanor." He slid his arm across the swing's worn back and closed his hand around her shoulder. "Eleanor—"

Her hand reached up and covered his, but she said nothing. When he leaned forward to look at her, he saw tears on her cheeks. Not tears like Letty's. Tears like Hermione's. He lifted his free hand, turned her face gently toward him, and kissed her. Then, as her tears—and his own— were still falling, he held her to him and slowly rocked the swing.

They had time, thank God. They had time.

Breinigsville, PA USA
21 June 2010
240337BV00001B/1/P